T0024890

Stranger in the Glade

Also by Susan K. Marlow

Circle C Beginnings
Andi's Pony Trouble
Andi's Indian Summer
Andi's Fair Surprise
Andi's Scary School Days
Andi's Lonely Little Foal
Andi's Circle C Christmas

Circle C Stepping Stones
Andi Saddles Up
Andi Under the Big Top
Andi Lassos Trouble
Andi to the Rescue
Andi Dreams of Gold
Andi Far from Home

Circle C Adventures
Andrea Carter and the Long Ride Home
Andrea Carter and the Dangerous Decision
Andrea Carter and the Family Secret
Andrea Carter and the San Francisco Smugglers
Andrea Carter and the Trouble with Treasure
Andrea Carter and the Price of Truth

Circle C Milestones
Thick as Thieves: An Andrea Carter Book
Heartbreak Trail: An Andrea Carter Book
The Last Ride: An Andrea Carter Book
Courageous Love: An Andrea Carter Book
Yosemite at Last: And Other Tales from Memory Creek Ranch
Stranger in the Glade: And More Tales from Memory Creek Ranch

CIRCLE C MILESTONES · 6

Stranger in the Glade

AND MORE TALES FROM MEMORY CREEK RANCH

AN ANDREA CARTER BOOK

Susan K. Marlow

KREGEL
PUBLICATIONS

Stranger in the Glade: And More Tales from Memory Creek Ranch
© 2022 by Susan K. Marlow
Revised and expanded edition. Previously independently published as *More Tales from Memory Creek Ranch*.

Published by Kregel Publications, a division of Kregel Inc., 2450 Oak Industrial Dr. NE, Grand Rapids, MI 49505.

All rights reserved. No part of this book may be reproduced, stored in a retrieval system, or transmitted in any form or by any means—electronic, mechanical, photocopy, recording, or otherwise—without written permission of the publisher, except for brief quotations in reviews.

Distribution of digital editions of this book in any format via the internet or any other means without the publisher's written permission or by license agreement is a violation of copyright law and is subject to substantial fines and penalties. Thank you for supporting the author's rights by purchasing only authorized editions.

The persons and events portrayed in this work are the creations of the author, and any resemblance to persons living or dead is purely coincidental.

Lyrics to "Auld Lang Syne" by Robert Burns, 1788. Public domain.

Scripture quotations are from the King James Version.

Cataloging-in-Publication Data is available from the Library of Congress.

ISBN 978-0-8254-4738-9, print
ISBN 978-0-8254-7793-5, epub
ISBN 978-0-8254-6944-2, Kindle

Printed in the United States of America
23 24 25 26 27 28 29 30 31 / 5 4 3 2

Gratitude

RECOGNIZING GOD'S UNMERITED FAVOR
AND EXPRESSING THANKFULNESS FOR HIS
GOOD GIFTS.

In every thing give thanks: for this is the will of God in
Christ Jesus concerning you.
—1 Thessalonians 5:18

The first story in this book opens three months after the final story in *Yosemite at Last: And Other Tales from Memory Creek Ranch* (book 5).

CONTENTS

Memory Creek Ranch, California, October 1887

I'm stumped. I don't know what to do about this situation, but I must make a decision soon.

CHAPTER 1

"I've got something for you," Riley called, stomping the dust from his boots. Smiling, he pushed open the backdoor screen, slipped through, and clicked it shut before the lazy fall flies could sneak in. "It's a letter."

Andi wiped her hands on her apron and shoved back a stubborn lock of dark, sweaty hair. Late summer heat had continued into October, settling over Memory Creek in a stifling cloud. "Who on earth would send me a letter?"

Riley shrugged. "I have no idea. Your name is scrawled across the envelope, but nothing else. I was on my way out of town when Toby Wright waved me down. He was getting ready to ride out to our ranch and seemed happy to save himself a trip in this blistering heat."

"I don't blame him," Andi said. "What does the letter say?"

"Andi!" Riley looked hurt. "I wouldn't open your private correspondence. All I know is that it has no stamp, so it's more like a message than a true letter." He held it out.

"I thought Toby worked for Sam Blake," Andi said, accepting the envelope. She jammed it into her apron pocket. "I didn't know he ran errands too."

Riley chuckled. "Anything for a dime."

"Did you pay Toby?" Andi asked, aghast. "He didn't carry that message far enough to earn a penny, much less a whole dime."

"We would've given him a much larger tip if he'd ridden all the way out here," Riley countered. He pointed at her apron pocket. "Aren't you going to read it?"

"I will when I get a chance to sit down." She swiped a dish towel across a plate and stacked it with the others. "I'm still wiping the noon dishes, and I have no idea what to prepare for supper."

Like always.

Andi's housekeeping and cooking skills had taken a nosedive when baby Jared entered their lives three months ago. Since her skills were already hovering near rock bottom, this new low was indeed dark.

A high, insistent wail broke through Andi's distressing thoughts about supper. The baby was awake and hungry.

"I'll tackle these dishes, sweetheart," Riley offered. "You take care of our precious son."

"Thanks." Andi gave her husband a grateful smile and vanished out of the kitchen as fast as her legs could carry her. *At last! I can rock Jared and read.* Her fingers brushed against the envelope in her apron pocket.

By the time she'd changed Jared, fed him, and settled him on her lap to rock back to sleep, Andi's curiosity had risen sky high. She pulled out the envelope and studied the handwriting.

Mrs. Andrea Prescott

Odd, she mused. It was a man's bold script, and it looked familiar. She couldn't place it, though. Anyway, what man would be writing to *her*?

Only one way to find out, I reckon. She tore the envelope open and unfolded a single sheet of thick, creamy stationery.

Andi,
If you and Riley could make time during the next few

days to come to town, I would very much like to see you.
I am in Fresno visiting my folks for two weeks, and then
I will be gone again.
   I remain, as always, your friend,
   Cory

Andi caught her breath. *Cory Blake!*

She had not seen Cory for over two years, not since she and Lucy had been rescued from Procopio's outlaw camp. Cory had wanted to see Andi then too. Their meeting had been awkward, and then he vanished.

"Where has he been all this time?" she wondered.

Jared squirmed, yanking Andi from her musings. She set aside the letter and lifted the baby over her shoulder to pat his back.

"Where has *who* been?" Riley asked, joining her. He held out his arms, and Andi gratefully handed over the baby.

"Cory. He's back in town." Puzzled by this unusual request, she looked up into Riley's face. "He wants to see us." She crumpled the letter into a wad and let it fall from her fingers. "Oh, Riley! What should we do?"

CHAPTER 2

Two years earlier
Fresno, California, May 1885

Seventeen-year-old Andi Carter swung out of her saddle and dropped to the dusty ground beside her chocolate palomino. "Whatever is the matter with you?" She still had half a mile to go before she reached town, and Shasta was not cooperating.

It took Andi less than five minutes to determine the problem. She let her colt's left front foot drop to the ground and slumped against his neck. "Well, isn't this swell."

Shasta had thrown a shoe somewhere along the road to town, and Andi had not even noticed until he started acting unhappy. "Some rider *I* am," she muttered, rubbing his neck. "I'm sorry for pushing you back there."

Shasta nuzzled her as if to say, *No hard feelings*, then blew a hot, horsey breath into her face.

Andi laughed. "I deserved that." She gathered up her colt's reins and began dogtrotting the last five hundred yards into town.

As she jogged, Andi wondered how she would keep this news from Chad. He'd reminded her half a dozen times this week to check Shasta's feet to see if he needed new shoes. She'd put off her brother's warnings until yesterday, when she finally brought Shasta to the ranch farrier. But Jake had quit for the day and was nowhere in sight. She'd missed him.

"Chad's gonna have my hide." Then a new idea perked Andi up. "Unless I solve this problem before I head home." She couldn't ride Shasta back to the ranch with a missing shoe, and she'd rather not go home until her colt had all four feet adequately protected.

She hurried down Inyo Street and turned onto J Street to pick up the items on Mother's shopping list. Afterward, she would cross to K Street and sweet-talk Sam Blake into shoeing Shasta at the livery pronto. Mr. Blake knew Andi was good for the payment.

"And big brother need never know." Andi put a spring into her step, entered the mercantile, and turned Mother's list over to Mr. Goodwin.

"It's good to see you, Andi," the shopkeeper greeted her from behind the counter. He grinned. "And congratulations."

Andi looked at him blankly.

"On your and Riley's courtship."

Heat exploded in Andi's cheeks. "Thank you, sir."

Where would Mr. Goodwin have heard about that? Only a handful of rescuers were with them last month up near Kings Canyon when Riley made his intentions known. Which one had blabbed to the shopkeeper?

Mr. Goodwin tied up several brown packages and tucked them into a large burlap sack. "I read about your courtship in the *Expositor* yesterday morning," he said cheerfully.

The newspaper? Andi managed a weak smile. "The paper must be mighty shy on news these days to include such a small item of interest."

The entire town would now know that she and Riley were courting. Tongues would wag, and advice would flow from one old biddy's lips to the other, all intended to reach Elizabeth Carter's ears in no time.

"That's our *Expositor*." Mr. Goodwin chuckled. "Might as well enjoy the attention."

Andi thanked the shopkeeper with a stiff nod, heaved the sack over her shoulder, and left the mercantile in a huff. Was nothing private?

Andi tied the sack around the saddle horn and headed for Blake's Livery. It was one block over, but she could not escape the sly looks and smiling faces. It appeared that anything a Carter did quickly became the talk of the town.

"How perfectly splendid to hear about your courtship," Mrs. Evans gushed, patting Andi on the arm. "Wedding bells are just around the corner. It's about time you grew up and—"

"Thank you, but I really must be on my way." Andi cut the woman off with a polite smile, gripped Shasta's reins, and walked faster.

Mrs. King waved to Andi halfway down K Street. She echoed Mrs. Evans's sentiments. "Growing up, are we?"

Groaning inwardly, Andi managed another smile and a quick nod. "Yes, ma'am." She ducked into Blake's Livery the minute the coast was clear. Then she peeked around the corner of the darkened livery out into the bright sunshine. "Safe at last." She sighed her relief.

"Safe from what?"

Andi whirled. Shasta blew out and shook his mane. "Ho, boy," she crooned. "You're fine. It's just Cory." She smiled at her friend. "Gossips."

"Ah," Cory replied. He took two steps toward her. "Is that why you're hiding in our livery?" He studied her with somber blue-gray eyes, as if he wasn't sure what to say.

No wonder. Today was the first time she had seen Cory since Chad and Ellie's engagement party back in April. When Cory had finally admitted that Justin was right—that Cory and Andi were not meant for each other—he accepted it with a crooked grin. He'd even thanked her for her honesty, and for her willingness to lay everything out in the open and not spare his feelings.

Cory didn't look thankful now. He looked positively grim.

"I'm wondering if you or your pa would be willing to replace a shoe," Andi blurted, hoping to ease the despondent look from her friend's face. He had assured her they would always be friends, but right now she felt like Judas, the betrayer.

"Sure," Cory nodded, suddenly all business. "I can do that for you. Bring Shasta on over."

The awkwardness of meeting after two months of silence dissolved like a vapor. Cory gathered his tools.

"I can run down to Justin's and visit so I'm not in your way," Andi offered. "It might take a while to stoke the forge and bend a shoe." The more she thought about it, the better this plan sounded. She didn't want her presence to cause her friend any more discomfort.

Cory shook his head. "Actually, I'd like to talk to you, so I'm glad I caught you in town."

Andi felt herself pale. He sounded serious. "What about?" She forced a chuckle. "Shasta is not for sale."

Cory didn't laugh. "It concerns the announcement I came across in the paper." He tied Shasta to a sturdy railing and lifted the colt's foot, avoiding Andi's gaze. "I thought everything would be fine after the party," he said softly. "I meant what I said when I told you God knows best."

He lowered Shasta's foot and looked at Andi. "The trouble is my heart is not in agreement with my decision. When I read about you and Riley officially courting, the reality of it hit me. I realized I care for you more than I ought to at this point." He took a deep breath then let it out. "I can't stay."

"What are you talking about?"

Cory dropped all pretense of shoeing Shasta. "I'm leaving Fresno. My folks think it's a good idea, and frankly, I'd like to see something of the world. I've never even been to San Francisco."

Andi wanted to interrupt this lunacy, but her tongue was tied in a knot. A lump found its way into her throat. How could Cory leave Fresno? How could he leave his father's livery business? Worse, it sounded like he was leaving because of *her*, because he still cared for her.

Cory caught the anguish in her eyes. "This is none of your doing, Andi. You were honest with me. Your brother was honest. I thought I was all right and could move on, but I can't. Not here. Not now. This is *my* problem to solve." He smiled. "You and Riley will do well together. Honest. But I need to find my own way."

"Where will you go?" Andi whispered through her tight throat.

Cory leaned against the thick, rough post holding up this section of the livery. "The Hawaiian Islands."

Andi stumbled backward in surprise. Cory leaped forward and caught her just before she fell over a barrel. "Take it easy." He steadied her against Shasta.

"The Hawaiian Islands?" She shook her head. "They're in the middle of the Pacific Ocean. You're not a sailor. What will you do?"

Cory laughed, and his eyes sparkled for the first time since Andi had walked into the livery. "I'm not going as a sailor. I'm traveling as a paid passenger. I've saved a lot of money. It will be fun."

He turned serious. "I have to do this, Andi. I'll probably be gone for at least six months, maybe longer. By then I hope to have my head and my heart speaking to each other again. I may or may not come back to Fresno, though. The summer heat in the valley sometimes gets to me."

"When are you leaving?"

"The end of the week."

Andi winced. "So soon?"

"Yes." Cory said no more. He turned around and gave his attention to replacing Shasta's missing shoe.

Andi sat on the barrel, frozen in thought. Cory was leaving. He had been such a big part of her life these past seventeen years. She wanted to say something to ease his departure, but she couldn't think of a thing.

Say nothing, a still, small voice whispered in her head. *Simply wish him well, go back to the ranch, and marry Riley.*

Sound advice from God's Spirit.

By the time Cory pounded the last nail into Shasta's new shoe, Andi was ready to leave. She took the colt's reins. "I'll pay your father the next time I come to town."

"You don't owe us anything," Cory said. "Consider it an early wedding gift."

"Thank you." Andi took a deep breath. "I wish you all the happiness in the world. The Hawaiian Islands sound exciting. Take care of yourself."

"I will." Cory held out his hand. "Good-bye, Andi."

Andi ignored his outstretched hand and brushed a kiss against his cheek. "Good-bye, Cory."

Then she turned and fled.

CHAPTER 3

Present day
Memory Creek Ranch, October 1887

Riley's hand on her shoulder brought Andi out of her mental brooding. "Are you all right?"

"I don't know," she whispered.

Andi didn't know how long Riley stayed beside her while her thoughts replayed her last meeting with Cory, but he was there when she returned to her present surroundings. The baby slept on, a picture of perfect contentment on his daddy's shoulder.

"What should we do?" she repeated her earlier question.

Riley smiled. "I say that you, Jared, and I go into town and see Cory, like he asked."

You, Jared, and I. A thrill shot through Andi at his words. She smiled back at her husband, glad to know she wouldn't have to endure a potentially awkward meeting without Riley and her baby along. "When shall we go?"

"I'm happy to rearrange any day to pay a visit to town," Riley answered cheerfully. "What about tomorrow morning? That way you won't have to agonize over what in the world the long-lost Cory Blake has been up to these past two years."

Andi nodded eagerly and relaxed . . . at least a little bit.

Andi had no idea why Cory wanted to see her and Riley. Her fingers fumbled as she dressed the baby in a cool cotton gown. She made sure her hair was neatly braided and wound around her head like a grown-up lady.

Riley donned his new plaid shirt with the pearl buttons, his birthday gift from Andi last January. His trousers were clean and pressed, and their buggy was in tiptop shape. He even gave his appaloosa a thorough grooming before hitching him up.

Andi raised an eyebrow at all these fancy doings.

"I won't meet Cory full of dust and dirt, and looking like a poor rancher," Riley explained, giving Dakota a final swipe with the brush.

Andi stepped off the porch with the baby in her arms. "But we *are* poor ranchers."

"Ah," Riley shot back, taking Jared from her, "but Cory doesn't know that." He helped Andi into the buggy, handing up the baby. She tucked her sweet little one safely in her arms to protect him from the rough road ahead.

Riley chattered nonstop during the hour and a half buggy ride into Fresno. Andi knew he was doing his best to keep her from thinking about the upcoming meeting. Listening to Riley and answering his questions about which colt they should train next or how many setting hens she'd discovered kept her mind where it should stay—on ranch matters.

Before Andi knew it, the horse was clip-clopping down Inyo Street. Riley turned onto K Street and reined Dakota to a smooth stop in front of the Blake residence, which butted up against the livery.

Riley took the baby, helped Andi down, and handed Jared back. She smiled and held the baby close. Riley's returning smile assured Andi that he knew holding her baby would keep her calm and ready for anything.

Riley didn't dillydally. He led Andi along the walk, past the two rows of blooming roses, which nearly every lady in the valley grew, and up the three wooden steps to the Blakes' front door. Raising his fist, Riley rapped on the door. "Here goes nothing," he whispered.

Andi didn't reply. Her throat felt too dry.

Cory's mother opened the door. "Oh, Andrea! I am so glad you accepted Cory's invitation to come for a visit while he's in town."

Andi relaxed. So much for Cory's cryptic letter about wanting to "see" her. He could have worded it in a way that would not have plunged Andi into a shaky past. Maybe something like, "My mother has invited you and Riley for a visit. It would be fun to see you again."

Andi shooed her thoughts away. "It's nice to see you, Mrs. Blake," she replied politely and took off her hat. It was close to falling off anyway. Jamming it over her thick braid never did the wide-brimmed hat any good.

Riley surrendered his hat as well.

Mrs. Blake gushed over Jared then ushered Andi and Riley into a small but homey sitting room. Sam Blake sat in an overstuffed chair reading the morning edition of the *Expositor*. He rose, greeted the visitors, then headed out back to his livery.

Just then, a tall, muscular young man tore around the corner from the kitchen. When he saw Andi, his eyes lit up. "Andi! It's so good to see you." He crossed the room and extended his hand. "I was hoping that you and Riley would accept my invite."

Andi took Cory's hand. "How are you?"

"Fine. Actually, better than fine." He looked at Jared then stuck out his hand to Riley. "Congratulations, old man. Boy or girl?"

The men shook hands. "A boy."

"Good for you!"

Andi stared at Cory. She barely recognized him. His straw-colored hair had darkened, and a neat beard covered the lower half of his face. His eyes were just as blue-gray as they had ever been, but sun wrinkles and laughter lines were everywhere. He showed no trace of the despondency he'd exhibited at their last meeting.

Cory had found peace.

Andi unlocked her tongue to ask the question burning in her mind. "Where have you been all these—"

"I know, I know." Cory sat down and motioned Andi and Riley to take the settee across from him. "You're full of questions. Where have I been? What have I been doing? Did I make it to the Hawaiian Islands?"

He winked at Andi. Somehow, his gesture didn't bother her at all. "Yes, I've seen the Islands. They are as beautiful as they say." He laughed. "But I didn't stay long. Too many bugs. And the heat? Sometimes worse than the valley. Too humid."

"Then what . . ." Andi's voice trailed off when Cory held up his hand.

"Hold your horses. I know you like to know everything all at once, but let me tell it in my own way."

Riley laughed and squeezed Andi's hand. "So true."

Andi ducked her head to hide her grin. These two knew her too well.

For the next twenty minutes, Cory wove a story of sailing, exploring, and adventuring during the summer of 1885. While it might have lasted for several years, Cory decided the sea and the Hawaiian Islands were not for him. Neither was the heat of California, so he made his way up the West coast to the state of Oregon.

"I discovered that I love the climate of the Pacific Northwest. Mild summers. Mild but rainy winters. They sure know how to grow trees in that country."

His gaze focused on Andi's startled reaction.

"Yes," he said, answering her unspoken question. "In September, I

19

decided to visit that town your friend Jenny Grant hailed from all those years ago. Tacoma, up in Washington Territory."

Andi's heart leaped hearing Jenny's name. What good times they'd had together as young girls! "I've missed Jenny. Is her family still in Tacoma?"

"Oh, yes," Cory nodded. "By then, God had washed me clean of all my despair and *Why, God?* questions, so when I showed up in Tacoma, it was like meeting old friends. Jenny invited me to stay with her family while I was there."

"Oh, my!" Andi could hardly contain her excitement at where this story might be headed. "What did you—"

"Andi," Riley warned quietly.

"Sorry," she whispered. But honestly! Cory was dragging this story out. She waited on tenterhooks for him to continue.

"Long story short, just for you," Cory finished, grinning at Andi. "Jenny and I tied the knot a few months later on New Year's Day, 1886."

Riley whistled. "A whirlwind courtship."

Cory looked sheepish. "What do you do when you feel God is telling you exactly what He has in mind? Jenny felt the same way, and her folks agreed, so why wait?"

Andi and Riley exchanged rueful glances. Mother and Justin had put the brakes on their own plans to be married too soon. They had waited over a year before tying their own knot.

"Jenny's pa helped me start up a livery business," Cory went on.

"In Tacoma?" Andi asked, now that she could talk without stammering.

"Yep." Cory's eyes glowed. "I love Puget Sound. Fishing for salmon. Crabbing off the dock. Not long ago, I snagged the strangest sea creature I've ever seen. Eight legs and—"

"They're called arms, not legs," a mock-scolding voice interrupted with a laugh. "An octopus has eight *arms*."

"Jenny!" Andi leaped up.

Jared wailed his surprise and waved his small fists. She laid the crying baby on Riley's lap and sprinted across the room into her red-haired friend's open arms.

Well, almost open arms. One arm supported a chubby, auburn-haired baby girl less than a year old. She sat perched on Jenny's hip.

Jenny bounced up and down on her toes. The baby added her outraged howls to Jared's wailing. Andi and Jenny shrieked their joy at seeing each other. The room exploded into an uproar.

Finally, Cory stepped in. "Come to Papa, Cissy." The child went readily into her father's arms. He turned to Riley and yelled over the din, "Let's take the babies outside and let them wail to their hearts' content. That way Andi and Jenny can catch up in peace."

Andi ignored the commotion. She gave Riley and the baby only a passing glance before hugging Jenny again. He was already on his way out the door. Cory was only footsteps behind him.

The door slammed shut.

"Jenny!" Andi grabbed her friend's shoulders and shook her. "Was it *your* idea to keep me in the dark about you and Cory until you decided to jump out and surprise me?"

Jenny doubled over in laughter. "You bet it was. I thought it would be the best surprise ever." She straightened and met Andi's gaze. "Was it?" Her wide, brown eyes turned serious. "Was it the best surprise ever?"

Andi didn't hesitate even a moment. "Oh, yes! I am *so* happy for you and Cory." Her heart overflowed with joy and thanksgiving. "My only sorrow is realizing that you and Cory and that perfectly adorable baby girl won't be living here in Fresno."

Jenny grabbed Andi's arm and led her over to the settee. No one else was in the room. Cory's mother had ducked into the kitchen. Coffee and cakes could be served later.

"The good news is that Cory, Celia, and I are here for two whole weeks." Jenny pulled Andi down beside her. "Oh, Andi! It's been ages. I want to see the Circle C again. I want to see where you and Riley live.

I want to cuddle your baby and let you bounce my baby on your knee. I don't want to waste even one minute of our stay here in the valley. I want it to feel just like old times before I return to Tacoma and have to be a grown-up, married lady again."

A smile spread across Andi's face. She couldn't wait to show off her house, the ranch, and Shasta. A bold thought made her catch her breath. She would challenge Cory to a horse race, for old time's sake. Right where they used to race time and time again, on the stretch of rangeland that was now Memory Creek ranch.

Andi released her breath in a long, happy sigh. "Oh, yes, Jenny. We'll have so much fun reliving old times."

———

As Riley, Andi, and baby Jared bumped their way back to Memory Creek ranch that evening, Andi's joy sang out softly:

> Should auld acquaintance be forgot
> And never brought to mind?
> Should auld acquaintance be forgot
> And days of auld lang syne?
> For auld lang syne, my dear,
> For auld lang syne,
> We'll take a cup of kindness yet
> For days of auld lang syne.

AN UNEXPECTED VISITOR

Memory Creek Ranch, March 1888

Every day brings unexpected reminders that God moves in mysterious ways.

CHAPTER 1

Andi Prescott was convinced that nothing was more beautiful or refreshing in the entire country than an early spring morning on Memory Creek ranch.

The Circle C came in a close second, but with her former home situated lower in elevation and closer to the valley, the Sierra foothills did not look quite as impressive as they did from her own back porch.

Andi paused in her daily sweeping and rested her chin on the top of the broom handle to drink in the March morning. The grass-covered foothills exploded in a green so brilliant that it hurt her eyes. Not far away, half a dozen new foals frolicked in the paddock.

"I will lift up mine eyes unto the hills, from whence cometh my help," she quoted softly, scanning the rolling foothills. She felt a moment's sadness for the townsfolk. When they swept their porches, they saw only the flat San Joaquin Valley and neighboring wood or brick buildings.

To the citizens of Fresno, the Sierra Nevada was a narrow, dark-purple range in the far distance. Andi sighed. "Justin and Melinda miss so much."

Then again, maybe they didn't miss the rangeland. Her brother and sister and their families didn't act like they noticed their loss. They seemed to enjoy the advantages of living in the middle of a busy town.

It's not a town any longer, Andi corrected herself. *It's a city*. Fresno had been officially incorporated three years ago and was growing too fast to keep track of. "Another reason I'm glad I live way out here," she told the mountains.

There were a *few* teensy-weensy disadvantages to being surrounded by oak-covered foothills. Riley brought up one of the major drawbacks with a wink and a smile whenever Andi forgot to add something to their weekly go-to-town list. "I can't head to town every time you need an ounce of baking chocolate or a sack of cornmeal," he teased.

True enough. So instead, Andi found herself dreaming up excuses to borrow something from the Circle C, which was only a leisurely thirty-minute ride away.

In recent days, however, Andi did not visit Mother or Ellie very often. She was especially busy this spring. Jared had discovered that crawling around on his hands and knees opened a whole new world. And the faster he crawled, the more of that world he could explore.

Andi had all she could do to pull the baby out of corners and run a finger inside his mouth every few minutes to find whatever it was he'd decided to taste. She became especially vigilant after Riley found a sharp splinter in Jared's mouth one evening. He held up the slobbery piece of wood and looked at Andi, eyes wide.

"Oh, no!" Andi cried, distressed. What kind of careless mother was she?

Riley did more than express his own dismay. He went to town the next day and returned before supper with a new carpet sweeper. "This should do the trick," he promised.

But even an expensive machine that swept the carpet could not find every bit of danger.

Wipe a dish, yank Jared out of a corner. Make the bed, keep Jared from crawling under it. Hang the laundry, run after Jared and pull a grass-hopper from his mouth.

The clatter of horses' hooves trotting up the driveway pulled Andi from her reflections. Broom in hand, she hurried around to the front of the house. Who had dropped by? Memory Creek was off the beaten path by many miles.

Was a Hollister neighbor stopping by to complain? Or a down-on-his-luck cowhand looking for work? "I hope not." She and Riley could barely afford to pay their current ranch hands.

Worse, her promised ride on Shasta would be delayed if she had to show hospitality to a guest. Andi had cleaned extra fast this morning, sweeping the carpet and flying through the wash. Diapers, sheets, and Riley's Sunday shirts hung crooked and wrinkled on the clothesline out back.

Andi hadn't ridden for three days, and she was itching to get back in the saddle. It was the one place where the baby would sit still for hours. Shasta, for all his youth and high spirits, always sensed when a little one was on his back and behaved like a perfect gentleman.

Andi relaxed when she identified the Circle C rider. "Howdy, Wyatt," she called. "What brings you to our neck of the ranch? You lookin' for Riley?"

She hoped not. Riley was out branding calves somewhere.

"Nope," Wyatt replied. "I got a message for *you*." He pulled his dappled gray horse to a stop near the porch and pushed back his wide-brimmed hat.

"You rode all the way up here to give me a message?"

Wyatt nodded. "It was no problem. Chad wanted me to flush out some strays up in the east pasture, so he asked me to stop by your spread."

Andi frowned. East pasture, indeed! She and Riley had owned Memory Creek ranch for nearly two years, but some folks couldn't stop thinking this little piece of heaven was still part of the Circle C. Over the years, Chad had sent ranch hands up to this special spot dozens of times to remind Andi that she'd better "get along home."

It looked like her brother was still doing it. "What does he want?" she asked with a sigh.

"Well, 'bout an hour ago, a spankin' new buggy pulled up to the Circle C. The lady asked for you, Miss Andi."

"A lady? What lady?" Andi's eyebrows shot up. "And why didn't Chad just send her up here?"

Wyatt shrugged. "I dunno. It ain't my place to question the boss, least-ways not about personal matters. The little lady had a couple o' young'uns with her. She looked a mite weary, so I expect your brother invited her to rest there while somebody fetched you."

She fumed. It appeared big brother was still fetching his younger sister hither and thither. "What if I had bread in the oven? Or a load of laundry to squeeze out and hang up? Am I supposed to drop everything and head to the ranch on Chad's say-so?"

Wyatt held up his hands in defense. "Don't shoot the messenger, Miss Andi."

Andi let out a cooling breath. The faithful ranch hand was right. He was just following Chad's orders. Besides, the idea of heading to the Circle C with Jared suddenly sounded like the perfect destination for a horseback ride.

Besides, she was curious about a lady and two children asking after her. "I'll ride over as soon as I get the baby up from his nap."

"I'd be pleased to saddle your horse, Miss Andi."

"Thanks, Wyatt. I appreciate that."

Wyatt touched the brim of his hat and nudged his mount around to the back of the house.

Andi swept the front porch in record time and put the broom away. Lending an ear to the bedroom door, she heard Jared snuffling and cooing as he woke from his morning nap.

"Hey, little man." She found the baby standing up and gripping the edge of his brass baby crib. He'd outgrown his cradle weeks ago, right after he'd gone head over heels and landed on the hardwood floor. "Would you like to go for a ride?"

Jared bounced and squealed his answer. Two pearl teeth showed in his wide smile. His hazel eyes sparkled.

Andi changed his diaper, drew a clean, white gown over his head, and hiked him up on her hip. As she passed through the kitchen, she remembered Riley. "I'd better leave a note."

She didn't know how long Riley would be busy with his ranch duties, but Carlos, who doubled as the ranch cook, took care of the noon meal. However, her husband might expect supper.

Andi had no idea of what she might fix for the evening meal. She scribbled a hasty note and left it lying in the middle of the table.

I rode to the Circle C. Come over for supper.

Andi knew she'd get an invitation for supper. Whoever this mystery guest was, she and her young ones would be pressed to stay for the evening meal. They would also be offered overnight lodging.

"No cooking tonight." This day was getting better and better.

When Andi carried Jared outside, Shasta was saddled, bridled, and stood tied to the hitching railing near the barn. Wyatt was long gone. Andi balanced Jared in the saddle and quickly swung up behind him. He shrieked his delight.

During the ride to the Circle C, Jared sat on Andi's lap and chewed on the ends of Shasta's reins. She held the baby with one arm around his tummy and directed her colt with her other hand.

Shasta behaved as always. Andi nudged the chocolate palomino into a lope. Jared crowed and waved his arms.

Half an hour later, the ranch came into view. The white stucco house with the red tile roof was surrounded by tall eucalyptus trees and valley oaks. The spreading branches were just beginning to burst with new leaves.

Andi's heart leaped as it always did when she saw her old home. How many times had she ridden over this final rise to see the house laid out like a jewel? The sight gave her a thrill. What a beautiful childhood she'd had in this home with her beloved family. And what joy knowing Jared would grow up in this wonderful extended family and visiting the Circle C often.

Thank You, Lord, she prayed . . . just because.

"*¡Buenos días!*" Diego greeted Andi when she reined Shasta to a stop in the yard. He took Jared and held onto Shasta's bridle while Andi dismounted. The baby put up his usual fuss. He never wanted to leave the back of a horse.

It tickled Riley to see his little son so determined to stay aboard, but Andi was never amused. Especially not today, when he was squalling in Diego's arms and she was about to meet a guest. The Circle C cowhands might laugh it off, but no guest wanted to see or hear a baby's tantrum.

"Hush, Jared." Andi took him from Diego.

Jared stretched out his arms toward Shasta and wailed louder.

Diego grinned. "I'll take care of your horse, *señorita*. You and the spirited *niñito* can go inside."

"*Gracias*, Diego," Andi yelled over Jared's screeching. Her sweet, contented baby was quickly growing into a small boy with a mind of his own.

Diego tugged on Shasta's reins and ambled toward a nearby paddock. "I remember such a one as your *niñito* many years ago." He laughed. "Only, *she* was a *niñita*."

Andi felt her face flame. Had she truly thrown tantrums as wild as Jared's? She glared at Diego's back then turned to her small son. "Jared Riley, that's enough."

He quieted down at his mother's no-nonsense tone and laid his head on her shoulder.

"Good boy," Andi whispered. But she had no idea how long Jared would stay quiet. She opened the screen door and slipped into the kitchen. "*Buenos días*, Luisa."

"*Buenos días. ¿Cómo está mi niñito guapo?*"

Andi smiled. Luisa always asked how her handsome little boy was. "Very vocal today," Andi replied in Spanish. "He's decided he can't be without a horse under him."

Luisa chuckled. "Just like his *mami* and his uncles."

Just then, Nila entered the kitchen. Her face usually lit up when she saw Jared, but not today. Her dark eyes were somber. She took Andi aside. "Your *mamá* would like to see you in the parlor *pronto, chiquita*."

Andi's stomach lurched at Nila's words and uneasy expression. Visions of a long-ago day in the same parlor but with a different visitor sprang to mind. It was the day she'd learned she had an older sister whom she never knew.

The day Katherine had arrived.

"What's the big secret, Nila? Surely, Mother isn't going to spring another surprise sister on me." Andi smiled to ease the fluttering in her stomach.

"No indeed, *chiquita*. This visitor you have met before." She pressed her lips together and hurried away, muttering in Spanish and clearly disturbed.

Oh, dear, Andi thought. What could have upset Nila so much that she turned and left before Andi could press her for answers?

She looked at Luisa, who shrugged and busied herself with the tea things.

Jared was getting heavy. Andi decided she'd best face this unknown guest so she could set the baby down. Whoever she was, Andi couldn't help but be glad. This invitation meant a ride with Jared and time with her family.

Best of all, it was a chance for Riley to enjoy Nila's excellent cuisine. *Instead of whatever I can find for supper.*

Andi hiked Jared higher on her hip and pushed through the swinging door into the dining room. It wasn't far to the parlor, where she heard childish voices along with a woman's soft murmurs.

She picked up her pace and reached the parlor's open doorway in no time. Peeking around the corner, she greeted her mother.

"Andrea," Mother said, rising from the settee, "you were able to get away. I'm so pleased."

"Wyatt gave me the message, and you know I'll always grab the chance to ride over here with Jared." Andi paused to study the young woman sitting across from Mother. "Howdy. Wyatt said you wanted to visit with me, and Nila says I've met you before."

The woman did look vaguely familiar, but Andi couldn't place her. Light-brown hair done up in a stylish bun, light-brown eyes. Tall and willowy.

She's probably a student from Miss Whitaker's Academy, who has come for a visit, Andi decided. Though why any of the academy's older students would ever choose to visit Andrea Carter—er, *Prescott*—was a mystery. *Florence maybe?*

Andi paused. Her stay in San Francisco had occurred a long time ago. She couldn't remember many of the older girls' names. Nor did she want to. Most of them didn't want anything to do with the younger girls.

This woman appeared to be the right age. It looked as if she'd married young and done well, if her clothes were any indication of her status. She also appeared to be the mother of two children.

The little boys sat wide-eyed and silent on the couch beside the stranger. The older boy wore a sailor suit typical of city folks. He was about two years old. The other boy was a baby who looked to be Jared's age. He was dressed just like Andi's son, in a white baby gown.

The woman rose and stretched out a long, slender hand. "I'm happy to see you," she gushed. "Thank you so much for coming over."

Andi shifted Jared to her other hip. "And you are . . ."

The stranger smiled at Andi's uneasiness. "Forgive me, Andrea. It's been so long since I saw you last. I'm Felicity Bradford."

CHAPTER 2

Felicity Bradford? Who in the world was Felicity—

It clicked. Andi didn't recognize the name Bradford, but she would never forget the name Felicity. The past rose before Andi like a foggy nightmare. Her back began to tingle. How many stripes had this wretched girl given her all those years ago? Three? No, four. She remembered the searing pain of every one of them.

And how many lashes had Felicity laid on Andi's beloved mare, Taffy?

"Andrea." Mother's voice broke through her daughter's reverie.

She jerked back to the present and took Felicity's outstretched hand. It was warm and soft. "Oh, yes. Hello." She couldn't bring herself to say anything ridiculous like, *It's good to see you.*

It was *not* good to see Felicity.

Andi's heart picked up speed, and she felt a droplet of sweat slip down the back of her neck. What did she do now? What could she say without choking?

Jared saved the day. He fussed to be put down. The baby loved Mother's parlor. The carpet was soft and bright. He liked to sit in the middle of the room and pick at the bright red roses in the weave. He could never pull them into his mouth but trying kept him busy for at least ten minutes.

Andi set Jared on the floor. She lingered over him much longer than was polite, hoping to find words that could pass over her numb tongue and through her frozen lips.

None came to mind.

When Andi straightened and faced her unexpected visitor, Felicity was still smiling. "You're probably wondering why I'm here."

Mostly, I'm wondering when you will leave, Andi thought, ashamed. But she couldn't help her uncharitable mindset.

She counted backward. Eight years was a long time, but apparently not long enough to erase the horrible week she'd spent evading Felicity Livingston's cruel treatment and sharp tongue. What kind of mischief was she up to now?

Worse . . . why had she come here to haunt Andi after all these years?

Thankfully, Andi had grown up a great deal during the past few years and didn't spout the next words that came to her lips. Words like, "Get out of here" were safely held at bay.

"You don't have to speak every thought that comes to mind," the preacher had exhorted his flock just last Sunday during the service. He was working his way through the epistle of James, and Andi remembered his admonition. It wasn't a verse, exactly, but more like a principle. A good one.

Today it saved Andi a load of embarrassment.

She finally managed a response. "I *am* a bit surprised to see you here after all these years."

Felicity laughed.

The sound ripped through Andi. She winced inwardly. It was the same laugh she'd heard while being taunted on the Lazy L ranch.

"I am very sure you *are* surprised," Felicity said quietly. "An unpleasant surprise, no doubt."

She took the words right out of Andi's mouth.

During the introductions, Mother had slipped away, no doubt arranging for tea and cookies. When Luisa appeared in the doorway, Andi's guess was confirmed. She shifted quickly into hostess. "*Gracias*, Luisa. Put the tray on the coffee table, please."

That broke the ice. Felicity took her seat between her two little boys.

"Would you like tea?" Andi asked.

Felicity nodded.

Andi poured a cup, trying hard to keep her hands from shaking. "Sugar? Cream? Lemon?" She'd been taught how to play hostess even during the most difficult of visits, which this one was gearing up to be.

"Two lumps, please," Felicity replied politely.

Andi passed her the teacup, poured a cup for herself, and sat down. She glanced at Jared, who was lying on his back playing with his toes. What a sweet boy!

"Andrea."

Andi snapped her attention back to the young woman.

"I will get right to the heart of the matter. I've come here to try to right a horrific wrong from my past." Felicity took a deep breath and clasped her hands in her lap. "I am no longer the cruel and selfish sixteen-year-old who caused you such grief when you were a child. I've changed, and I deeply regret the wrongs I did to you." She paused and swallowed. "Could you ever find it in your heart to forgive me?"

If Felicity had just announced she was flying to the moon tomorrow, Andi would not have been more surprised. The question caught her off guard. She never imagined she would hear Felicity Livingston admitting she was wrong or sorry about *anything*.

Andi sat stock-still, stunned. *Please fuss, Jared*, she pleaded silently. *Cry. Do something, so I can use you as an excuse to move.*

Jared kicked his feet, rolled over, and smiled at his mama.

Even as Christ forgave you, so also do ye.

The verse echoed in Andi's head. She'd had plenty of practice forgiving people—her brothers a few years ago and her cousin Daniel—so the concept was still fresh. But forgive Felicity? She looked at her lap. *I can't.*

Yes, you can. God's gentle prodding slipped into her mind. *If you can forgive your family and especially Daniel for what happened to Taffy, you can forgive anyone. It's a choice you have to make.*

Andi bit her lip. True enough. She raised her head and looked Felicity full in her face. "Yes, Felicity. I choose to forgive you." She took a deep breath. "But it might take more time to *feel* that forgiveness. Thank you for asking."

Felicity blinked and brushed her hand across her cheeks. Clearly, she'd been afraid Andi might hold her actions against her for the rest of their lives. "Oh, I do thank you, Andrea. You can't know what a load you've taken off my conscience. My husband is a devoted Christ-follower, and he's been helping me learn ways to live out my new faith."

Andi's eyebrows shot up. Better and better. Well, maybe Felicity's confession was sincere, after all. If so, Andi might be able to call her a friend someday.

The baby seated next to Felicity set up a howl and started crawling into her lap. "This is Timothy," she explained. "He's eight months old. And Charles is two years. I'm married to Tobias Bradford. He pastors a large church in Bakersfield."

Could this day bring any more surprises? Felicity married to a preacher. Felicity a mother to a couple of handsome little boys.

The baby fussed louder. He sounded hungry. Andi had no idea what to offer him. Felicity's tight-fitting bodice was clearly not designed for easy access to feed a hungry baby.

"Oh, Timothy," she chided. "You're always hungry." She smiled. "Forgive me, Andrea. Let me get the boys settled."

Felicity handed Charles a cookie and fished around in a large carpet-bag that sat at her feet. An instant later, she drew out an oddly shaped glass bottle that held a length of rubber tubing inside. The tube ended in a nipple.

The baby went wild with joy and anticipation. He gurgled and clapped his hands. Felicity set the glass bottle in his lap. Timothy grabbed the nipple and popped it in his mouth, sucking greedily on the contents.

Andi was flabbergasted. Never in her life had she seen a baby drink out of a bottle. Bottles were for orphan calves. Or for lambs. Sometimes an orphan foal could be coaxed to accept this unnatural way of eating.

Just then, Jared let out a squall Andi recognized immediately. It was well past his lunch time. He crawled over to Andi and tried to pull him-self up by the folds of her split skirt.

"Hey, little man," Andi crooned, lifting him into her lap. "Do you want your lunch too?" Jared snuggled right down, wriggling in delight at the idea of his soon-to-be-filled belly.

Felicity sucked in a breath, and her cheeks flamed. "You don't . . ." She licked her lips. "I mean . . . surely not. You don't feed him yourself, do you?"

Andi looked at her blankly. "How else would he get fed?"

"My *dear* Andrea," Felicity said. "We live in modern times now. Only poor peasants feed their own babies." She pointed to the toddler. "Charles drank from a bottle right from birth, and now Timothy does too."

Andi peered at the clear liquid Timothy was slurping. "That doesn't look like milk to me."

Felicity laughed. "Bottles hold many kinds of nourishing fluids. He's having sugared water to hold him off until I can prepare his milk."

Sugared water? How could that possibly be good for a baby?

"Prepare his milk?" Andi frowned, stumped. "What kind of milk? Cow's milk? Goat's milk?" She'd heard tales of goat's milk saving babies' lives if their mother died, but Felicity was alive and well.

Maybe she knew something Andi didn't. "Do you have a cow in your backyard? Does someone milk her and pour it into that glass bottle?"

"Goodness no, Andrea!" Another peal of laughter.

Andi felt herself redden.

"I use canned milk, of course," Felicity explained. "It is all the rage for us modern mothers. Bottle feeding is the only way we women can keep our figures and not have to fiddle around with corsets and bodices and—"

She cleared her throat. "Well, this way I can feed the baby anywhere without . . ." Her voice trailed off. "As you can see, babies like Timothy can feed themselves with this small wonder. It's called 'The Little Cherub,' and it truly is."

Feed themselves? Where was the fun in that? Andi did not like the idea of handing over her precious baby to fend for himself. How would he get cuddled and rocked? She peeked down at her baby boy. He was sound asleep. Her heart squeezed in sympathy for the two little boys flanking Felicity.

"The bottles are easy to take care of too," Felicity said. "I read in *Mrs. Beeton's Household Management* book that I need only wash the nipples every two to three weeks." Her mouth turned down in a small pout. "Tobias doesn't agree, however. He has instructed our housekeeper to clean the nipples and tubing much more often."

Andi bit her lip. The thought of letting Jared suck on a stick he found outside was bad enough. How did a person wash out spoiled, leftover milk from that narrow tubing?

She did not ask. Instead, she tried to think of something nice to say. "The bottle does seem handy," she finally ventured. Felicity no doubt considered Andi a hayseed next to a pastor's highfalutin wife.

"It is," Felicity gushed. "I don't know what I would do without my Little Cherub."

There was no need to say anything more about feeding babies. Andi asked a question about Reverend Bradford's church, and Felicity prattled on for the rest of the afternoon.

Riley arrived just before supper, and Andi made all the proper introductions. Thankfully, Mother called them for the meal soon afterward. Supper could not end soon enough for Andi. She was polite but relieved when Riley announced he needed to get back to the ranch to finish up the evening chores.

Andi bid Felicity a forced but pleasant good-bye, and she and Riley took Jared home.

Riley remained quiet most of the way back to Memory Creek. He knew the history of Andi's tragic adventure as a young girl, and he'd never had a high opinion of selfish Miss Felicity Livingston. "I'm happy to learn she's come to Christ and has turned over a new leaf," he told Andi, nudging Dakota closer to Shasta so they could talk.

"I'm glad too," Andi replied.

She *was* glad, although she and Felicity would never become close friends. For one thing, Bakersfield was over one hundred miles away. *Thank goodness.*

Andi breathed a sigh of relief. It was enough to accept Felicity's apologetic embrace and realize her own willingness to forgive her old enemy had gone a long way toward giving them both a good day.

She prayed fervently that today's visit would close the door on Felicity Livingston Bradford once and for all.

Historical Note

The Little Cherub bottle of the Victorian Era (19th century) was also called Mummie's Darling, the Princess, and the Alexandria. However, this banjo-shaped, hard-to-clean glass bottle became known as the "murder bottle," and rightly so. Nobody knew much about hygiene back then, but it didn't take a lot of knowledge to figure out that the narrow tubing and the shape of the bottle made it nearly impossible to keep clean. Doctors condemned their use, but mothers continued to use them for decades. Is it any wonder that half of all babies born during this era did not live to see their first birthday? The "murder bottle" stands guilty as one of the causes for these deaths.

Memory Creek Ranch, April 1888

It hasn't been easy going from being a daughter of the wealthiest ranching family in California to struggling to make ends meet on our own ranch.

CHAPTER 1

Two more weeks. That's what the calendar told her. "I must have been out of my mind to give in to Riley and Chad like that," Andi berated herself.

"It's good money," Riley had convinced her ten days ago. "I'm not sure how I'm going to pay Joey, Matt, and Carlos this month unless I take Chad up on his offer."

Andi winced hearing the truth. Life would have been a lot easier if Riley had stayed on permanently as Chad's foreman. It wasn't as if big brother hadn't offered her husband the position. He had, more than once. Occasionally, Chad begged.

Riley was happy to supplement their income with part-time work on the Circle C, but he was unwilling to trade his independence on their own Memory Creek for a secure foreman's position. The downside of this picture-perfect ranch was all the hard work for so little return.

And the bills must be paid.

"But a cattle drive to San Diego?" Andi had moaned.

"Ramrodding for Chad is an honor," Riley insisted. "He promised me a tidy sum if I'd do it. Mitch has too many irons in the fire these days to go along."

"Chad trusts you," Andi said. "I know how important it is to have a trusted second-in-command." Boy, did she know! The one cattle drive Andi had begged to be included on had nearly ended in disaster five years ago.

"I'll bring home enough money from this one trail drive to keep us through the rest of the year, including wages for the men. We have three hands now, you know." He winked.

"I know."

So, it was settled. Riley left the ranch in his wife's capable hands and drove two dozen of their own steers toward the Circle C on the first day of April. Andi had pasted a smile on her face and waved good-bye, hiking nine-month-old Jared higher on her hip.

"It's going to be a long month," she muttered as he disappeared between the hills.

"You can always stay with your mother and Ellie if it gets too lonely out here. The cowhands can look after things," Riley had suggested when he prepared to leave ten days ago.

Now, with two weeks left before his return—maybe longer if the cattle drive hit a snag—Andi considered his idea. Another spring rainstorm was keeping her indoors with nothing to do and nothing to look forward to except more cloudy, soggy days.

Yet, run home to Mother just because she was bored? Andi set her jaw. "I can't."

A tickle in the back of the grown-up part of her mind told her she was in charge. Matt consulted her every couple of days. Carlos kept her appraised about the milk cow and the cookshack supplies. And Joey?

Their new young cowhand couldn't remember where he left his lasso half the time and needed Andi's firm direction.

Being a rancher's wife was a sight more work than being a rancher's daughter . . . or a rancher's sister.

At least she didn't have to leave Jared alone in order to tend the chores. The men banded together to keep "Miz Prescott" supplied with fresh eggs and milk. They cleaned the chicken coop, checked that the new colts and fillies were safe in their paddocks, and looked after the rest of the livestock. Joey made sure she always had stove wood stacked neatly on the back porch. All that on top of their regular ranch duties.

In return, Andi baked pies for the faithful hands.

Matt returned an empty pie tin one late Saturday afternoon. "If ya don't mind, the boys and me are thinkin' of headin' to town. The weather's cleared up some, and most of the chores are done." He pulled off his wide-brimmed hat and twisted it around and around in his large, rough hands. "Carlos milked the cow a little early."

"Why should I mind?" Andi asked in surprise. "You boys have outdone yourselves keeping up this place. I've barely had to lift a finger. Riley will be pleased when I tell him."

"Shucks, ma'am," Matt said, reddening. "Ain't no trouble a'tall. We promised the boss we'd look after you and the young'un."

"You three go on and have a good time." Andi paused. A sudden, horrible thought came to mind. Did they want their pay? She scrambled to think if any payroll dollars were left in the lock box. "Do you need—"

"No, ma'am," Matt interrupted. "The boss paid us a bit to tide us over 'til he gets back from the drive."

Andi gave Matt a sunny, relieved smile. "Wonderful. Well, then, goodbye. Will you be back by morning to milk, or shall I? I do know how to milk a cow, feed the horses, and even collect the eggs," she teased.

Matt chuckled. "Ah, Miz Prescott, don't worry none about that. We'll be back in plenty o' time. Can we fetch you anything from town?"

"No, thanks. I'm fine." Andi shut the door and returned to ironing the baby's gowns. It didn't take long, and Jared woke up from his nap soon afterward. She took him outside to enjoy a little sunshine and sit on Shasta for a few minutes.

The late afternoon sun shone down bright and hot, but new clouds were piling up behind the foothills. Andi could just see their fluffy tops. The wind was picking up too.

She sighed. "Another rainy evening."

Andi knew she should welcome these rare spring storms. They had turned Memory Creek ranch green and lush, and more rain would keep the rangeland that way. The new calves and foals grew quickly with all the rich, fresh fodder.

"Rain as much as you like," she hollered at the clouds.

It wasn't until nightfall, when the rain started coming down in torrents, that Andi changed her mind about welcoming the rain. How lonely it was out here in the dark by herself during a storm! She jumped at an unexpected clap of thunder. "Just what I need," she said with a shaky laugh. "A thunderstorm on top of everything else."

Thankfully, Jared didn't wake up. She peeked at him, added another blanket, and then quietly closed the bedroom door behind her.

Another boom of thunder and a loud thumping sound sent Andi's heart into her throat. She turned up all four lamps in the sitting room. Shadows vanished, dispelling some of her fears. "I'm a wife and a mother now," she told herself firmly. "I won't let a little thunder and lightning scare me like they did when I was a child."

She sat down in the rocking chair and pulled the lamp closer. Her fingers trembled as she reached for the Bible and her nightly reading.

Thump, thump. Thump, thump, thump.

The noise set Tucker growling and plunged Andi into another bout of worry. *I will trust and not be afraid. I will trust and not be afraid.* "Shh," she scolded the dog. "It's just the wind blowing the stove wood across the porch."

Tucker lay down at Andi's command but stayed alert.

So did Andi. She stayed so alert that she knew she would not sleep a wink until the hands returned later tonight and retired to the bunkhouse. Or until the storm passed, but it might last all night.

More thumping and then a loud banging propelled Andi from the rocking chair. Her heart slammed against the inside of her chest. That was no storm. Nor was it the random sounds of stove wood rolling across the porch. She found the rifle Riley always kept loaded and tiptoed through the dimly lit kitchen.

Bang, bang, bang. "Anybody home?" a weak voice called.

Tucker growled.

"Help . . . please . . ."

Andi heard a thud, like someone collapsing to the porch floor, and then everything was still.

CHAPTER 2

He blew back into my life like an unwanted whirlwind.

With shaking hands, Andi unbolted the back door and opened it a crack. Rain pattered the porch roof like drumbeats. The wind whistled. A dark mound lay curled up on the porch, covered by a soaking wet rain poncho.

Andi waited while Tucker slipped through the opening to investigate. He circled the pile of soaked outerwear then looked up at Andi.

Taking Tucker's reaction as a good sign, she leaned the rifle up against the counter, lit a lantern, and stepped outside. The wind immediately whipped her hair in all directions so that she could barely see.

Andi wished with all her heart that the men had not gone into town tonight. Given a choice, she would have stepped over the huddled figure and raced to the bunkhouse for help. But that choice was no longer available, especially when the pale-yellow lantern light showed more than just mud and water. A dark pool had formed under the heap of clothing.

Blood?

The pile moved.

Andi jumped backward, clutching her housecoat around her middle. "Who are you?" she demanded. "Where did you come from? What are you doing on my porch?"

There was no answer, at least none that Andi could make out. The pile of rags moaned softly and struggled to speak. "Help . . . me."

Andi was conflicted. The last time she had helped an injured stranger, the wounded but friendly TJ Silver had transformed into con artist Troy Swanson, her despicable brother-in-law. Andi had been cured forever from wanting to help another injured man like Troy.

But here she was again, only this time Andi had no one to advise her. She could not go after Riley or Chad. They were hundreds of miles away. She couldn't call for the cowhands or even for Mother or Mitch.

She also knew she couldn't leave the stranger lying outside on her porch. He would surely die, probably before the night was out, if she did not bring him inside.

Andi shivered. *Inside my home, where my baby is sleeping.*

It was a shame this filthy, injured man could not make it to the barn. She would gladly offer him shelter, so long as he stayed far away from her, but it was clear he had no strength.

With a quick prayer for wisdom and courage, Andi put the lantern down and dragged the man over the threshold. It was surprisingly easy. The rain and blood made him slippery.

Once inside, she slammed the door shut and stepped back. *Now what?* She couldn't stay here alone, not with this strange man lying on her kitchen floor. She must take Jared and go to the Circle C to bring back help.

Another boom of thunder told Andi she was stuck here, at least until morning. She took two deep breaths to still her racing heart and realized this injured stranger was no danger to her or to her baby. He could barely move.

Questions flooded Andi's mind. *What happened? Who are you? How did you make your way miles from nowhere to my ranch? Do you have a horse?*

"What happened?" Andi asked, swallowing hard. It was the question foremost on her mind.

"Shot," the stranger managed from his prone position. "The bullet went in and out, but the blood . . ." His voice trailed off.

Andi squatted next to the soaked pile of man and rags. "Mister, wake up." She shook his shoulder. "You can't stay here. You have to—"

"You said you'd help me if I ever needed it." The wounded man raised his head. He sucked in a shallow, painful breath and looked Andi in the eyes. "Little lady, I need help *now.*" His head dropped to the floor and he passed out.

Andi shot to her feet and backed away, nearly crashing into the table. A wave of dizziness threatened to overwhelm her. She clutched the table's edge to steady herself.

The man had lost consciousness before he told Andi his name, but she didn't need him to. She knew exactly who he was.

Jed Hatton.

———

The dark hours passed at a snail's pace. Andi stirred the cookstove to life and boiled a kettle of water. She rummaged through her rag basket and found enough clean strips to stuff into the bullet holes and hopefully staunch the copious flow of blood.

She had treated bullet wounds before, but knowing she held this man's life in her hands made her weak with worry. What if the bleeding would not stop? What if he died?

Good riddance! Chad's would-be reaction echoed loud and clear in

Andi's mind. *That criminal has lived on borrowed time long enough. Let him meet his Maker.*

Maybe Chad would say that, but would he be right? Should she let Jed die? He was certainly guilty of many crimes. Like a bad penny, this rough outlaw kept turning up in Andi's life. It wasn't enough that he'd used her as a hostage when she was just a child. Jed had also been part of the Mexican Procopio's band when she and Lucy had been kidnapped three years ago.

Would Jed never go away?

Andi shook her head. As much as she wanted to let the outlaw die, it was the law's job to carry out the verdict, not hers. She would tend Jed . . . and then turn him in.

Strengthened by the knowledge that she would do what she could and leave the rest to the Almighty, Andi rolled Jed over and began to peel away the layers of muddy coverings. It didn't take long to discover the source of the bleeding. Just as Jed had said, the bullet had gone clean through a belly wound on his left side. Blood oozed from both openings.

Andi closed her eyes, breathed deeply, and began to wash away the filth, the dried blood, and the sweat. Jed coughed, and blood spurted from the bullet holes. She pressed clean rags on the wounds and held them firmly in place.

Then she remembered the yarrow plants out back. Soaking wet, their leaves and flowers worked wonders to stop bleeding. Right now, the wild foliage covered the Sierra foothills in a yellow blanket.

Andi grabbed the lantern and darted outside in her housecoat. It took only a few minutes to pull handfuls, but she returned to the house dripping wet and shivering. She found a spare housecoat and went to work on Jed.

Andi loosened his clothing and covered the bloody holes with yarrow and clean rags. Then she wrapped Jed's belly in long strips to hold everything in place. As a final touch to her inept nursing skills, Andi found a pillow and a blanket.

She settled the wounded man on the floor and sat back on her heels, drained. "It's the best I can do," she said. *Lord Jesus, keep him alive according to Your will.*

She didn't expect a response, but she was mistaken.

"Much . . . obliged." Jed's soiled fingers made their way to Andi's hand and gave it a weak squeeze. Then his fingers loosened, and he fell into a deep sleep.

Andi stayed by the outlaw's side until she made sure he would not bleed to death all over her kitchen floor. The yarrow and tight rags had done the trick, however. It wasn't long before Jed's pale face began to show a flush of color.

"Thank God," Andi breathed a grateful prayer. "And thank You for keeping Jared asleep."

The baby didn't often sleep through the night. He was a hungry, growing boy, but tonight was clearly the exception. Andi felt weak with relief. Jared would have distracted her from what needed to be done.

She took time to thoroughly wash her hands, remove her soiled housecoat, and change into a clean nightgown. Then she checked Jed Hatton once more, turned down the lamps, and tiptoed to her room.

Jared lay sound asleep in his crib. His rosebud lips made noisy sucking motions, then his face twisted into an expression Andi knew well. He was getting ready to wake up and demand to be fed.

Before he cried, Andi lifted the baby from his blankets and tucked him into bed beside her. Even if he wasn't hungry, she wanted to keep Jared close by for the rest of this topsy-turvy night.

Andi knew she wouldn't sleep. Cuddling her baby would give her a chance to rest, pray, and think of what in the world she would do about the injured outlaw tomorrow.

CHAPTER 3

I'm pretty sure Jed Hatton and I are remembering the same events somewhat differently.

Light was streaming through her bedroom window when Andi awoke the next morning. With a start, she sat up in bed. Her gaze immediately went to Jared, who slept on.

"I can't believe I fell asleep." She stroked Jared's cheek and listened. The house was silent, except for the rooster's early crowing. Relief flooded Andi. The storm must have ended during the night. She could send one of the cowhands to the Circle C or ride over herself.

Andi slipped from her bed and changed into her favorite work clothes, a plaid shirt and dark split skirt. The skirt fell just below her knees, giving her plenty of room to move and keep from tripping. Her fingers flew, plaiting her dark, waist-length hair into a long braid, which she carelessly flung behind her shoulder.

Although she itched to check on her injured guest, Andi took time to pile pillows on either side of Jared to keep him from rolling out of bed. She pressed a kiss to his blond, wavy hair. "I'll be right back, little man."

Making her way from the bedroom, Andi passed through the sitting room and into the kitchen. Jed Hatton lay on the floor exactly where she had left him. Tucker sat close by, not moving. When he saw Andi, his tail thumped twice. Then he returned to guard duty.

Andi caught her breath. Was Jed Hatton alive? She watched his chest barely rise and fall. Yes, he was alive, at least for the time being. Andi let out the breath she'd been holding.

Moooo.

Andi turned her attention away from the injured man and looked out the kitchen window. Rosie was bawling to be milked. Where were those ranch hands? They should have returned from town by now.

The cow bellowed again, more insistent. Andi grabbed a pail off the counter and headed outside. "Matt!" she hollered. "Carlos! Joey!" Had they spent the night in Fresno?

No answer. Andi didn't take the time to ponder why the hired help had not come home. She milked Rosie and turned her out to graze. Collecting the eggs could wait. She hated leaving Jared alone for even a minute.

Loud wails and frantic barking greeted Andi when she entered the kitchen. "Jared!" She set the pail on the counter, leaped over Jed, and raced to the bedroom.

Despite the care she'd taken, Jared had awakened and crawled up and over the pillows—and right out of bed. An angry-red bump showed on his forehead. He sat on the throw rug, screaming at the top of his lungs. "*Mamama!*"

Tucker circled Jared, whining and yipping. The poor dog seemed at a loss to know what to do.

"Quiet, Tucker," she commanded. Then she picked Jared up and consoled him. "Shh. Mama's here." She changed his diaper and gown, snuggled him close to feed him, and afterward carried him into the kitchen. Tucker stayed close at her heels.

"Mornin', little lady."

Andi stopped short. Jed sat at the table, pale and drawn. His arms leaned heavily against the tabletop, holding himself upright. His teeth clamped down on his lower lip.

He's in pain, Andi thought. "How did you—"

"Don't wanna lie on the floor like a dog," Jed said between gritted teeth. "Figured I could at least make it to a sittin' position." He sounded proud of himself. "Don't s'pose you got any whiskey 'round here."

Andi shook her head. "Even if I did, I wouldn't give it to *you*." The thought of a drunken outlaw terrified her.

Jed managed a weak smile. "Still spunky, ain't ya?"

More frightened than she cared to admit, Andi plopped Jared into his wooden high chair and gave him a hunk of dry toast from yesterday. He grabbed it and started gnawing, perfectly content to stare at the strange man sitting at his mama's kitchen table.

Unbidden tears sprang to Andi's eyes. The enormity of this situation threatened to engulf her. She whirled on Jed. "What are you doing here?"

Jed laid one hand against his wounded belly. "Lookin' for you."

"What?" Andi snapped. "Why?" It was either snap or sob, and she chose the former. "When you helped me get away from Benita back at the camp, I promised to say a good word at your trial, *not* tend your wounds or hide you from the law."

"It ain't the law that's after me, little lady."

"Don't call me that!"

Jed nodded. "As you like. Actually, I wanna turn myself in. I been runnin' too long."

"Fine. I'll ride into town right now and get Justin."

"No!" Jed's bloodshot eyes widened.

Jared whimpered.

Andi shushed him gently, turned back to Jed, and clenched her fists. "Do you think you can stop me? You're trussed up and weaker than a newborn filly from loss of blood."

"I ain't foolin', Andrea. You can't leave this house." He paused. "And if you got any hired help, they'd best stick to the bunkhouse and not show their faces."

The fear in Jed's voice froze her blood. Fear for whom? Himself? Did he think she would run off and let him die? No, it must be something else. Was he afraid for *her*?

"The hands went to town yesterday," she whispered, catching his fear, "but they're not back yet."

Andi collapsed into the other chair, spent. "Please tell me. I've already been outside. I milked the cow. What's going on? Why can't I leave? And why are you so afraid?"

CHAPTER 4

Jed didn't answer. One minute he was supporting himself against the tabletop. The next minute his body slumped, and he slowly began to slide off the chair.

Andi caught Jed just in time and steadied him until he could catch his breath. "You've got to lie down," she told him.

"Not . . . the floor," he pleaded.

"This way." Andi strained to support the heavy man across the kitchen and into the main room. Nearly collapsing under his weight, she let him drop onto the settee.

"Much obliged," Jed muttered before passing out.

Every nerve screamed at Andi to grab Jared and get away. Gallop to the Circle C. Chad wasn't there, but Mitch was. Sid too, plus a dozen ranch hands who had not gone on the cattle drive. They would all be eager to apprehend Jed Hatton.

I ain't foolin', Andrea. You can't leave this house. Jed's ominous warning returned, shattering Andi's intentions to run to the Circle C. She frowned at the sick, filthy man lying on her settee.

"All right, Mr. Jed Hatton," she whispered. "I won't leave until you wake up and tell me what on earth is going on."

Andi stayed indoors. A feeling she couldn't explain underscored Jed's warning. She peeked through the curtains every so often but saw nothing out of the ordinary.

No ranch hands either. Where in the world could they be?

After breakfast, Jared crawled around, played with his blocks and soft toys, and pestered the dog. During the baby's morning nap, Andi cooked broth, hoping Jed would soon come around. She figured he was too ornery to lie abed longer than a few hours.

Jed woke up just before noon and pushed himself high enough to guzzle the hot broth Andi brought him. "It's right tasty, little la—" He caught himself. "Andrea."

Andi dragged the hassock close to the settee and sat down. The baby was sleeping. It was time to get to the bottom of this before Jed drifted off for another nap, or before Jared needed her attention. "I want to know, Mr. Hatton—"

"Jed," he corrected, slurping down the last few drops.

"Fine. I want to know, Jed, what you are doing here. This is not an easy ranch to find. I also want to know who shot you and why I can't leave my house." She drew a deep breath. "Is it some new plan to rob me? Or kidnap me and my son?"

Andi would not allow either plan to succeed. Riley's rifle beckoned her. If Jed tried any funny business, she would finish the job someone else had started.

"No." Jed burst into hacking coughs. The last drop of broth must have lodged in his windpipe. His face twisted in agony before the spell passed. "I came to warn you, little lady"—he ignored Andi's furious look—"but gettin' shot slowed me down." He shook his head. "Now, it's mos' likely too late."

"Warn me about what?"

"Not *what*," Jed corrected. "*Who*. Mateo Vega."

"Vega?" Andi's thoughts spun. "He's dead. I shot him." She squeezed her eyes shut. "I shot him at close range and didn't miss." After that she had flung the derringer far and wide and run for her life.

Her eyes opened. "You're mistaken."

"Ain't no mistake about it," Jed insisted. "Vega's comin' for you. I've known it for some time. He won't stop 'til you're dead, girl. Don't you get it?"

No, she didn't. "But why?" Her voice cracked.

"Vega hates you with a burnin' hatred. You and that Ramón fella tricked him. He don't like being made a fool of, and he's got a long memory. It didn't take much figurin' to learn where you live. You're a Carter. Your family's all over the place. A few questions here. A coin there. People talk."

"How did he put Ramón and Riley together . . ." Andi's words trailed off as a memory unfolded. Vega, holding her in a crushing grip and telling her to scream all she wanted. The imposter would not come to her aid.

The air left Andi's lungs as the memory clicked into place. She had screamed Riley's name. "Oh, no," she whispered.

"'Fraid so, little lady." Jed nodded. "Those left in camp saw you ride off with him that night. Vega learned that you and Ramón got hitched. He knows you have a son."

Andi's heart pounded against the inside of her chest. "But why now? It's been three years."

Her thoughts twirled faster than a tornado. Procopio had been shot dead. Benita had fled. Nobody was left of that outlaw camp. The sheriff had assured Andi that those who escaped justice had scurried back to Mexico, never to return.

Jared woke up just then. Andi shot up from the hassock. She couldn't pick up her baby fast enough. Her whole body shook as she changed his diaper and sat down to feed him. Rocking back and forth on the bed, she blinked back anxious tears.

Oh, dear God, Andi prayed silently. *Riley's not here to protect us. I don't know what to do. Please, show me. How can I save Jared and myself?*

When she returned to the sitting room with Jared, she expected to find Jed out cold, but he lay propped up in silence, watching her. She sat down on the hassock.

"Three years ain't that long," Jed said, answering Andi's question as if she'd never left the room. "Not when a fella's plannin' revenge." He scratched at his scruffy whiskers. "I didn't stick around after I shot Benita. I got outta camp before the posse raided it. But most of those scoundrels got away, including Vega. I heard he crawled back to Mexico and laid low for a couple of years. That belly wound you gave him took months to heal. It still bothers him. He carries the pain around every live-long day. It fires his hate."

Andi wrapped her arms around Jared and held him tight. He squirmed and squealed, wanting to be free. She finally set him down, and he gave her a wide, drooly smile.

"Fine lookin' young'un." Jed fixed Jared with a protective gaze. "Wouldn't want nothin' bad to happen to you and the boy." He looked at Andi. "Or to your fella."

Andi's fists curled in her lap. "Tell me what Vega's planning and how you know about it."

Jed nodded. "You know the sayin' that 'birds of a feather flock together'? Well, I can't seem to keep myself outta trouble. A few months back, I took up with some of Vega's old crew. We did odd jobs, robbed a few stage-coaches. Felt like old times." He paused.

Andi steamed. Old times, indeed. "Go on," she forced out between clenched teeth.

"That's how I found out about Vega's plans. Scared me spitless. That snake is purt-near as crafty as the first one in the Garden. Smooth talker, but pure evil."

He drew a deep breath. "He's gunnin' for you and your man, little lady. When you're dead, he plans to take your baby and disappear over the border. He's got some kinda deal with Benita."

Andi cried out, startling Jared, who burst into tears. She left her place on the hassock and snatched him up. "I have to get to the Circle C. I can't stay here."

Jed sat up, then fell back against the settee. "You *can't.* That's what I'm tryin' to tell you. I meant to get here a couple of days ago and make sure y'all made it to your folks' fancy spread. But I got bushwhacked. Purty sure it was Vega's *compadres.* It put me in a real hurry to find you. It also tells me that Vega's men are watchin' this place. It's the only explanation for why your hired help ain't back. I don't know where your fella is, but if he shows up, he's a dead man."

Andi sat back down. "He's ramrodding a cattle drive with my brother and their hands."

Jed nodded. "Good. He's safe for now. But your hired help either got waylaid or . . ." His words trailed away.

"Or they're *dead,*" Andi finished in horror. Her empty stomach turned over. She'd forgotten to eat breakfast. She closed her eyes and cried out, "What do I do, Lord?"

Jed reached out a dirty hand and patted Andi's knee. "Not to worry, little lady. I got a plan."

CHAPTER 5

Jed's words did not instill confidence in Andi. This wounded, weaker-than-a-kitten outlaw had a plan? "What sort of half-baked plan might that be?" she blurted.

Jed gave her a pain-filled grin, taking no offense at her sassy retort. "You ain't changed a bit, little lady."

Andi rolled her eyes, giving up on Jed Hatton's worn-out way of addressing her.

"You are still the spunkiest little gal I ever laid eyes on. I remember when you was just a young'un, sittin' on that horse. Mad enough to spit nails, and me holdin' that pistol on you." He chuckled, which made him wince and clutch his belly.

Andi ducked her head. "That was a long time ago."

"It was *yesterday*," Jed said softly. "I ain't never forgot you and your spunky ways. That's why I couldn't let Benita hurt you back at Procopio's camp, and that's why I ain't gonna let Vega kill you now or take your baby."

Andi looked up. Jed held her gaze. His eyes were glassy. Was it from fever or tears? She looked at her lap to spare him embarrassment. This conversation was getting far too personal.

Jed was not finished. "Sometimes, little lady, on those long, lonely days wanderin' from one part of the country to another, I thought about gettin' myself hitched. I was hopin' I might get me a daughter who grew up to be just like you." He sighed. "But I never got 'round to it."

Andi squirmed. What could she say to that? Never in her wildest dreams could she imagine herself as the daughter of a thieving, murdering, hostage-taking outlaw. And who would marry such a man? She couldn't say what she was thinking, so she smiled brightly and said, "I'll get you some more broth."

When she returned with the broth, Jed was asleep.

———

Jed Hatton would not explain his plan to get Andi and Jared out of this dangerous fix. When she prodded, he clamped his dry, cracked lips together and shook his head. "Not to worry," he kept insisting. "I got a plan."

But Andi *did* worry. The day dragged until she demanded, "What are these ruffians of yours waiting for? If they know I'm here, what's the holdup?"

Jed shrugged. He had lost some of his enthusiasm for talk and looked as if he was feeling worse than this morning. Andi laid a hand across his forehead and found it warm to the touch.

"They're waitin' for Vega." Jed eyed her. "He'll skin his *compadres* alive if he doesn't get to personally take care of you himself. I reckon his men are only watchin' to make sure you don't leave."

Everything inside Andi curled into a ball of dread. *Oh, Riley! Will I ever see you again? If Vega kills me, will you ever see Jared again?*

Jed dozed off and on the rest of the afternoon.

Andi worked her way through chores she'd put off for weeks. She threw her whole heart into mending Riley's shirts. She stirred cornmeal into boiling water for something to eat, and then she scrubbed the kitchen floor. She washed away the dirt, mud, and blood from the spot where Jed had spent last night.

One time when she peeked out the kitchen window, a saddled sorrel horse walked by, cropping grass. Jed's horse. The gelding didn't appear to be suffering under his saddle, so she let him be. Did she have a choice?

Jed's warning had driven spikes of fear into Andi's belly whenever she thought about stepping foot outside. Thank goodness Shasta and the other horses were out on the range these bright spring days. The mares and foals were secure in their paddocks with rich fodder and plenty of water. The cow needed milking, but something told Andi that Rosie's udder would have to stay full this evening.

When Jed roused, the western sun was dipping lower in the sky. He appeared to have regained his strength. "Where's that dog of yours?" he asked, looking around.

"Tucker," Andi called.

Wagging his tail, Tucker came out from the bedroom. With Riley gone, the dog always slept on the rug near his master's bed.

"Does he have a collar?" Jed asked gruffly.

Andi nodded. She opened her mouth to ask why, but Jed glared at her. "Get it. The dog is part of my plan." He drew a short breath. "I need paper, pencil, and string too."

Andi complied wordlessly. What was he up to?

By the time dusky shadows settled over the ranch, Jed had written a note, wrapped the scrap of paper around Tucker's collar, and tied it up with a piece of string. "There. Call it a wild guess, but I reckon this-here dog is smarter than he looks."

"He is," Andi agreed. "Tucker followed us to Procopio's camp. Then he led Riley, the sheriff, and his posse back to the secret hideout."

Jed double-checked to make sure the string was securely fastened. "I figured. There's no chance your fella found that camp on his own." He smiled. "Let's see if your dog can find the Circle C."

Andi's eyebrows shot up. "What did you write?"

"Ain't your worry, little lady. Just tell the dog to hightail it to the Circle C. I got a feelin' Vega will be here soon."

Shivers exploded up and down Andi's arms. What did Jed mean when he said it was not her worry? This entire affair revolved around her and Jared. The look on Jed's face warned her not to ask questions.

She knelt beside Tucker, hugged him, and led him to the back door. "Find Mitch," she commanded, pushing open the screen door.

Tucker wagged his tail and yipped.

"Mitch. Now!" She pointed toward the hills. "Go."

Tucker leaped off the porch and was soon out of sight. Whatever the note said, her family would soon know about it. Hopefully, it said, *Come to Memory Creek, guns blazing.*

No, that was folly. Anybody approaching the ranch would be picked off in the same way Jed had been. Maybe that's why he chose a small, fast dog to slip between the rolling hills. Some might even mistake Tucker for a coyote.

No matter how hard Andi pressed, Jed would not disclose the contents of the note. She finally gave up, fed Jared and herself the cornmeal mush, and put the baby to bed. Then she returned to the kitchen to clean up.

"Andrea."

She crossed to the sitting room, wiping her hands on a dish towel. The sun had set, and shadows from the dimly lit lamps danced on the walls. Jed's face looked gray. He lay weakly against the settee's pillows.

"Are you feeling all right?" she asked.

He ignored her question and pointed to the kitchen. "Go back to the kitchen and dump the rest of the broth down the drain. Then stow whatever's left of supper. Make it look like you haven't been cookin'."

"But—"

"Do it!"

Andi whirled at Jed's rough command and did what he said. While she was sweeping up the last of the crumbs, she noticed the rifle. It was leaning against the counter near the back door, exactly where she'd left it the night before. It might come in handy, just in case.

The clattering of horses' hooves galloping up the drive sent Andi's heart to her throat. Whoever the riders were, they were coming *here*, and they were coming fast. She dropped the broom and snatched up the rifle.

"Horses," she exclaimed, tearing into the sitting room.

Jed appeared more alert than she'd seen him all day. He put a finger to his lips and motioned her to his side. "I'm only gonna say this once, so listen and do exactly what I tell you. No questions asked." His eyes pleaded with her to obey.

Andi bit her lip and nodded.

Jed glanced at the rifle. "That piece of iron is your last resort. Vega ain't comin' alone. Hopefully, you won't need it, but you can keep it if it makes you feel better."

Andi clutched the barrel. It made her feel a *lot* better.

"Now, little lady," Jed whispered. "Go into your room, pick up your baby, and slide under the bed as far back as you can go. Then keep that young'un quiet."

Andi stared at Jed, stunned. *This* was the big plan? Was he out of his mind? Keeping Jared quiet was not a problem. He was down for the night, but how was hiding under the bed a good idea?

"I'll take care of Vega," Jed said. "Trust me." When Andi hesitated, he sat up and jabbed a finger toward the bedroom. "Go. Now! And no matter what you hear, don't come out."

Andi backed up. *Trust him*, a little voice said in her head.

She turned and fled.

CHAPTER 6

Jared made whimpering noises, but Andi managed to get them both under the bed without too much trouble. It was a tight fit. Her shoulders scraped the bedstead overhead, and she could barely turn over. She kept her shirt loose in case she needed to quiet Jared in a hurry.

The rifle lay just beyond her fingertips. Jed was right. It was useless from under here.

Crash!

A door flew open, banging against the wall. Front door? Kitchen door? Andi didn't know, and she couldn't see a thing. It was pitch black in this cramped, stuffy cave. The quilt coverlet touched the floor on both sides of the bed. She strained her ears to hear what was going on.

Somebody had broken into her home. Judging by the stomping, more invaders than one evil Mexican outlaw had joined the raid.

Crash!

The heavy kitchen table had surely been overturned. More crashing . . . loud banging . . . then the tinkling of a thousand pieces of glass.

Andi winced. How many windows had they broken? She cuddled Jared closer, praying the commotion would not awaken him. If he cried, all was lost.

A curse cut through the sounds of destruction, then a shout in Spanish for *mas luz*, more light.

"*Ven aquí, Vega. Encontré a Jed.*"

Andi caught her breath. They had found Jed and were calling Vega into the house. She sent up a prayer for his safety, and for her own.

"*¿Dónde está ella?*" When Jed didn't tell them where Andi was, the sound of a brutal slap resounded through the house. "*¡Dígame!*"

Jed moaned. "I don't know."

"*¡Dígame!*" Vega shrieked, insisting again that Jed tell him.

Andi heard the dull thud of a fist against flesh and Jed's breath whooshing out. She bit her lip to keep from screaming.

"I swear, Vega, I don't know. She ain't here."

Vega cursed his *compadres* then screamed, "Did you not watch her?"

"*Sí, jefe*. We saw her this morning. She went in and out of the barn with a pail."

Andi paled. Vega's men had seen her. They could have killed her right then.

A ripping sound broke into Andi's thoughts. "I see that the wildcat tended your injuries, *señor*," Vega said. "She *is* here. Where have you hidden her?"

Jed groaned. "No, Vega. She's gone. I don't know where."

"*¡Eso es imposible, jefe!*" Vega's *compadre* sounded scared.

He was right. It was impossible that Andi could have left without Vega's men seeing her. Her throat went dry with fear. They would find her if they searched long enough.

"This . . . evening," Jed wheezed. "She left just . . . before dusk. Dressed in gray." He coughed and fell silent.

"Search the barn," Vega snapped. "The bunkhouse. The outhouse. Turn them all upside down." He lowered his voice until Andi could barely hear. "I shall have her, *señor*. If you value your life, you will tell me where she went." Another blow. More slaps.

"All right," Jed wheezed. "No more. I'll tell you."

Andi held her breath. *No! Please no!*

Jed coughed and wheezed. "I tried to keep her here. Told her your men would catch her. But she left. I couldn't stop her, not laid up like this."

For the first time since those animals had invaded her home, Andi heard silence. Vega seemed to be pondering.

His *compadres* returned out of breath. "We searched everywhere, *jefe*. The bunkhouse is deserted. The barn is empty."

"She is not lurking in the outhouse either," another man added.

"It hasn't been that long," Jed rasped. "A few minutes before . . . before you came tearin' inside."

"We would have seen her," one of the men insisted.

"You think so . . . *compadre*?" Jed's words were growing softer. "That . . . little gal probably knows every trail and hidden path for miles around. This is her ranch." He sucked in a breath. "Betcha she snuck out . . . right under your noses. Grabbed a horse from a back paddock and rode off."

Vega swore at his men. "*¡Estupidos!*"

Yes, you're all stupid, Andi agreed. *And dangerous.*

"Where did she go?" Vega barked. "Tell me now, or I will kill you."

Jed coughed. "The Circle C."

"You are certain of this?"

"Where else would she go? It's the . . . only safe place for . . . thousands of acres," Jed said, panting. "Betcha she went for her brothers." More wheezing. "She took the baby and slipped away in the evening shadows . . . just like a wraith."

Andi listened with growing admiration. Jed Hatton was an accomplished liar.

"No!" Another curse from Vega. "I will not lose her."

"You can catch her . . . if you go quick. She hasn't got much of a . . . head start." He coughed. "And you know where she's headed."

Vega stomped back and forth, spewing oaths in Spanish. Finally, he hissed, "That little wildcat will not escape me *this* time." He raised his voice. "*¡Vámonos, compadres! ¡De prisa!*"

Yes, please hurry, Andi pleaded silently. *Hurry and leave.*

"What of Jed?" one of the men inquired.

"Leave him," Vega ordered. "He is of no use and will not live through the night."

Tramping and crashing, Vega and his men ravaged their way one last time through Andi's house. She clapped a hand over her mouth to keep from crying out. They were destroying her things.

When heavy footsteps came near the bed, she tightened her hold on Jared. *Please, God, don't let them find us!* A whimper from Jared sent Andi's heart racing.

The footsteps just beyond her hiding place slowed. "*¿Oíste eso?*" a snarly voice asked.

"Hear *what*?" Neither voice belonged to Vega.

"That noise."

The man snorted. "You're imagining things. The girl and her kid are miles from here, just like Jed told the *jefe*."

The men ripped the quilt from the bed. Andi saw muddy boots and torn trouser cuffs from where she lay curled and trembling. Then came the sound of a knife ripping through Andi's beautiful quilt, the one she'd worked on piece by piece and kept in her hope chest. It hurt as much as if the blade were ripping her heart.

Silent tears dripped down Andi's cheeks and splashed on the floor. Would these wild beasts never leave?

After what seemed like hours but must have been only a few minutes, footsteps headed for the kitchen. "It will take no time at all to catch the wildcat. When I do, I will drag her here to see what I have done to her precious home." Vega laughed. "Then I will kill her and take the child."

The back door slammed shut, and a desolate silence fell.

Andi let out a long, shuddering breath. It was a wonder that the men had searched the outbuildings and slammed their way through closets and cupboards, but they had never peeked under the bed.

God truly had His hand on her little family tonight.

———

Andi didn't know how long she lay, cramped and aching, in her tight hiding place. Jared awoke much later with a hungry cry. She fed him and hushed him back to sleep. She listened for any sound, any hint of the outlaws' return.

And she prayed.

Her heart overflowed with gratitude not only to God but also to the injured man who lay dying in the other room. Lying under the bed for hours, too scared to sleep and with nothing to do but think, Andi pieced together Jed Hatton's plan to protect her and Jared.

The note on Tucker's collar most certainly warned her family not to come near Memory Creek tonight, not at any cost. Instead, it probably told them to be on the lookout for Vega and his band, and that Jed would send them soon.

Andi smiled in the dark. Recognizing Vega's dark mood from his ranting and cursing, she knew he would plunge headfirst after her without considering that he might have been tricked. Mateo Vega was always the volatile member of the outlaw band, not the smart one.

That honor fell to the long-deceased Tomaso Procopio Rodendo.

When Andi felt sure Vega and his *compañeros* would not be returning, she made her way out from under the bed. Stiff and sore, she slowly rose. She settled Jared in his crib and covered him. "Sleep well, precious baby," she whispered.

Then she turned away in search of her rescuer.

It took time to find him. Andi dared not light a lamp. What if Vega had left a lone watchman? She tiptoed out of her room and felt her way into the sitting room.

Crunch, crunch. She stepped on broken glass and winced. Even if she wanted a light, it appeared Vega and his band had broken the lamps in a fit of rage. Andi reached out in the darkness until her fingers touched the edge of the settee.

"Jed?" she whispered. "Are you all right?"

There was no answer, not even a moan.

Blind as a bat and helpless in her own home, Andi made the dangerous decision to find a lantern. Her fancy glass lamps might be broken, but who would bother with a lantern? She crept to the kitchen and found it on the floor, overturned but undamaged. She lit it, turned it down to the lowest setting, and hurried back to the outlaw's side.

"Oh, no!" Andi threw a hand over her mouth to squelch her shock. Jed was hardly recognizable. His eyes had swelled shut, and his nose looked broken. He lay unconscious, barely breathing.

She set the dim lantern on the floor and gently pulled Jed's shirt away. She gasped at the damage Vega and his men had done. The cloth wrappings had been ripped away from his wounds, and fresh blood streamed from the holes. Dark bruises showed on his stomach, chest, and around his neck.

"That . . . that . . . *devil*," Andi whispered.

Not even the best doctors in California could save him. It was only a matter of time before Jed Hatton succumbed to his wounds.

He did this to protect me, she thought.

Sobs rose from within Andi's gut with such strength that she couldn't quiet them. She tried. It was dangerous to make noise tonight, but she couldn't stop crying. She buried her head in her arms against the settee and wept. "Please, God, don't let him die."

Andi felt something stroke her hair. "Hey, none of that, little lady."

Her head snapped up.

"My plan . . . worked." Jed's words came in snatches from between swollen and cracked lips. He sounded pleased.

Andi rubbed away her tears. "Don't talk," she begged. "Just lie still."

Each breath Jed took sapped him of energy. "I gotta ask you . . . somethin'." He closed his eyes and grimaced.

"What is it?" Andi asked softly.

"I . . ." He swallowed, as if searching for just the right words. "I told you I . . . wanted to turn myself in."

"Yes, you did."

"I'm tired of runnin' from the law." He sucked in another agonizing breath. "Tired of runnin' from God." He patted her arm. "I told Him so too."

Andi sat still, daring to hope. What was Jed saying?

"Can I ask you somethin' . . . little lady?" Talking was becoming more difficult. For sure, Jed's ribs were broken. His voice fell to a labored whisper.

"Ask me anything." Andi leaned her ear close to his lips to catch his next words.

"Will that Christ you're always prayin' to remember me if I ask Him? I got a hankerin' to see them . . . golden streets."

Andi held Jed's hand. "The thief on the cross asked the same thing, 'Remember me,' and Jesus said, 'Today you will be with me in Paradise.'"

Jed let out a slow breath. "That's what I want. Will you help me ask Him?"

"Of course." Through tears, Andi choked out a short yet powerful prayer. Jed tightened his grip on her hand, a silent way of saying "amen" when he was too weak for words. When she looked up, he had fallen asleep. An expression of peace showed on his battered face.

Andi held Jed's hand until his fluttering heart slowed and then stilled. Tears coursed down her cheeks. Jed had saved her life and the life of her son. When she finally untangled her fingers from around his cold, stiff hand, she bent over and kissed his forehead.

"Good-bye, Jed Hatton. I will never forget you. We'll meet again someday in Heaven."

CHAPTER 7

When he arrived at Memory Creek, Mitch Carter found his sister curled up in a ball, fast asleep and keeping vigil over the earthly remains of the outlaw Jed Hatton. Justice had come full circle, and Mitch was glad this whole ordeal could finally be put behind their family for good.

He glanced around Andi's house and shook his head. The gray shadows cast by the just-rising sun could not hide the devastation Vega and his *compañeros* had brought to this small home.

Mitch sighed. Thankfully, everything could be repaired or replaced. Vega would never again come after his sister, his nephew, or his brother-in-law. Thank God Riley was away on the cattle drive with Chad for at least another two weeks.

Mitch planned to make it his personal goal to set the house back in order and see to it that Riley's young wife was happy and cheerful again. Memory Creek ranch would look just as it did the day Riley rode off to join Chad.

Hopefully, Riley would never learn the full account of the horror that had unfolded here. Andi would share the story with him, of course, but without the evidence of a shattered home or the man sprawled out dead on the settee of their sitting room, Riley would have a hard time visualizing it.

Which was exactly what Mitch intended.

He squatted next to Andi and laid a gentle hand on her dark, tangled hair. "Hey, Sis. It's morning."

Andi woke with a start. She spared a quick glance at what used to be Jed then turned and flung her arms around her brother's neck. "Oh, Mitch! I'm so glad you're here. It means everything turned out all right."

"Yes," Mitch said, helping his sister to her feet. "Everything turned out exactly as it should. Vega and two of his men are dead. The rest are headed to jail, where they will never hurt anyone again . . . especially you."

"Vega's dead?" Andi's blue eyes were wide and scared. "You're certain?"

Mitch nodded. "I personally made sure this time."

Andi let out a long, shuddering breath and slumped against Mitch. "Thank God."

"I'll tell you all about it on the way back to the Circle C." He hugged her. "Let's go. You're not coming back to Memory Creek until we've cleaned up the mess and put your house back in order. Your ranch hands can't wait to get started."

"They're all right? Vega didn't . . . didn't . . ." She swallowed.

"No, he didn't kill them," Mitch answered cheerfully. "Vega or his men knocked them out and dumped them in a deep gully. They were shaken to the core, especially young Joey."

"I bet," Andi said.

"They'll get over it and have quite a story to tell their grandkids someday. Their ordeal has made them more than eager to help set Memory Creek in order."

Gratitude for her family and their loyal ranch hands welled up inside Andi. "Thank you," she whispered.

Mitch nodded at Jed's still form. "The family will take care of the burying too."

Andi nodded as a Bible verse swirled in her thoughts. *Greater love hath no man than this, that a man lay down his life for his friends.* "He saved my life, Mitch. And Jared's." She smiled. "In the end, he saved his own life too."

"Huh?"

Andi squeezed his arm. "I'll tell you about it later, but first, let me get the baby and then we can leave."

Mitch chuckled. "Mother's fixing your favorite breakfast. Waffles and hot chocolate."

Andi gave Mitch the little-girl smile he knew so well. "Well then, what are we waiting for?"

ALL IN A DAY'S WORK

Memory Creek Ranch, July 1888

Jared is just beginning to walk. Two steps forward and down he goes. It's so funny to watch him.

"Mamama!"

Andi swiped at the sweaty tangle of hair that kept getting in her way. "Mama's right here," she called to the chubby toddler.

One. Two. Three steps, and plop! Jared sat down on his padded bottom. Andi laughed.

It was not easy for Jared to navigate the smooth floor of their little house. He had an even tougher time learning to walk on the rough yard outside. He'd turned one year old two weeks ago, and oh my! Her little boy was in such a hurry to grow up.

"Slow down, little man," Andi warned him.

Don't grow up so fast, she begged silently. Had only a year passed since she'd spent a centuries-long day birthing this sweet baby?

Jared looked up and smiled. Slobber ran down his chin, evidence of the two new teeth he was cutting. He yanked at the dry, golden grass and tried to stuff it in his mouth.

Andi dropped the hoe she was using and hurried over to her son. "You are not a horse." She ran a finger around the inside of his mouth and pulled the grass stems loose.

At the word "horse," Jared's eyes lit up. "Hohohoho," he burbled, bouncing with each sound. He lifted his arms.

"Sorry," Andi told him. "No horsey rides this morning. I have these tomato plants to tend before they wither and dry up. And you—" She picked Jared up and carried him back to his quilt, which lay spread out under the thick, wide branches of a valley oak. Even in the stifling July heat, the shade felt cool and refreshing. "Stay on your quilt."

Piling a stuffed dog, a wooden horse, and three rattles in his lap, she left Jared and hurried for a bucket. *Water, water, water!* The kitchen garden screamed for a drink three or four times a day. Andi had no choice but to haul numerous buckets of water from the pump to pour on each plant.

Her hard work was paying off this year. Despite caring for an active little boy, Andi's garden rewarded her with all the peas, beans, onions, corn, potatoes, and tomatoes her family could eat. She had never been a farmer, but she discovered she loved working with the plants.

Plants did not kick or bite. Plants did not complain. They were never in a hurry. Vegetables waited patiently until Andi came out to weed and water them. She liked to pick the orange-and-black beetles from the potato leaves and put them in a jar. Then for fun, she'd call the chickens and watch them gorge themselves on the plump bugs.

Andi enjoyed her garden. She did not, however, enjoy lugging water, but it must be done. She dropped another empty bucket under the pump and gripped the handle. A dozen pumps later, the bucket was full . . . and heavy.

Just then, Tucker bounded through the open barn doors and ran around Andi's legs, barking a greeting. She almost tripped. "For goodness' sake," she scolded. "What have you been up to in there? You seem mighty pleased with yourself."

Tucker yipped an affirmative and trotted off to see the baby. Andi watched the two of them with a contented smile. Tucker loved children and babies, and Jared adored the dog.

Her little boy's deep belly laugh made Andi laugh too. Both of Jared's hands were clutching the dog's black-and-white fur. "Do me a favor,

Tucker," she called when she reached the garden. "Keep Jared on the quilt. I don't want him eating dead grass, bugs, or dirt."

She didn't expect Tucker to understand, but he seemed to sense the correct order of things and the baby's boundaries. A high-pitched scream of rage ten minutes later told Andi that Tucker was taking his babysitting duties seriously.

Andi dumped the last of a bucketful of water on a wilting tomato plant and turned to see the commotion. Tucker's teeth held the hem of Jared's gown. Step by careful step, the dog was dragging the baby back to the quilt. When the small collie reached his goal, he let go. Then he sat back on his haunches and looked at Andi for approval.

Andi doubled over with laughter. Jared was a sight. His hands and face were covered with dirt and tears. Tucker had dragged him along on his belly.

"No-no-no!" Jared wailed.

"Good dog!" Andi called from across the yard.

An hour later, Andi finished her garden work. The plants were hoed, weeded, and watered. She let out a long, satisfied breath and imagined the vegetables breathed easier too.

She raised a hand to her forehead and glanced up at the sun. It would soon be midday. Time to go inside and throw something together for dinner before Riley came home. She wrinkled her forehead in thought. Or was he eating with the men today? She grinned.

Oh, yes. That's right. It's just Jared and me today. Easy.

She left the hoe and bucket near a row of shoulder-high corn and headed for the pump. A quick, cool wash in the trough would be welcome. She glanced toward the oak tree. Tucker was still minding the baby. What a good dog!

Andi got the pump going and cupped her hands under the stream of cool water. *Ahh!* How good it felt. She turned around just in time to see Tucker lunge to his feet. The fur on the back of his neck stood up straight. His tail was rigid.

What in the world?

Jared had figured out how to push himself to his feet. He stood for a moment catching his balance then wobbled toward the edge of the blanket. One step. Two steps—

Growling, Tucker leaped at Jared and knocked him down. He gripped the baby's gown in his teeth. Jared screamed in fear and pain.

"No, Tucker," Andi ordered. "Leave the baby alone. He's on the quilt."

Tucker did not obey. His teeth stayed in Jared's gown, keeping him in one place. No matter how hard the baby wriggled and thrashed, he couldn't get loose. He screamed louder.

"For goodness' sake, Tucker!" Andi yelled. "What do you think you're—"

Andi broke off the scolding with a gasp. A bigger-than-life rattlesnake lay coiled only a foot or two away from the quilt. It lifted its head. Its rattle buzzed. "Oh, no! Please, God, no!"

Before Andi could rush to Jared's rescue, Tucker backed up. Jared howled and squirmed, but Tucker did not let go. He dragged him farther and farther away from the deadly reptile.

Rip! Jared's gown tore, and Tucker lost his grip. He left the baby crying in the dirt and raced back to the rattlesnake.

Jared sat on the ground screaming his anger. He was safe for the moment, so Andi let him cry. She dashed back to the garden and snatched up the hoe. When she returned, the snake had uncoiled itself. It slithered leisurely across the yard and away from the tree, as if it had all the time in the world.

Tucker followed, snapping at the snake's tail. He leaped out of the way when the rattler struck out at him. Back and forth they went, as if they were playing a bizarre, deadly game of tag.

"Tucker, back!" Andi commanded. She didn't want the rattlesnake to bite their dog. Years ago, a Circle C ranch dog had been bitten. No matter how much care their foreman gave, the faithful dog had succumbed to the snake's venom. Andi had cried for days afterward.

Now that Jared was out of danger, Tucker obeyed. He returned to

Andi's side and waited while she watched the huge rattlesnake make its way toward the paddock. Then he whined as if to say, *You're letting it get away!*

Jared sobbed in the background. Andi gripped the hoe and put his crying out of her mind. She could not let this snake lurk around their ranch. Who knew when it would pop out from under a rock and grab one of the barn kittens or a chick? *Or my baby!*

Andi followed the snake. It ignored her and slowly nosed its way toward the tall, dry grass. Stretched out, this big boy looked five feet long and didn't seem to care that someone was stalking it.

Andi saw the big bulge in the middle of its belly and knew why Mr. Rattler hadn't been too serious about coming after the baby or Tucker. A valley gopher had no doubt found its way into the snake's stomach a short time earlier today.

Its last meal, Andi vowed. She tiptoed faster and had no trouble keeping up with the meandering snake. "God, give me strength!"

Whack! Down came the hoe just inches behind the snake's head.

Whack! Andi brought the hoe down a second time and then a third, until the head was completely severed from the snake's body.

When she was sure the snake and its head had parted company, Andi dropped the hoe and ran for Jared. "Shh, shh," she crooned, picking him up. "Mama's here." She rubbed his back while he snuffled and hiccupped in her neck.

"Mamama," he whimpered.

"Shh." Andi held the baby and made her way back to her kill. "Stay back, Tucker. Don't go near it."

The dead rattlesnake's body continued to writhe, contracting and relaxing its useless muscles. The head twitched too.

Andi shivered. Even dead, a rattlesnake was dangerous. Its lifeless fangs could suddenly jerk and plunge into an unsuspecting person's hand, or Tucker's nose. She and her dog would stay far away from this snake until the muscle spasms ceased for good.

She turned and slowly headed for the house. Andi stopped at the pump and cleaned the dirt from Jared. She checked him from head to toe to make sure the snake had not touched him.

Later, after Jared had eaten his noon meal and was down for his nap, Andi returned to the rattlesnake. She buried the snake's head then sliced off its rattle as a souvenir to show Riley when he came home this evening.

Andi held up the rattle and gave a low whistle. Ten segments! This was indeed a huge, old snake. She admired the rattle for a few moments before dropping it into her pocket. Then she dragged the rest of the reptile far away from the yard.

A stray thought slipped into Andi's mind just before she tossed the snake into the field. *Rattlesnake stew?* She shook her head. Not today. The turkey vultures could feast on this fellow.

She sent up a quiet prayer of thanksgiving for God's protection. Then she smiled. "And thank *you*, Tucker." She reached down and scratched the dog behind his ears. "I reckon it's all in a day's work for you and me."

Memory Creek Ranch, October 1888

It's been at least two years since Riley and I returned to the hidden glade he showed me when we were first married.

CHAPTER 1

September passed into October without a hint of cooler temperatures. The garden dried up, and the harvest was over. Andi and Riley devoured the fresh vegetables faster than she could preserve them, which was fine with her. Up here on Memory Creek ranch, Andi need only wait until the hot weather passed before she planted again.

For now, however, she wanted to take a day off and ride far and wide.

"Riley!" A splendid idea took root in her mind.

Riley paused from bouncing Jared on his knees in yet another before-bedtime horsey-ride. "What?"

"Tomorrow is Saturday." Andi set aside her sewing basket and gave her husband a pleading look. "Can the hands take care of the ranch? I have the most urgent desire to go riding."

"Don't you and Jared ride every afternoon?"

Andi slumped. "Yes, but it's not the same. I want the three of us to go on a long ride clear to the Banded Rocks." Before Riley could reply, she plunged on. "I'll pack a picnic lunch. We haven't been to our secret glade for so long, not since you showed it to me."

Riley gave Andi an apologetic look. "I always meant to take you back. I really did, but Chad kept me too busy working those first few months to spare even a day. Then came the winter rains, and then you were carrying Jared and . . ." He shrugged.

"I know." Andi nodded. The last couple years had flown by. "Jared's walking now. He would love to splash in the pond, especially since Memory Creek is barely a trickle this fall. Please, Riley?"

Riley ignored Jared's horsey-ride demand and chewed on his lip for what seemed to Andi like hours. She knew he was weighing the loss of a whole day preparing the ranch for the next season. Taking off meant losing money, and the good Lord knew they couldn't afford many days like that.

Or was Riley worried about leaving Memory Creek in the care of their three ranch hands? That didn't make sense. Riley often left the ranch in Matt's, Carlos's, and Joey's hands when he worked for Chad. They could run Memory Creek nearly as well as Riley.

Riley gave Jared one last wild horsey ride then rose and threw him high in the air. "You're absolutely right." He caught Jared and set him down. "I've a hankering to see our secret glade, not to mention escape the last of summer's heat."

Andi jumped up and threw her arms around Riley's neck. "Oh, thank you! I can't wait!"

———

Shasta and Dakota pranced and whinnied the next morning, mirroring their riders' enthusiasm. The sun had barely topped the Sierras when Riley tacked up the horses and tied them to the hitching rail. Then he slipped into the combined bunkhouse and cookhouse for a word with his ranch hands.

By the time Riley emerged from giving last-minute instructions, Andi was ready with enough food stashed in the burlap sack to last them all day. She'd filled their canteens with cold lemonade and tied a couple of bedrolls behind their saddles to use as picnic blankets.

Jared was wild with excitement. He toddled around the yard, ducking between the horses' legs and babbling, "Horseys, Mama, Daddy," over and over.

When Andi mounted, she had her hands full controlling her feisty gelding and steadying Jared. The baby wouldn't sit still. He reached for the reins and screeched when Andi peeled his fingers away.

Riley took charge of the grub sack and canteens, plus the canteens for the horses. Water sources were few and far between this time of year. "Are you ready to ride, my princess?" He grinned his anticipation.

"Indeed, I am, my knight in shining armor," she answered.

Ten minutes into their trip, Andi knew Shasta wanted to race. His quivering muscles and the tug on his bit told Andi the young horse was eager for a good gallop. She wanted to race too. "We can't," she scolded him. "I can't take off anytime I please. I have a baby in my arms."

Not for anything would Andi put Jared in danger. She curbed her desire to race and held Shasta to a smooth, relaxed lope. "Another time, my friend." She leaned past Jared and consoled Shasta with a gentle stroke on his neck.

Riley chuckled. "It's killing you not to ride hard and fast, isn't it?" He slowed Dakota, and Andi followed suit on Shasta. "Gallop ahead if you like. Jared can ride with me." Without breaking the appaloosa's stride, Riley reached over and scooped Jared into his saddle. "We'll meet you at the Banded Rocks."

Andi grinned her thanks and nudged Shasta. The chocolate palomino needed no further urging. He broke into a gallop like the one that had won Mitch the Fourth of July race the year Jared was born. Andi's hat flew from her head, nearly choking her with its stampede string. She didn't look back, but she heard Riley cheering her on in the distance.

On and on Shasta carried Andi. The Banded Rocks drew closer. Their towering, striated bands gleamed orange, yellow, and pink in the sunlight.

When she finally slowed Shasta to a cooling lope, then to a walk, both she and her gelding were breathing hard.

"Oh, wasn't that fun!" She stroked Shasta, who shook his mane and whinnied his agreement.

When Riley showed up nearly an hour later, Andi was dozing in the shade, leaning against a solid rock cliff. Shasta nickered a greeting to Dakota, and Andi's eyes flew open. "I can't remember where we go from here," she said. "It's been too long, and I only saw it once. Besides, I was skeptical at the time and didn't pay much attention to where you were taking me."

"I remember." Riley dismounted and looped Dakota's reins over a branch next to Shasta. He dumped the contents of two canteens into his hat and gave both horses a drink. Then he untied the bedrolls and grub sack and heaved them over his left shoulder. He looped all four canteens over his other shoulder. "I'll refill these at the pond before we leave. Shasta and Dakota will appreciate another drink before we head home this afternoon."

Andi hiked Jared up on her hip. "I've got the baby. Let's go see our glade."

Riley set off through the winding cliffs and narrow passageways of the Banded Rocks. The sudden switch from scorching heat to cool shade was a blessed relief. "It's like living in the middle of an *Arabian Nights* story," she told Riley in a hushed whisper.

He nodded but didn't respond. His attention was fixed on the landmarks so he did not lose his family in the maze of rugged, ages-old boulders and sky-high cliffs.

Shivers of delight skittered up Andi's neck. Would they round a corner and come face-to-face with an impenetrable cliff wall? *Open sesame,* she commanded silently. Riley would think her silly if she said those magic words out loud. Instead, she imagined Ali Baba running from the forty thieves and a genie billowing up in front of their little family.

Yes, she decided, a truly secret hideaway. Best of all, it was their very own. No one else knew about it.

Andi was still imagining genies and Ali Baba and secret caves when *smack*! She plowed into Riley, nearly losing her balance. He had stopped in front of the low, nearly hidden entrance that led to their special glade.

"Oops, sorry." She hugged Jared and whispered, "We're almost there, sweetie."

"I'll go first." Riley smiled at Andi's dreamy look. "Then you can guide Jared, and I'll pull him out." He ducked into the narrow opening, dragging the canteens, grub sack, and bedrolls behind him.

When his feet disappeared, Andi didn't hesitate. She set Jared down. He was small enough to scamper through on his hands and knees without scraping his head. "Your turn, little man. Follow Daddy."

"No." He clutched Andi's skirt. "Dark."

"It's all right, sweetie. I'll stay right with you." She dropped to her hands and knees and pulled Jared down beside her. He wouldn't budge.

"Riley!" Andi called, ducking her head in the tunnel. "Call Jared, will you?" She could see the light at the other end, but no Riley. "Riley!"

No answer.

Where could he be? Why had he left her alone to coax a scared little boy to move along?

Andi crammed herself against one side of the tunnel, opening up just enough room to keep Jared by her side. Gently pushing and cajoling the baby, Andi inched her way through the rocky enclosure. Jared whimpered the entire time. She couldn't wait to free herself from this narrow, damp tomb.

"Riley!" she blurted when she and Jared emerged from the tunnel and into the bright light of the glade. "Why didn't you—"

The rest of Andi's words stuck in her throat. A grizzled old man with wild hair and a gray-streaked beard held Riley around the neck with one arm. His other hand gripped a long-bladed knife. The point touched Riley's neck.

"Don't make no sudden moves, missy."

CHAPTER 2

Andi froze in her crouched position. One hand reached for Jared, but he slipped away.

"Daddy!" Jared toddled forward and threw his arms around Riley's legs. "Up!"

The old man's eyes opened wide. "What the . . ." His knife hand relaxed.

With the speed of a striking rattlesnake, Riley twisted out from the man's grip. He flung Jared toward Andi. "Keep him away!" Then he clamped his fingers around the man's wrist and squeezed. The old man fought to keep the knife, but Riley's youth and strength worked in his favor. The knife dropped to the ground.

Riley pounced and came up brandishing the weapon. "What's the matter with you, old man?" he hollered, panting. Sweat beaded his forehead.

The man staggered backward, breathing hard. He lost his footing and landed on his backside with a painful grunt.

Riley sprang forward, pinning one of the man's shoulders to the ground. The knife never wavered. Riley placed the point against his neck. "Explain yourself. What are you doing here, and why did you jump me?"

Hard brown eyes didn't blink. "I don't have to explain nothin', youngster. This here's my place. You're the intruders." He paused. "Couldn't trust what was coming through that tunnel."

"A woman and a baby," Riley said through gritted teeth. "If you'd given me a chance to explain before jumping me, I would have told you." His voice shook. "Instead, you stuck a knife to my throat. Not exactly welcoming."

Andi held Jared close. She heard fury and fear in Riley's voice. She wanted to turn tail and crawl back the way she'd come, but she couldn't leave her husband behind to face this crazy old man on his own.

"That's all?" The old man scowled.

"Yes. Just my wife, myself, and our little boy. We came to the glade for"—he paused to let his words sink in—"a picnic."

At Riley's words, the fight left the old man. He let out a long, slow breath and went limp. "I'm sorry about scaring you. You never know who or what might be sneaking up on a body. I reacted. Let me up. I won't hurt you."

Riley shook his head. "Not until you explain who you are and how you found this place."

"I could ask the same thing of you, sonny. This glade is a secret from most folks." When Riley kept the knife close, the man sighed and gave in. "My name is Elijah Hunt. A Yokut Indian showed me and my friend this place nigh on forty years ago." He brought his thick, gray eyebrows together. "What's *your* story?"

Riley exchanged glances with Andi. When she nodded, he withdrew the knife and rolled off Elijah. "Riley Prescott. My wife, Andrea, and our son, Jared. I found this glade by accident a few years ago."

Elijah sat up and brushed the grass and dirt from his arms. "You don't say." He pointed at the small, rocky opening. "Through that tiny peephole?"

Riley shrugged. "I was following a coyote and he vanished. I wanted to find out where he went." He looked around. "I found out, all right."

"That's an awful tight fit, sonny." Elijah squinted at the opening. "Seems to me you'd want to enter through a passageway big enough to bring your horses. That way, the poor critters could get a drink." He turned and whistled.

Andi's eyes opened wide when a small, white donkey clip-clopped out from behind the bushes on the other side of the glade. "How in the world did you bring a donkey in here?"

"Horsey!" Jared yelled, clapping his hands.

"There's a bigger but more secret way into this glade than that tunnel of yours," Elijah told them. "It's farther north, with plenty of twists and turns. If you don't know the exact route through the maze, you could get lost forever. The Yokut tribe used it back in the day."

His face turned sorrowful. "I reckon none of them are left to remember it now. Leastways, I've not seen another soul, except you folks, since I found my way back here a couple of years ago."

Andi counted backward in her head. Elijah Hunt must have returned not long after Riley showed her the glade. "Your way back from *where*?" she asked, lowering Jared to the ground. He was heavy, and this old man didn't seem quite as frightening now as when he was armed with that long blade.

Jared toddled toward the donkey.

"No, Jared," Andi said.

Elijah waved Andi's concern away. "Captain Avery wouldn't hurt a flea. Don't worry about your boy." He pointed to the burlap sack. "Is that what I think it is?"

Andi had lost her fear, but Riley still looked wary. After all, he'd been jumped and held at knife point not too many minutes before. "What do you think it is?" he countered gruffly.

Elijah chuckled. "Well, sonny, you said you were on a picnic. I'm thinking there's some mighty tasty grub in that sack for a fella who's had to put up with his own cooking for far too long."

Andi grinned. Even *her* cooking would probably taste like heaven to this old man. "You're right," she told him.

He rubbed his hands together, looking as excited as if he'd just discovered the mother lode of gold. "How about we work out a trade? You share your picnic lunch with me, and I'll share my story with you."

Riley looked at Andi. She smiled and nodded.

"Well, then"—Riley held out his hand—"I reckon you got yourself a deal."

CHAPTER 3

Elijah helped Andi and Riley haul their grub sack, bedrolls, and canteens across the lush green grass toward the pond. He found a shady spot under a willow tree, whose long branches hung like tendrils over the pond. A drake and his mate splashed into the water, quacking their protest at the rude intrusion. Three ducklings plunged in after their parents.

The old man watched in eager anticipation while Riley spread out the bedrolls and Andi unpacked the food. His dark gaze lingered on the chicken sandwiches Andi unwrapped and laid out on cloth napkins.

Then came half a dozen bruised and partially squished Circle C peaches, followed by a tied-up bundle of sugar cookies. "My mother's best recipe," she explained. "But they're a little crumbly after our long ride."

Riley handed a canteen to Elijah.

"Land o' Goshen!" Elijah exclaimed after taking a long pull on the canteen. "It's real lemonade." He looked sheepish. "I'm even sorrier now for not being more neighborly."

Andi had already forgiven the old man's harsh welcome. Jared showed no fear either. He plopped himself down next to Elijah and helped himself to part of his sandwich.

"You're a cute little beggar," Elijah said, handing him a cookie.

During the meal, Riley relaxed. He reached into his waistband and withdrew the knife. "I reckon I should return this to you."

"Thanks." Elijah accepted Riley's goodwill gesture with a nod. "I don't know when I've feasted so well. Not for many years, anyway. There's nothing like a woman's home cooking." His eyes grew soft, as if remembering another woman's cooking. He sprawled out on the bedroll and propped his head up on his elbow.

Not far away, Jared had succumbed to the early afternoon warmth. He slumbered in perfect peace to the sounds of frogs singing and crickets chirping. High overhead, an eagle soared.

"I reckon it's my turn to tell you how I first came to this glade." Elijah took a deep breath. "Where to begin?" He paused, pondering his words. "Since the afternoon's passing, I'll try to keep my story short. It's a whopper, and there's some that might not believe it all. But it's true. Every last word."

Riley propped himself up against the trunk of the willow tree. Andi joined him, yawning. She leaned on Riley's chest, eyes bright with eagerness. There was nothing she liked better than a good story, especially a tale of mystery and intrigue. She knew that anything having to do with this secret glade was worth the hearing.

"I was a young whippersnapper back in forty-nine," Elijah said. "Didn't care a whit about anything but finding gold, hoping to spend it on having me the time of my life. I teamed up with a serious young fella, since there's safety in numbers in the gold fields. Jimmy was ten years my junior and fresh off the ship his father captained. He'd heard about the gold rush and couldn't wait to strike it rich."

Elijah chuckled. "That young fella was full of life. He had more energy than two of me. We made a good team prospecting along the American River. In no time, we became rich."

"I heard most miners never struck it rich," Riley remarked.

Elijah scratched his beard and nodded. "You heard right, sonny, but that came later. Jim and me were part of the first wave. A fella could reach into the river in those days and pick up nuggets."

Andi opened her mouth to scoff, but Elijah held up his hand. "I told you this story would be hard to believe, ma'am, but it's true. Jimmy and me had sacks of nuggets, a couple of really good pokes. Once a month we made our way out of the hills and into San Francisco for supplies."

Elijah's eyes turned dark with remembrance. "Like I said, Jimmy was a serious sort, a real God-fearing kid. I figured I'd better watch out for him in Frisco. Instead, it turned out he had to watch out for me." He sat up, crossed his legs, and hung his arms over his knees. "I couldn't stay away from the Barbary Coast. Ever heard of it?"

Andi bit her lip and nodded. Cousin Daniel had found himself in parts of the Barbary Coast when he took a holiday in the city instead of returning to the ranch. The dark streets were crowded with thieves, gamblers, cutthroats, and drunken sailors.

And liquor. Lots of liquor. Enough to get a person knocked out, robbed, and even killed. Daniel had barely made it out of the Barbary Coast alive.

"Jimmy refused to go near the Barbary Coast and begged me to leave it alone. I laughed at his scaredy-cat ways and goody-goody upbringing. I liked the danger, the excitement, the women, and the whiskey. My young friend chose to hang around a shop instead."

He chuckled. "And not just *any* general store. This mercantile was run by a blue-eyed spitfire. Her folks had either died or gone back east, but there she was, one of the few women in that rowdy city. She was eking out a living selling supplies to rough miners like myself and Jimmy, and to even worse riffraff."

Prickles tickled the back of Andi's neck. She shivered. Why did some of this story sound familiar?

"Are you all right?" Riley whispered.

"I'm fine."

Elijah stretched, helped himself to another crumbly sugar cookie, and popped it in his mouth. He followed up with a swallow of lemonade. "Didn't take me long to figure out that Jimmy was head over heels in love with this female shopkeeper." He slapped his knee and started laughing. "So, we took to visiting Frisco *twice* a month. That wasn't good for me, though. Jimmy dragged me out of a few rough places, but I never went along quietly."

"Did you ever find all the gold you wanted?" Andi couldn't help asking. She remembered being so caught up with gold fever that she and Cory dragged sacks of fool's gold around, thinking it was the real thing.

"That we did, Miz Prescott." Elijah nodded. "Then Jimmy started pushing us to find a safe place to stash our pokes. I liked spending mine, but it made me a prime target for cutthroats.

"After about a year, the gold fields got too crowded. Gold got scarcer. Murderers, thieves, and claim jumpers were running rampant. Jimmy told me he was done prospecting. He had bigger-than-the-sky dreams. He wanted to buy a huge parcel of land, settle down with that shopkeeper gal, and raise horses, cattle, and a passel of kids."

Andi caught her breath. *It couldn't be.* She pushed the similarities between Elijah's story and her own family's history into a corner of her mind. It wasn't possible that the stories could be related. Thousands of miners had roamed the gold country for years and years. The smart ones became railroad tycoons or bankers or ranchers. The others wandered up and down the state and found another way to make a living.

Curiosity spurred Andi to ask, "Did your friend ever buy his ranch?"

Elijah turned a sorrowful look on Andi. "I never got a chance to find out." He bowed his head. "We traveled south for new diggings in the southern Sierra. I was looking for more gold. Jimmy was looking for the perfect spot to build his ranching empire."

He snorted. "Jimmy and his dreams. Anyway, long about this time, we helped an abused Yokut escape his slavery to some white miner. It was Jimmy's idea." The old man shook his head at the memory. "We almost got ourselves shot. Miners don't appreciate folks spiriting away what they think is theirs."

Slavery? A Yokut? Andi swallowed. "I remember some Yokut families who lived on our ranch. They had to live out of sight for fear somebody would take their scalps for the five-dollar bounty."

Elijah pierced her with a sharp, dark-brown gaze. "Exactly. Jimmy nearly burst a blood vessel hearing about that poor Indian's plight. Young hothead," he muttered. "We escaped by the skin of our teeth and headed this direction." He waved to take in the glade.

"In return for our help, the Yokut showed us the secret entrance into this glade. Said his tribe had often come here, but they hadn't used it for some time. With the white men pushing them nearly to extinction, most had fled deeper into the mountains."

"So, you buried your gold *here*?" Andi asked breathlessly. "In this glade?"

"You betcha." Elijah slapped his knee. "Nobody would ever find it in this forgotten place. Jimmy and me memorized the twists and turns so we'd never forget the way in or out. We didn't want to end up like other miners, those fools who buried their gold and never found it again."

By now, Riley was caught up in Elijah's tale. When the old man paused and chomped on a leftover sandwich, Riley looked ready to jump down his throat in anticipation. "So?" He eyed him. "What happened?"

Elijah grinned. "That's the problem with you youngsters. No patience. No matter. We'd no sooner buried our pokes when Jimmy announced he was heading to San Francisco to ask that pretty little shopkeeper for her hand in marriage. I wasn't surprised. No sirree.

"'Lijah,' he said, 'you're comin' with me. I want you to see the look on Beth's face when I pop the question.'

"'Sure thing, Jimmy.' I was happy to agree. That little shopkeeper gal could cook as good as she could sell mining supplies. I never said no to a home-cooked meal." Elijah's eyes turned misty. He swiped a hand across his face and grew silent.

Andi leaned forward. What had happened? Had his friend Jimmy been killed? Had Beth refused to marry him? The questions danced on the tip of her tongue, but Riley's gentle pressure on her arm kept her words inside. Instead, she peeked at Jared, who was beginning to stir.

When the old man gained control over his emotions, he shook his head. "Sorry about my momentary lapse. It always breaks me up to remember what happened."

Whatever had happened that day in San Francisco, Elijah seemed reluctant to bring it up. But he couldn't end the story now! Andi's whole body quivered wanting to hear more. Elijah Hunt certainly knew how to spin a tale.

"You don't need to tell us if it's painful," Riley said quietly.

Andi stiffened and turned to gape at her husband. *He does too!* her glare shouted.

Elijah saw Andi's scowl and chuckled. The tension eased. "I see you're a little spitfire too, Miz Prescott. Just like Jimmy's gal. Don't worry. A deal's a deal."

He shifted his position and settled back to finish his tale.

CHAPTER 4

"We got to Frisco with half a day to spare. Jimmy was going to find a pretty ring for his pretty little gal. That was not how *I* wanted to spend the afternoon, so he told me to meet him at six o'clock sharp at the mercantile.

"'Not a minute past six,' Jimmy insisted. 'We'll all go out to supper. Beth is not going to cook for us on the day I plan to ask for her hand.' He looked me straight in the eye and made me promise not to go to the Barbary Coast. I laughed him off and promised to be back at six."

A feeling of dread settled in Andi's belly. She knew before Elijah spoke what he was going to say.

"I never met Jimmy at six," the old man said with deep regret. "I never saw my friend again. Instead, I woke up in the stinking hold of a whaling ship, seasick and aching all over. Especially my head."

"You were shanghaied!" Andi exclaimed, sick to her stomach.

She knew the horror of almost being shanghaied when she and her friend Jenny had been kidnapped and readied for a trip to the Orient. Seven years was a long time, but her mouth went dry at the memory.

The dark, dank warehouse basement . . . the leering sailors . . . the terror . . . the hopelessness of thinking she'd never see her family again. She moaned.

"Hey." Riley wrapped an arm around her and squeezed. "It's all right."

Jared woke with a loud wail, dispelling the memory. Andi pulled the baby into her arms and returned to her safe spot close to Riley. Jared cuddled down, still sleepy, and popped his thumb in his mouth. His hazel eyes stared at Elijah.

Elijah smiled at Jared then looked at Andi. "It appears that a landlubber like you knows what I'm talking about."

"I do," she whispered but said no more.

"Shanghaiing is worse than any story you've heard." His hands curled into fists. "I spent over thirty years at sea repenting of my foolish ways. The sea is a harsh taskmaster. Every splash of the waves against the hull reminded me of what a fool I'd been. Every harsh stroke of the whip on my back. The endless days at sea. The horror of a whale almost turning our ship into splinters."

Elijah was trembling now, his fists white from clenching. "Not an hour went by, day or night, when I didn't wish I'd heeded my friend's warning about wasting my gold on drink, cards, and loose women. I shed an ocean's worth of tears that first year, but the God of the sea was silent. I reckon He figured I needed to learn my lesson.

"When I realized there was no leaving the ship—at least leaving it alive—I settled in and accepted my fate," Elijah went on. "I eventually rose through the ranks and ended up as bo'sun."

Andi wrinkled her forehead. She knew what shanghaied meant, but she knew nothing else about sailing ships. She was happy to be an ignorant landlubber.

"The bo'sun's in charge of the deck crew," Elijah explained at her confused look. "It's a sight better to be in charge of the crew than it is *being* the crew. I learned everything there is to know about seamanship. Captain Avery liked what he saw, and life got a bit easier after that."

Andi chuckled. Now she knew how the white donkey had gotten his name.

He shrugged. "I kept the *Scandia* in tiptop shape the last ten years of my service. When I finally stepped off the ship in San Francisco again, everything had changed. I was sixty-seven years old and an old man."

Elijah looked older than sixty-seven, Andi decided. Life at sea had aged him tremendously.

"I wanted to make things right with my old friend, to apologize for not keeping my promise to meet him that day." He sniffed. "I wondered if Jimmy had ever married that bright-eyed miss or if he bought land to create his dream ranch."

Tears stung Andi's eyes. "Were you ever able to find out?" This was the saddest story she had ever heard. No matter how it ended, Elijah Hunt deserved to spend the rest of his days in this peaceful glade.

STRANGER IN THE GLADE

Elijah nodded. "After a fashion. I spent the next several months poking around San Francisco, trying to find clues of where Jimmy might have gone. The little gal's shop was no more. A bakery stood in its place. I looked up old records, but I couldn't find anything. Trouble is, I'd forgotten Jimmy's last name."

Andi gasped. "That would make it almost impossible to trace him."

Elijah chuckled. "You got that right, Miz Prescott. I traveled up and down the valley, asking about ranchers, especially as I got closer to this area. Jimmy had liked what he saw around these parts, so maybe he'd bought some land, an old Spanish land grant or something."

He picked up a cookie and wolfed it down. "Right good cookies, Miz Prescott."

"Thank you." Inside, Andi was impatient for Elijah to finish his story. She had a wild, crazy notion of where it might end. If he would only hurry and confirm her suspicions!

"I finally learned of a rich rancher, one of the wealthiest in the state, but he died back in seventy-four, while I was at sea. There was no use trying to connect my old friend Jimmy with this James Carter fella."

Goosebumps exploded all over Andi's arms. "James Carter was my father."

CHAPTER 5

"Your friend Jimmy was my father," Andi repeated in a choked voice. "My mother is Elizabeth. She ran a mercantile business in San Francisco before she married Father. He left his own father's ship with a blessing and hit the gold fields, hoping to strike it rich. I heard the story dozens of times growing up, but there was never any mention of a friend named Elijah."

Elijah stared at Andi, white-faced. "I don't blame Jimmy for that," he whispered. "I was dead to him." His shoulders slumped. "I spent the last few years since coming ashore looking for the secret way into this glade. I packed up supplies on Captain Avery—the donkey, not the sea captain—and wandered around until I found my way in.

"Jimmy's stash of gold was gone, but I dug my poke up right where we'd buried it. He hadn't touched even one nugget. Left it all for me, even though he must have figured I was dead. A true, God-fearing man."

Tears splashed down Andi's cheeks in hot, salty streams. This man had told her things about Father she had never known. Mother probably knew Elijah, but she would have assumed, like Father, that Elijah had perished.

"Come to the ranch, Mr. Hunt," Andi blurted through her tears. "Father died when I was a small child, but Mother is there. You would remember her. Her eyes are still blue, and they snap when somebody's in trouble."

Andi was laughing and crying at the same time. "Won't you please come and show Mother you're alive? You can meet the whole family. Your friend Jimmy realized his dream. He married Mother, built a ranching empire, and had a passel of kids. Three boys and three girls. I'm the youngest."

Elijah's eyes crinkled with sudden mirth. "I should have guessed. I saw right away that you're a spitfire, and you've got Beth's eyes." His voice dropped. "Yep, I should have guessed." He straightened and held Andi's fervent gaze. "No, Miz Prescott. You go back to your father's ranch and tell her yourself."

"But she'd love to see you."

"No." Elijah stayed firm. "I'm happy here. I dug up my poke after I arrived, then bought enough supplies to hold me over until I breathe my last. I'm a tired old man. I just like to sit and watch the critters. I've coaxed wild bunnies to eat out of my hand. Can't ask for more than that."

Andi held her tongue. Her pleadings would do no good. Elijah Hunt had his mind made up.

"I'm not lonely, and I have all I need. I want to rest and enjoy God's handiwork." He cracked a smile through his gray beard. "However, if you two and your little boy want to visit me sometimes, I'd give you a warmer welcome than I did today. I could share stories of the South Seas, the Hawaiian Islands, and the rest of the Pacific that would curl your toes and keep you awake at night." He chuckled.

Riley smiled. "We would like that very much."

"We sure would," Andi said eagerly.

"God has gifted this old sinner with the unexpected," Elijah said. "Seeing Jimmy's daughter and his grandson is a blessing." He nodded at Andi's questioning look. "Yep, Miz Prescott, the Union Gospel Mission in Frisco helped me find Christ when I returned from the sea. I was worn out and didn't know what to do with my life after thirty-some years."

"Oh, that's wonderful news!" Andi grinned. "Father would be so pleased."

"I reckon so." Elijah drew a deep, satisfied breath. "On the day you come to visit and find that I've breathed my last, I'd like you to bury me here." He looked around. "Right under this willow. Then I want you to send what's left of my gold to the mission in the city. I'd like to pay them back for showing me the path to true riches."

Andi nodded. "We promise."

Jared was wide awake now, fussing for something to eat. He refused the bruised and squishy peach and latched on to a cookie Elijah held out. Giving the old man a smile, he stuffed the treat into his mouth.

"We'd best be going," Riley said, glancing at the sky.

Andi sighed. She was not ready to leave. She wanted to hear another adventure story right now. But she followed Riley's gaze and was forced to agree they must head home quickly. The sun was already dipping behind the glade's western cliff.

"Wish I could show you that other way out," Elijah offered when Andi dragged an unwilling Jared into the narrow cleft. "But like I said, it's a long way north of here."

"Another time perhaps." Riley grinned. "Andi's probably already planning our next visit."

"I am!" Andi hollered up from the opening. Then she ducked inside and began the short crawl back to the cliff maze. Her heart thrummed with elation.

What a story she had for Sunday dinner tomorrow!

Circle C Ranch, January 1889

I recently heard someone say that the poor get their ice in the winter, while the rich get theirs in the summer. Well, the Circle C crew and Riley are harvesting ice this week, so I guess that makes Memory Creek ranch rich.

CHAPTER 1

"I'm putting together a crew to harvest ice this week." Chad brought up his newest project during the middle of dessert and coffee one blustery Sunday afternoon. "Do you want to go along, Riley?"

Andi paused with a forkful of apple pie halfway to her mouth. Did Riley want to go along? She smirked. Of course, he did. He had finished building a small icehouse last fall and couldn't wait to fill it up with big blocks of ice.

Andi couldn't wait for their own icehouse to fill too. Hauling ice all the way from the Circle C was a bothersome task that, when Riley forgot, resulted in spoiled milk and bad meat. With their own icehouse close by, Jared's milk would stay fresh. She could keep leftover beef longer than a day.

A convenient icehouse nearby was a luxury Andi had lived without for far too long.

"I most certainly do want to join you." Riley's eyes lit up. "How big a crew are you taking?"

"A dozen men, half a dozen wagons," Chad replied. "We'll see how thick the ice is up at Mirror Lake. I'd like to go back a couple more times if the mountain weather stays cold."

"Sounds good."

Chad chuckled. "It will sound even better when you hear I'm paying wages. It's not easy work."

Big brother was always roping Riley into "just one more job" around the Circle C. He seemed to forget that Riley had his own ranch to run. This time, however, Andi had no objections. The extra money would be a godsend during these slow winter months, along with the bonus of all that ice.

"If you can spare a hired hand or two," Chad went on, "I could use them."

Riley nodded. "I'll see who I can pry loose. At least one hand needs to stay behind and manage Memory Creek, though. I don't like leaving Andi alone, especially overnight."

Andi ducked her head and pretended to scrape imaginary pie crumbs from her plate. Ever since Jed Hatton's ill-fated appearance last spring, Riley had become extra vigilant about making sure his wife and young son were not left on their own.

If he knew all the ugly details about that night, Andi thought grimly, *he would probably sell the ranch to Chad, ask for a full-time job, and move us to the Circle C.*

The Carter family had shielded Riley from the harsh details and rallied around Andi to put things back in order. By the time Riley returned from the cattle drive, she was able to tell the story without falling apart.

"How long will you all be gone?" Andi asked. She was not afraid to stay on Memory Creek, but spending the dark, rainy days alone with a rambunctious toddler sent her spirits drooping.

"A week, maybe longer," Chad answered. "It depends on how smoothly things go. A couple days to get up there. Two or three days to mark the ice, saw the blocks, and load them. I want to fill six or seven big wagons with ice blocks. Then a couple days to get home." He shrugged, which meant he was giving her a wild guess.

Andi's spirits sank to her toes. A week or more in this winter gloom! Well, perhaps she and Jared could go riding to pass the time.

A low, uncertain whistle from Riley yanked Andi back to the conversation. "I dunno, Chad. That's a long time for me to be away."

Big brother appeared to have anticipated Riley's reluctance. "Ellie is coming along to cook for the harvest crew. Mother is watching Susie." He winked at his wife.

Ellie smiled at Andi. "Perhaps you'd like to come along and help with the cooking."

Andi's heart leaped to her throat. Her eyes widened. "W-what?" she stammered. "Me?"

"Well, she's not asking Melinda," Chad joked.

"Indeed not," Melinda chimed in. Laughter rippled around the table. Everyone knew that Melinda would not go on such a trip.

There was nothing Andi would rather do. A holiday in the mountains, snow dusting the tall pines and firs, being with Riley and—

Her thoughts came to a screeching halt. "What about the baby? Jared's too little to go along." She slumped in disappointment.

"I would be delighted to keep him," Mother offered. "He and Susie get along so well. Honestly, it's easier to mind two little ones who can play together than to chase after one child." She smiled. "With Luisa and Nila to help, it would be no trouble at all."

Andi couldn't believe her ears. Mother was willing to watch two babies? "But a week or more? Jared has never even been away from me overnight."

Mother clucked her tongue, just like Aunt Rebecca used to do. "It's high time Jared learns to be comfortable spending the night with me. Besides, the Circle C is his second home. He'll be too busy playing to miss you, Andrea."

Andi's feelings went to war. On the one hand, this trip would break up the winter. She could spend time with Riley and get to know her sister-in-law Ellie better. Riley's eager expression showed that he was all for it.

Plus, Mother was right. Jared would not miss Andi. He loved his grandmother, and he adored his cousin.

On the other hand . . .

She glanced at Jared. He sat in the wooden high chair with what was left of his apple pie. Chubby fists squished the filling and crust into an inedible mush. Some of the pie had made its way into his sandy-blond hair. When he saw his mama looking at him, he grinned. "More."

"It's all gone," she told him.

Jared went back to rubbing the tray back and forth, spreading apple goo and crust in every direction.

Andi's heart melted. Could she really leave her baby for several days? She looked at Riley.

"It will be fun." His hazel eyes held an imploring look. He really wanted Andi to come along.

She squeezed his hand. "I'd love to."

CHAPTER 2

Mirror Lake, Yosemite Valley, January 1889

Brrr! Andi crossed her arms and buried her mittened hands under her armpits. Her breath exhaled in a frosty cloud. "How much farther?" she asked between chattering teeth.

Riley flicked the reins over the backs of Ranger and Buster to hurry them along. The horses had no trouble pulling the large box wagon over the snow-packed road. They snorted, tossed their heads, and stepped higher. "Not long. It's only a couple more hours to the lake."

A couple more *hours?* Andi turned around on the high wagon seat and looked at an identical high-sided wagon several yards behind them. Ellie sat hunched over, clutching a heavy blanket around her shoulders. She looked as chilled as Andi felt. Five more wagons crowded with Circle C ranch hands, ice-harvesting equipment, and supplies strung out in a dark line behind Chad and Ellie's wagon.

What was I thinking, coming up here to freeze to death?

Andi tried to quash her momentary regret for agreeing to this lunacy. Singing "Jingle Bells" and watching the road transform into a lacy-white winter wonderland had worn off hours ago. After all, this was the same road she and Riley had traveled during their honeymoon two and a half years ago.

Billowing dust had prevented Andi from seeing the sheer drop-offs during her first trip into the Yosemite Valley. This time, though, the day was crisp and cold, and Andi could see for miles. The wintry Wawona Road edged too close to the precipice for her comfort.

She slipped a mittened hand into Riley's coat pocket and nestled closer. "If I'd known Mirror Lake is way up in the Yosemite Valley, I might have declined to come along."

"And miss spending last night at the Wawona Hotel?" Riley chuckled. "Just like old times."

"Not quite." Andi shivered. "We were rousted out of bed hours before dawn by Chad's banging. A cup of coffee and a cold piece of coffeecake is not my idea of a predawn breakfast."

Riley refused to be discouraged by his wife's last-minute jitters. He slapped the reins and broke into his own version of "Jingle Bells."

> A day or two ago,
> I thought I'd take a ride,
> And soon my sweet wife, Andi,
> Was seated by my side;
> Our horse was fast and true,
> But misfortune seemed his lot;
> He threw us in a drifted bank,

And then we got upsot.

Andi heard laughter from behind and reddened. "I'd much rather be thrown into a snowbank than plunged over these cliffs." She huffed. "Besides, this isn't a sleigh ride in thick snow. It's a wagon ride along a well-used winter road."

Riley didn't respond. He was too busy singing. When he finally stopped for breath, Ellie's voice, high and clear, took up the song with a verse of her own invention.

> A wagonload of ice,
> Is what Chad thinks we need;
> But he'll learn very quickly that
> The men he's got to feed.
> We ladies came along
> To help the menfolk out,
> They better treat us right or they'll go
> Hungry without doubt.

Andi was laughing too hard to join in the "Jingle Bells" chorus. Her chills melted away along with her uncertainty about the trip.

Before it seemed possible, two hours had passed, and the wagons pulled into an enormous clearing near ice-covered Mirror Lake. Two small log cabins with stone chimneys sat near the edge of the forest.

By the time Riley reined in his horses and set the wagon brake, Chad was already on the ground. He jogged up to their wagon. "Looks like we have the place to ourselves." His smile showed his relief that his crew would not have to compete with others to saw the ice. "We're a little early in the season," he went on, "but if we wait too long, this small lake will be crawling with ice men."

Riley had never harvested ice, but he looked eager to begin. "Just tell me what to do, boss."

"With Mitch managing the ranch, you're my right-hand man." Chad thumped him on the back when Riley climbed down. "We'll set ourselves up in that cabin." He pointed to the one on the left. "The men can crowd into the other. See to it."

Riley nodded and set to work.

Chad cupped his gloved hands to his mouth and bellowed orders. "Daylight's wastin', men. Let's get the gear unloaded."

The Circle C hands, along with Joey from Memory Creek, jumped at Chad's command and quickly unpacked the wagons. Ice-harvesting equipment—spiked horseshoes, scrapers, pickaxes, chisels, saws, and large ice tongs—began to pile up near the edge of the lake.

Chad had brought along a horse-drawn ice cutter with double blades to mark the ice quickly and uniformly. Two men heaved the plow-like contraption from a wagon and set it down near the shoreline. It would soon be hitched to a horse, and the men would get to work marking the ice.

While Chad supervised the ice-harvesting equipment, Riley waved two men over and put them in charge of unloading the rest of the supplies. "Store the perishable items outside but hang the beef high enough to keep it out of the predators' reach." He indicated a likely tree. "The rest of the food goes in the left-hand cabin, where the ladies will soon prepare our grub." He grinned at Andi. "Isn't that so?"

Andi filled her arms with blankets and smiled at Riley. It was only mid-morning, but breakfast seemed like hours and hours ago. "With Ellie supervising, even *I* can cook something edible this week."

Riley laughed, kissed his wife, and returned to supervising the hands.

Ellie came up beside Andi. Her arms overflowed with bedding. They tramped through the snow until they reached the cabin. "I can't wait to get started," Ellie said. "Chad intended to bring Cook along on this venture, but I talked him into letting me cook instead." She lowered her voice. "I love to cook but sometimes feel like I'm underfoot in the Circle C kitchen. This is my chance to be in charge."

"That's fine with me," Andi said. "Like Riley told Chad, just tell me what to do."

CHAPTER 3

Giggling like schoolgirls, Andi and Ellie opened the door to what would be their home for the next few days.

Andi's laughter died in her throat. "Oh, dear."

This was not a cabin. It was a dark, empty shack. Recollections of another mountain shack slammed into Andi's mind—she and her friends trying to turn a hovel into a place of rest and healing for Andi's injured brother. "At least that other hut had beds," she murmured in disgust.

Ellie's gaze swept the dark interior. She said nothing.

When Andi's eyes adjusted to the gloom, she realized the shack was not entirely empty. A dusty cookstove stood in one corner. There were no beds, but several large grizzly-bear rugs lay rolled up and pushed against one wall. The floors were dirty but made of wooden planks.

"A pile of blankets on a thick bearskin rug can be just as comfortable as a bed," Andi suggested.

"I agree," Ellie said. "We will make the best of it. After all, it's a line shack, not the Wawona Hotel. And it's sure better than a tent." She cocked her head at Andi. "Did you know I lived in a tent until I was eight or nine years old?"

Andi's eyes widened. "Really? No, I didn't know."

Ellie nodded. "The spring rains sometimes poured under the tent flap and turned the dirt floor into mud. It was awful." She made a face. "After Mama died, Pa bought a broken-down ranch. Jem and I slept in the attic. It felt like heaven." She looked at the ceiling. "I listened to the rain drum on the roof and wriggled with joy that no water could seep into this real house."

Andi marveled. Her sister-in-law had come a long way from a poor gold-miner's family to marrying the richest rancher in the state.

Ellie sighed. "It's funny how memories can pop up when you least expect them." She pointed to three shuttered, glass-paned windows and changed the subject. "We'll get one of the men to open the shutters from the outside." She stepped across the threshold and dropped her load of bedding near the bearskins.

Andi quietly followed suit. She knew next to nothing about Ellianna Coulter Carter, only that she and Chad had first met when they were children. Chad never tired of retelling boyhood tales of his adventures in an old gold mine, but he'd kept mighty silent about Ellie after they began courting.

I hope Ellie likes to talk while she cooks, Andi thought. *She probably has a million stories about the gold fields.*

Andi had only one gold tale to relate, and it was an embarrassing story. Ellie would never mistake a chunk of fool's gold for the real thing, like Andi and Cory had done all those years ago. Ellie would know the difference with a glance.

A slight pressure on her arm brought Andi out of her musings and back to the cabin's dim interior. "I'm sorry. Did you say something?"

Ellie nodded. "Find me some firewood. We need to heat the stove and light the fireplace. The men will soon be cold and hungry. Let's fix them a meal that will stick to their ribs."

—·—

Andi watched her spunky sister-in-law with growing admiration. By the time noon rolled around, Ellie had organized the food stocks, aired out the cabin, and fired up the balky cookstove like an expert. She had even gone next door and worked on the second cabin. "When the men collapse tonight, their bunkhouse will be nice and warm," she told Andi.

Was there anything Ellianna could not accomplish?

The twelve ranch hands, plus the Carters and the Prescotts, crowded into the main cabin for the noon meal. They sat in front of the fireplace's cheerful flames and ate heated beans, fried apples in bacon grease, and sourdough biscuits.

Wyatt, a longtime Circle C hand, praised the ladies. "The grub's mighty good at this ice camp."

"Andi made the biscuits," Ellie deferred to her. "I simply opened the cans, heated the beans, and added a bit of flavoring. We didn't have time to go all out."

Twenty minutes later, Chad headed for the door. "Back to work."

"We'll have something even heartier for supper," Ellie promised when the men filed out. "Happy ice cutting!" she yelled after them.

Andi looked around at the leftover mess and sighed. Tin plates and utensils lay spread all over the floor, where the men had plopped to devour the food. She spent the next few minutes gathering the dishes and stacking them on the narrow counter near the cookstove. "The only water I know of is sitting in our canteens," she said. "How will we wash up this mess? Shall I start collecting snow?"

"It's a lot of work to heat snow." Then Ellie snapped her fingers. "How about this? I'll get supper started while you head for the lake. Bring back a couple buckets of water."

"The lake is a sheet of ice."

"Not for long. Why don't you go outside and see what the men are doing? I bet they're close to sawing the first block. After that, you'll see a dark square of open water."

Andi agreed to give it a try. She found two empty buckets and made her way outside. The afternoon sun shone down in a blaze of light against the snow but offered little warmth. She shivered and wrapped the scarf tighter around her face. In spite of the bitter cold, some of the men had peeled off their sheepskin coats. Others were hatless.

Clearly, harvesting ice was hard work.

Curious, Andi walked to the lake's edge. The inch of snow she'd seen earlier had been scraped off this part of the lake before the men stopped for lunch. Chad and the Circle C blacksmith, Jake, were busy with a horse. When Jake lifted a hoof, Andi wondered if the horse had lost a shoe.

She wandered over. To her surprise, Jake was nailing a spiked horseshoe on each of the horse's feet. A minute later, Chad hitched the horse to the ice cutter and led the animal out onto the icy expanse.

Joey took his seat on the cutter to add weight to the blades. Another man held the cutter's handles from behind to keep everything going in a straight line. "Ready, Chad!" he hollered.

Andi watched the blades score grooves two feet apart in the ice. The horse plodded along as securely as if he was plowing a furrow in the dirt. Not far away, four men held saws, waiting to begin the serious cutting. Others held long pikes, splitting bars, and ice hooks.

Riley held an auger and was hard at work boring into the ice.

Andi put down the empty buckets and stepped gingerly onto the lake. The horse wore ice spikes, but her boots had nothing to keep her from slipping and sliding. She held out her arms for balance and carefully made her way to where Riley bent over the auger, turning it for all he was worth. Sweat beaded his forehead.

"Why are you boring a hole in the ice?" She shaded her eyes against the glare.

"Chad wants to know . . . the thickness . . . of the ice," Riley answered between breaths. A few more turns and the auger broke through. "Finally." He wiped his forehead. Then he pulled out the auger and poked a measuring iron down the hole. Its bent edge caught the bottom of ice.

Riley peered at the measuring stick and grinned. "Twelve inches. That's good news."

After marking the first row, Chad turned the horse around and marked the next row, then the next. Back and forth, the three men and the horse plowed.

While Chad's team marked the ice, Wyatt stationed two men near the corner where Riley had bored the hole. Their tall, iron ice chisels slammed into the grooves. *Crunch, crunch, crunch.* Ice chunks flew everywhere. A few minutes later, water began seeping up and onto the surface.

One of the men hurried over, ice saw in hand. The saw with its wide handle was nearly as tall as he was. He inserted the toothy blade into the groove and began cutting back and forth.

Andi backed up, her mission to fill her water buckets forgotten. So much work for a single block of ice! She had never given thought to how ice was harvested. Circle C ice was stored in a large icehouse around back. Growing up, she and Cory raided the icehouse and chipped off ice for lemonade or to make ice cream. She never imagined how much work it was to bring the ice home.

Wyatt chuckled at Andi's expression. "Don't worry, Miss Andi. Only the first block is stubborn. Once we get it out, things will go much faster."

Andi was not convinced. "If you say so."

Wyatt motioned Diego over. The Mexican ranch hand took what looked like a pitchfork with extra-heavy tines and started cutting into the fourth side. The block broke free, bobbing up and down in the water. Wyatt and Riley took two giant ice tongs and together hauled the first block out of the hole and onto the lake's frozen surface.

Chad strolled up just then and glanced into the hole. "Good work. Back a wagon down here with a ramp, and let's start loading ice." He turned to Andi. "What are you doing here?"

"Ellie sent me for water."

He looked around. "How did you plan on carrying it?"

A hot flush crept up Andi's neck. She slipped and slid to the lakeshore, grabbed the buckets, and returned for the icy water. When she'd filled the buckets, she took two steps toward shore, slipped, and landed on her backside. Water spilled everywhere. "Ouch!"

Riley and Chad reached Andi at the same time. "Little sister, why didn't you ask someone to carry the water?"

Riley lifted Andi from the ice and drew her into a quick hug. "Wrong question, Chad," he admonished his brother-in-law. "Why didn't one of us offer?"

CHAPTER 4

Later that evening, the cabin rang with laughter and merriment. Although weary from this first day's ice harvesting, the men had accomplished a lot. One wagon was filled with good-sized blocks. Another wagon was half full before Chad called it quits at seven o'clock.

With their bellies full of thick, hot stew and biscuits, the group lounged on the floor cracking jokes and telling tall tales. To Andi, it felt like an indoor cattle drive, with the massive stone fireplace replacing the campfire. Instead of watching over 1,000 cattle, the crew cared for a dozen horses, blanketing them against the freezing night air and making sure the grain bags fit over their noses without spilling.

Chad chased the men out of their cabin about ten o'clock. "Get some sleep," he ordered. "We'll be up before dawn."

When the last man backed out the door, grinning his thanks at Andi and Ellie for supper, Chad shut it and headed for a quiet corner. He spread the bearskin rug out, piled two or three blankets on top, crawled inside, and pulled another grizzly bearskin over the top. "G'night."

Riley followed his brother-in-law's example, and within minutes the men were out cold.

"I had no idea sawing ice was such strenuous work," Andi remarked. "I'm tired, but not like they are." She sat on a furry bearskin rug a few feet from the fire, enjoying its warmth and the snapping and crackling.

Ellie added more wood and relaxed next to Andi. "I'm not ready to sleep either. Too much excitement, I guess." She clasped her arms around her knees and stared at the fire. "Have you thought about Jared today?"

Andi started. "No, I haven't." *What kind of a mother am I?* she wondered silently.

Ellie must have heard the guilt in Andi's voice. "It's all right. I confess I haven't spared a minute to think about Susie. It means we both trust your mother to look after our babies. She's probably spoiling them rotten, snuggling them all night when Susie, at least, should be sleeping in her own bed."

Ellie's words warmed Andi clear through. Yes, Mother would do that, especially if Jared whimpered for his mama.

"Your mother is special, Andi. Much more than simply my mother-in-law." Ellie took a deep breath. "It was hard to lose my own mama to influenza. I felt her loss for many years, even though Aunt Rose stepped in." She paused.

Andi waited on tenterhooks. Perhaps this snippet of Ellie's heart might unlock more revelations. Andi wanted to know everything about her sister-in-law.

"It wasn't the same," Ellie continued. "Aunt Rose tried, but she couldn't fill Mama's shoes. Nobody could, at least not until I met your mother. After one meeting, my thoughts whirled continually. I adored her. I loved your beautiful family. When Chad asked for my hand in marriage, I had to make sure I was marrying because I loved *him* and not just so I could have your mother."

"I know Chad loves *you*," Andi said softly. "Whenever you came to dinner, it was a wonderful time. No table banging or roaring about this or that ranch tragedy." She giggled. "Melinda and I wished you two would have found each other years earlier. Meals would have been much more pleasant."

Ellie covered her mouth to keep her laughter inside. Chad and Riley needed their sleep.

Andi gathered her courage and asked the question she had wondered about for a long time. "So, how did you and Chad finally get together? Big brother has always been close-mouthed about the details. Everybody knows you accepted the position of schoolmistress when Miss Hall retired, but apart from that, I don't know anything." She sighed. "I'm just the little sister."

"Don't say that, Andi. You're not 'just' the little sister. Oh, if you only knew!"

Andi narrowed her eyes. "If only I knew *what*?"

Ellie found a more comfortable spot on the bearskin and smiled. "Let me start at the beginning."

Andi nodded eagerly, wide awake.

"You knew the schoolboard was hiring a new teacher, right?" Ellie said.

"Of course. I danced a little jig when Justin told me they'd found an older, unmarried woman to take the school. I didn't care how old you were. I was thrilled that I didn't have to do it."

"Did Justin also tell you that my brother, Jem, sent Chad a telegram to let him know I was coming?"

"No." Andi's eyes grew wide. "Why would your brother do that?"

"Jem didn't want me to be left alone and friendless in a new city. He hoped Chad would remember our time together as children and make me feel welcome." Ellie shrugged. "It was a silly gesture. Twenty years is too long. But I can't say I didn't feel a twinge of disappointment when Justin met me at the depot instead of Chad."

"Chad was probably up to his eyebrows in ranch work," Andi said. "He's not too keen on running to town if he doesn't have to."

Ellie nodded. "That's exactly what Justin told me. I felt better when he said Chad would greet me at his earliest opportunity. He was anxious to hear news about Jem."

Andi sat up, enthralled. "Did he meet you?"

"Yes, but most likely out of obligation to Jem. I spent a thoroughly miserable first week with my class. Some of the children were delightful, but more than a few gave me nothing but trouble until I established my position."

A grateful smile crept over Andi's lips. How glad she was that Ellianna Coulter had rescued her from having to endure teaching a long, miserable school year.

The fire had burned down to embers. Andi pulled a blanket around her shoulders, while Ellie stirred up the coals and threw on more wood. The sparks quickly burst into a friendly orange blaze.

"Chad entered the schoolhouse one day during an after-school row between two boys. I could barely manage them. He stepped in and pulled them apart. Then he gave them a stern warning and sent them on their way."

Ellie's cheeks turned red, and not from her nearness to the fire. "I was embarrassed that this stranger had witnessed my inability to maintain discipline. When I found the nerve to glance at him, I saw penetrating blue eyes, black hair, and—surprisingly—a look that quickly put me at ease."

"Chad's looks never put *me* at ease," Andi whispered. "They always put me on my guard." She giggled. "He must have fallen head over heels in love with you that very day."

"Perhaps." Ellie's eyes twinkled. "I liked him at once, more than I should have, I suppose. After all, he was Jem's friend not mine. We sat in my classroom and chatted for nearly an hour. I shared all the news about Jem, Pa, and Goldtown. When I said I must get back to the boarding-house or miss supper, Chad invited me for supper at the ranch."

Andi grinned. "I remember when he brought you home. Just like that, with no warning, we were entertaining the new teacher for supper. I was *very* curious about you, but Chad flashed me a warning look, so I kept quiet the entire meal."

"I know. On the way back to town, I asked Chad about you." Ellie broke into a wide smile. "You are not just the little sister, Andi. You're *Chad's* little sister and very precious to him. I learned how much your brother adores you and how protective he is."

Andi ducked her head. "Hmm. You must be referring to the trick riding he wouldn't let me do. You say *protective*. I say *bossy*."

"Yes," Ellie went on. "He was dead set against letting you take foolish chances, but I helped him see reason. By the time he dropped me at the boardinghouse, he looked thoughtful. He did admit that his new wrangler, Riley, was a cautious fellow."

Andi's thoughts spun faster than a whirlwind. She had been convinced that Mother's thawing, Riley's prudence, and her own wistful pleading had changed Chad's mind about letting her learn to trick ride. How could a new spinster schoolteacher, one whom Chad barely knew, have had such an influence on her brother right from the start?

She gasped. "It was *you*? You convinced Chad to soften his opinion about my trick riding with Riley?"

"I wouldn't say it quite that way." Ellie laughed softly. "I merely offered Chad a few ideas to think over, along with a reminder about his own scrapes during his time in Goldtown. I was secretly pleased when I learned you and Riley were trick riding, after all."

Andi shook her head. "Here I thought Chad gave in because he finally figured I was old enough to make my own decisions." She reached out and gave Ellie a hug. "Thanks. You are the first person I've ever met who could talk Chad into doing something he doesn't want to do."

"My dear husband is a handful at times, but he's not too hard to manage." Ellie winked. "Don't tell him I said that."

"Never!" Andi promised.

As much as she wanted to hear more stories from Ellie, a sudden yawn convinced Andi it was time to turn in. She and Ellie must rise early with Chad and Riley. The men needed a hot, hearty breakfast before they ventured outside to work on the dark, frozen lake.

Andi gathered her pile of woolen blankets closer and snuggled up next to the grizzly bearskin's massive head. It made a good pillow. She had slept on a bearskin rug before, and it wasn't a bad way to spend the night. "Night, Ellie," she whispered, closing her eyes.

"G'night." A dull clunk and the hiss of sparks flying upward told Andi that Ellie had added more wood to the fire before retiring. This auburn-haired woman was Chad's joy.

Andi fell asleep with a sigh of gratefulness for all God had done for her family.

CHAPTER 5

The next morning flew by in a flurry of activity. The men knew their roles and dug into the ice harvest with gusto. After sawing through the grooves Chad's cutter marked out, the longer blocks were cut into shorter lengths with hard, quick blows by long-handled chisels. Other men separated the blocks and sent them floating away from the main ice.

Whenever she could, Andi slipped outside to watch. Large sections of the lake had turned black with open water. Using tall pike poles, a human-powered assembly line poked and prodded the short blocks along the icy edge. They floated from the center of the lake to shore, where other men used ice tongs to haul the blocks out of the water, up a ramp, and into the back of the wagons.

Riley and Wyatt heaved and hauled each block, stopping often to rest.

"What's the matter?" Andi asked her husband, peering over the side of the wagon. It was half full. "Why all the huffing and puffing?"

These were two strong men used to throwing calves, tossing grain sacks, and hauling piles of fence posts. Surely, this small, two-foot block of ice couldn't weigh that much.

Wyatt grinned at Riley, who nodded. The older ranch hand gave Andi his ice tongs. "Give it a try, Miss Andi."

Happy to be outside in the fresh, new morning, Andi grinned and snatched the tongs. They were awkward, but she had watched Mr. Graff, the iceman, grab blocks of ice and haul them into Goodwin's Mercantile many times. He made it look easy.

The iceman's blocks were much smaller than these, of course, but how hard could it be? Andi opened the tongs and closed them around an ice block sitting at the bottom of the ramp. "This one's next?"

Riley crossed his arms and leaned against the wagon bed. "Yep."

Andi took a deep breath, steadied the ice tongs, and pulled.

Nothing happened. The block did not move even a fraction of an inch.

Andi's brow furrowed. What was wrong? The ground and ramp were slippery. The men had covered both with water. During the night, a slick, frozen surface had formed, over which they could slide the blocks. How hard could this be?

She took another breath, braced her feet, and yanked harder.

The block moved a couple of inches.

"What's the matter with this ice?" she demanded, annoyed.

"Not a thing," Riley chuckled. "But it weighs nearly two hundred pounds. Wyatt and I have to work together to get this one rascally piece of ice settled in the wagon."

Andi looked at the block of ice. She looked at her ice tongs. She looked at the ramp and the wagon. Then she loosened the tongs and handed them back to Wyatt with a sheepish grin. "The joke's on me. I had no idea ice weighed so—"

A startled shriek, followed by a loud splash, sent chills skittering up Andi's neck. "Oh, no!" She whirled toward the lake. A splash meant only one thing. Either a horse or a man had fallen in. Last night, the men had jested about last year's ice harvest, when one of the hands, Roy, had taken the "polar plunge."

It was no laughing matter for Andi to witness a worker slip and fall into the dark, black water. Who had gone in? Chad? *Oh, please, God, no!* She ran to the shore but stayed away from the drama playing out on the ice a hundred yards away.

Riley and Wyatt had already responded, ice blocks and tongs forgotten. They were halfway to the scene of the accident. The men scurried like ants. In a matter of seconds, two of them had their hands around the victim's arms and were hauling him out of the lake. He emerged and lay on the ice.

Andi shaded her eyes, trying to identify the half-frozen man, but he was too far away. Four men lifted the limp body and began to carry him toward shore. Andi turned tail and raced for the cabin.

"Ellie!" She barged inside. "Lay out the bearskins and blankets. Somebody fell in the lake."

Ellie wiped her hands on her apron and sprang into action. Together, she and Andi spread out a bearskin and piled blankets near the fire. Andi stirred up the flames and added more wood. The cabin was warm, but whoever had fallen in needed more heat.

Two minutes later, the men piled into the cabin, stamping their boots free of snow and carrying the shaking, shivering ranch hand. "Put him down by the fire," Ellie ordered. "Strip off those wet clothes and wrap him in warm blankets."

Andi's hand flew to her mouth when she saw who it was. "Joey!" Her voice came out as a squeak. Young, green Joey. He'd begged to come along. "I'd like the experience," he argued, and Riley agreed.

In no time, Joey's boots, sopping-wet coat, flannel shirt, and heavy trousers had been removed. He shivered uncontrollably in front of the blazing fire. His eyes were closed, and he flopped his head back and forth.

Chad sucked in a sharp breath. "Uh-oh."

Under Joey's trousers, his woolen long johns showed a deep cut just below his knee. Thick, dark blood oozed. His hands fumbled. He mumbled, but his words were slurred. "C-c-cold," he stammered.

"Get him out of those," Chad ordered. "The icy water has slowed the blood loss, but right now he needs to warm up. We'll deal with his wound later."

The men hopped to it. A minute later, Joey was wrapped securely in a blanket cocoon. Riley covered Joey's head with a woolen cap and pulled the young man into his arms. Together, they sat in front of the fire until Joey's shivering lessened.

Andi sat down next to the pair and turned stricken eyes to her husband. "What happened?"

"I don't know."

"Nobody knows for sure," Chad answered from Riley's other side.

"One minute, the boy was sawing ice. The next instant he screamed. When I turned around, he was in the water."

Riley looked up at the men who had brought Joey inside. "Did any of you see what happened?"

Diego shook his head. "No, *señor*. We were keeping our eyes on our own tools." The others nodded their agreement.

Ellie stooped down just then. She held a tin mug of hot, sweet tea. "Get him to drink this. It will help."

Joey's eyes opened, and he didn't protest when Andi encouraged him to sip the tea. Slowly, he drained the mug. He managed a slight smile for Andi. "Th-thank you." Then he coughed and lay back against Riley's arms.

"Can you talk?" Riley asked. "What happened?"

"M-my own . . . f-fault. G-goin' too fast. Saw . . . s-slipped. Hurt like f-fire. Felt the c-cold water but d-don't remember anything else." He let out a long, shaky breath. "Th-thanks for c-comin' after me."

Andi stared at Joey. He could have drowned. What if he'd been swept under the ice?

Riley shook her. "Andi, we're going to look at his wound. Get a lantern. We need more light."

Andi didn't move. The last thing she wanted to see was a blood-oozing wound on Joey's leg. It reminded her too much of the endless night when Mitch had been shot. It reminded her of Jed Hatton's battered face and body.

No, she couldn't do this. Not again.

CHAPTER 6

In the end, Ellie brought the lantern and tended Joey's long, deep cut. The rest of the crew had gone back to work. Joey would be fine, Chad insisted, and daylight was wasting. Work would keep the rest of them from brooding over the hapless young man.

While Ellie took over the nursing, Andi fried up a triple batch of doughnuts. "Please, God," she whispered as she mixed flour, butter, sugar, and eggs, "don't let me botch these. The men need this treat." She swallowed. "And so do I."

God answered Andi's prayer. An hour later, she called out the door, "Doughnuts!"

The men dropped their saws, ice chisels, pikes, and tongs and came running. Between refilling cups of hot, black coffee and offering seconds and thirds to the shivering, worried men, Andi had her hands full.

The men lingered over their doughnuts and coffee, chatting with Joey. He reclined near the fireplace, beaming at all the attention. He lifted the blanket and showed off his thickly wrapped leg. "Miz Carter did a bang-up job sewing me together," he insisted. "I'll be back in the saddle in no time."

Andi paled at Joey's boasting. She'd glanced at the ragged wound before turning quickly away just as Ellie was finishing the last of several stitches. Joey had not cried out, but his agonized expression told Andi everything. He'd had a close call.

That evening, the aroma of beef and rich gravy filled the cabin. Like the night before, the ice-harvesting crew scraped their tin plates clean. They didn't stay late into the night but hustled off to their own quarters.

When the door shut, Chad sighed. He glanced to where Joey lay sleeping then turned back to his family. "Six of the seven wagons are filled to the brim. That's enough ice for this first trip. Joey will need to ride in the back of the empty wagon. I'll leave the tools and supplies here and come back next week."

No one disagreed. Andi wanted Joey out of the wilderness and back to Memory Creek as fast as possible. It was warmer in the foothills, and Carlos would be happy to pamper the young cowhand until he was back on his feet. Andi planned to look after him too.

Chad rose. "I'll let the men know we're pulling out before dawn." Just before he opened the door, he turned to Riley. "We'll unload these wagons into your new icehouse."

"No need, Chad," Riley protested. "I can wait."

"I insist. Your icehouse is not very big, and I want you and Andi to have a full measure."

Riley opened his mouth to protest, but Andi clapped her hand over it. "That's real nice of you, big brother," she told Chad. "We accept."

Chad burst into laughter, and Ellie giggled. Riley peeled his wife's fingers away from his mouth. "I reckon so," he gave in, chuckling.

"Shh," Andi warned. "We don't want to wake Joey up."

The two families muffled their high spirits and readied themselves for the night. Chad loaded up the fireplace, Andi and Ellie spread bearskins and blankets near the warmth, and Riley took one last look at Joey. He hadn't moved.

As much as Andi craved another occasion to sit up and learn more about her sister-in-law's younger life, it was too late tonight. Perhaps now that the "ice was broken," Ellie and little Susie could ride over for tea more often. Spring in California was just around the corner.

Andi curled up under the blanket, rested her head on the grizzly's furry pillow, and drifted off to sleep to the crackle and snap of the fire.

MOONGLOW

Memory Creek Ranch, March 1889

The winter rains are finally behind us. Even one day of rain is too much rain for me, because when it comes down it drowns everything.

CHAPTER 1

Most California ranchers and farmers appreciated the heavy rains, especially small ranchers like Riley Prescott, who lived in the foothills far from the irrigation ditches in the valley.

Riley lived for the rain. A late-spring storm set him nearly turning cartwheels for joy. A spring rainstorm transformed his drying rangeland into a green haze overnight. He was in an especially good humor the last week in March. He smiled, tickled Jared, and lavished Andi with hugs and kisses.

It was going to be a good haying year.

Andi tried to catch some of her husband's enthusiasm, but it was hard. She had never seen so much rain, not in all her twenty-one years. The horses wallowed in paddocks that resembled mucky pigsties. No matter how often Riley tried to keep their best stock clean, it was a losing battle.

Especially when the horses turned around five minutes after their grooming and rolled in the mud.

"Riley." Andi was in the middle of wiping breakfast dishes and happened to glance out the window. She never tired of seeing the foothills covered in bright green, with the snow-capped Sierra rising behind them.

"Hmm?" He sat at the kitchen table, scribbling notes, happy as a colt in a clover field.

"There's snow on the hills."

"It's only March," Riley reminded her without looking up.

Andi turned around. "I don't mean way up on the Sierras at five thousand feet. I mean there's snow on *our* foothills. The ones only a few miles away."

That caught Riley's attention. He pushed back his chair and joined Andi at the window. "Well, what do you know? There's a light dusting." He grinned. "All the more runoff for the rangeland."

Andi shivered. She was a California girl through and through. Snow practically in her backyard meant it was freezing cold outside. "It will probably stay like this all day," she remarked sourly and shoved an extra stick of wood in the cookstove.

"Uh-huh," Riley answered, but his thoughts appeared miles away.

He didn't mind the snow, the cold, the rain, or even the mud these days. He was too busy lining up a buyer for Moonglow, their four-year-old colt. Riley had spent the last two weeks telegraphing ads to be placed in big-city newspapers like Oakland, San Jose, and San Francisco. He refused to consider any buyer from the valley, not even the businessman from Modesto who offered Riley two hundred dollars for Moonglow, sight unseen.

"I'm holding out for a buyer from the city," Riley explained when Andi asked why he hadn't taken the two hundred. "Moonglow is special."

"*All* horses are special to you," Andi cut in, laughing.

"True," Riley admitted. "If we're patient, word will get around. Folks pay well for Circle C stock, especially a stallion with Moonglow's pedigree. Plus, city folks pay more than valley folks."

Riley had a point. Memory Creek had no selling reputation of its own, not yet anyway, but the Circle C? Chad could name his own price.

Riley's patience paid off. A telegram from a wealthy horse buyer in San Jose had arrived yesterday. His message was short and to the point: "Ready Circle C Moonglow for 11 a.m. tomorrow. If satisfied I will pay your asking price."

This morning, Riley had risen with the rooster and hurried to the barn to clean, groom, and clip that big boy to look like the champion he would someday become.

"Come out and see what I've done with Moonglow," he urged Andi after the dishes were wiped and Jared was cleaned up and ready for the day.

She glanced at the warm stove. Cookies were on her to-do list this morning, not tiptoeing around the muddy yard to avoid the puddles. Freezing half to death was not on her list either.

Riley gave her such a pleading look that she gave in. "All right. I reckon it will be the last time we'll see him, and he is magnificent."

A few minutes later, Andi and Riley stood next to the stall railing and admired their stunning silver buckskin. The colt's light-silver coat glistened, even in the dim light of the barn. He shook his sooty-black mane and swished his black tail. Four identical black stockings finished this masterpiece of God's creation.

Riley lifted Jared to the top railing. The toddler stuck his fingers at Moonglow. "Horsey!"

The young horse snuffled, snorted, and blew on Jared's fingers like a gentleman. Moonglow was not only good horseflesh but also gentle. He extended his head over the railing for a rub.

Andi scratched him under his forelock, Moonglow's favorite spot. His eyelids grew heavy, and he relaxed into drowsiness.

It seemed like only yesterday—not four whole years ago—since Chad had turned Moonglow over to Riley. Big brother had sold the week-old foal cheap to his new wrangler, but not because he didn't have good breeding. Circle C Moonglow came from excellent stock and came with the papers to prove it.

Unfortunately, the newborn colt had been handed a rough start to life. His dam succumbed to a strange wasting disease and had to be put down, leaving little Moonglow without a mama. Chad didn't think the foal would ever amount to much.

When Riley offered to care for the foal day and night, Chad agreed. "If you save him, I'll trade him for a double eagle," he promised.

Riley quickly agreed. Twenty dollars was a lot of money for a hired hand to spend, but he saw the potential. If this little colt could be saved, he would be worth a goodly sum one day.

Andi occasionally dropped by to see Riley's progress with the sickly foal, but she agreed with her brother. This little fella looked like a lost cause.

The joke was on Andi and Chad. Riley saved Moonglow and handed over the double eagle. The stunning silver buckskin colt joined the newly-weds as a sprightly yearling when they moved to Memory Creek ranch.

Riley planned to turn his twenty-dollar investment into a five-hundred-dollar sale for his silver beauty. He stuck to his guns, declining offers from stockmen all over the valley for two hundred, two-fifty, or even three hundred dollars.

He advertised as far away as Nevada and Arizona, and a certain Mr. Thomas replied. He would arrive at eleven o'clock. Riley was giddy with anticipation.

Eleven o'clock came and went. The clock struck twelve, and Riley picked at his lunch. By two o'clock in the afternoon, his elation had turned to gloom. He moped around the house, glancing out the front window every time the clock struck the quarter hour.

Andi sympathized. Riley had about a million things to do today, but here he was, waiting around for a rich, fancy horse buyer. "I wonder what happened to Mr. Thomas," he muttered. "His wire stated eleven o'clock." He poured himself a cup of coffee and slumped at the kitchen table.

Andi offered him a cookie.

"No thanks." Riley sighed. "I reckon he changed his mind. I'd best get out to the range and finish up with those steers. I can't leave them all to Matt and the boys."

Andi saw movement through the front window. "Maybe that's Mr. Thomas now." She crossed into the sitting room. A buggy circled one of the hills leading up to the ranch. Their driveway curved, so it was always a surprise when a visitor seemed to pop out from nowhere.

"Hallelujah!" Riley sprang from his chair, nearly knocking over his coffee. "It's about time." He pushed through the front door and hailed the driver. "Howdy. Mr. Thomas, I presume?"

Andi stepped outside on the porch and stood next to her husband. "I really hope it's not him," she whispered, and for good reason. The buggy had stopped a few yards from the porch steps. Mud caked the rims, the spokes, and the sides.

Riley didn't say anything, but his jaw twitched.

"Yes, I am he." Scowling, the man stepped down from the buggy.

Andi caught her breath. Mr. Thomas was in worse shape than the rig. Moonglow's potential buyer was splattered with mud from his fancy suit collar to his sleeves. Andi's gaze drifted to his boots. Mud caked them clear past the tops.

"I'm Riley Prescott." He shook Mr. Thomas's hand. "What happened, sir?"

The man glowered at him. "I'll have you know, young fella, that my rig got stuck clear up past the axle on one of your confounded muddy roads."

Just then, Andi heard Jared crying. *Thank goodness!*

She ducked into the house, where she could listen to the conversation yet escape the older man's exasperated expression. She left the screen door shut and the front door open. She did not want to miss any of this, not even if the cold outside air dropped the house's temperature a dozen degrees.

"Mama!" Jared ran up to Andi and threw his arms around her legs. "Up."

Andi picked up her son, shushed him, and listened.

Mr. Thomas went on and on about his horrific ride out to the middle of nowhere. "Then, just when I thought I'd conquered the quicksand road, it reached up and grabbed my horse and buggy, pulling us nearly to our deaths."

Mr. Thomas was a master with words. He painted a picture that made Andi cringe. She knew the very spot he was ranting about. So did Riley.

The recent rains had turned one section of the road to Memory Creek especially soft. Worse, the soft spot gave no warning. One minute an unsuspecting person was driving along at a nice pace. Then with no warning, he was sucked into thick, sticky mud up to the axle.

Their own buggy had recently fallen into the trap one Sunday afternoon on the way to Carter Sunday dinner. Riley had to go back to Memory Creek for a couple of horses to pull the rig out. After that, Andi and Riley avoided that particular spot.

How unfortunate that Mr. Thomas had found it. From the sound of things, he had ended up stuck as badly as she and Riley had been. "If not for a cowboy, I think his name was Matt, I would still be stranded." He grunted. "My hat is still stuck back there."

"Your muddy trip will be worth it when you see Moonglow," Riley assured him. "He has the potential to be a stallion you'll be proud to own."

Mr. Thomas grunted again. Not a good sign.

It's not our fault the roads are a muddy mess, Andi wanted to holler through the screen door. She didn't. Instead, she threw a quick prayer up toward heaven. *Please don't let Riley be talked down from the five hundred dollars just because a grumpy old man is annoyed.*

Five hundred dollars bought a lot of feed and ranch tools. It also helped pay the three ranch hands, who depended on Andi and Riley for their bread and board. Speaking of bread, she added, *Thank You that I don't have to cook for the ranch hands like other small ranchers' wives do.*

Their cowhands would probably starve to death if they depended on Andi's cooking skills. She had improved greatly since her first days of marriage, but cooking was a labor of love for her family.

Carlos, one of the ranch hands, had doubled as ranch cook since a few weeks before Jared's birth. Riley bought the supplies. In exchange for milking the cow, Carlos took all the milk he wanted. Everybody stayed happy, especially Riley, who sometimes ate with his men.

Mr. Thomas acknowledged Riley's cheerful assurances about Moonglow with a gruff nod and another grunt. The two of them disappeared around the side of the house, headed for the back yard and Moonglow's stall.

CHAPTER 2

"Come on, Jared. I want to hear Mr. Thomas's gasp of wonder when he sees our gorgeous stallion." Excitement stirred as Andi bundled her little one against the chilly wind, threw a cloak around her shoulders, and slipped out the back door.

Andi heard a gasp, all right. However, the breath of air coming from Mr. Thomas's lungs sounded more like a soldier gasping out his final breath.

What in the world? Hugging Jared close, she tiptoed around muddy patches and headed for the barn. When Riley gasped, Andi ignored the puddles and splashed right through them. She almost ran into the two men hurrying from the barn.

Riley's face showed his horror. The men rushed around the side of the barn and headed straight for Moonglow's paddock. Why would they go back there?

After Riley had groomed Moonglow until he shone like glistening silver, he locked him in his stall. Two sturdy planks blocked the wide opening into his paddock. Riley did not want Moonglow to dirty even one hoof before Mr. Thomas took him away.

Andi rounded the corner of the barn and stopped short. She gasped too. She couldn't help it. "Oh, no!"

Her shout didn't faze the men. They stood slack-jawed at the sight of

Moonglow. He had somehow managed to escape his stall. Right now, he was splashing around in a huge mud puddle as if it were the finest sport in the world. He tossed his mane. Dirty-brown water flew everywhere.

"Moonglow! Stop that this instant," Riley commanded. "Come here."

The colt ignored Riley. For one horrible minute, Andi thought Moonglow might lie down and roll in the extra-thick mucky mess. What had gotten into the finest colt this side of the Circle C?

After his first gasp, Mr. Thomas remained speechless. His dark eyes seemed to bug out of his head. He stood next to the paddock fence stiffer than a fence post.

Tears stung Andi's eyes. All of Riley's hard work to make Moonglow beautiful had gone down the drain. *This sale is over*, she mourned silently. Mr. Thomas would not consider the horse worth a plugged nickel, much less five hundred dollars. Riley would have to start all over again, placing expensive ads to find a new buyer.

Andi's shoulders sagged. The Carter family might own the richest ranch in the entire state of California, but Riley and Andi certainly did not. Riley's earnings from last spring's cattle drive had gone a long way toward keeping their heads above water that year. This spring, a sale like this would bring in needed cash for wages and spring supplies.

Andi hugged Jared closer and watched the beautiful, long-legged prize colt turn into a filthy-looking scrub horse, the kind that went for twenty-five dollars at the livestock auction.

Jared fussed to be put down. He reached for Riley. "Daddy-daddy-daddy," he burbled.

Riley usually melted when Jared called to him, but not today. His gaze stayed fixed on Moonglow. "Spirited, isn't he?" Riley ventured, red-faced.

Mr. Thomas's eyebrows met in the middle of his forehead. "Champion colt, you say?"

Riley chewed on his lip. "Yes, sir." He didn't sound as confident about that as he had this morning. "He's from the best Circle C lines. I have his papers if you want to verify it."

Then the worst happened. Tired of splashing, Moonglow decided to go all in and give himself a mud bath. He lay down and began to roll until his glistening silver coat turned muddy brown.

"I don't know what's gotten into him," Riley whispered.

Andi didn't know either. Riley never locked Moonglow inside his stall. He didn't have to. Moonglow rarely stepped outside during a storm to muddy his precious, princely hooves. So, why had the colt chosen *today* to misbehave, especially on such an important day?

The splintered planks told Andi that Moonglow was a strong, well-muscled colt. For sure, he had not enjoyed being locked up, not even for his own good.

Andi flicked Mr. Thomas a sidelong glance. He looked annoyed and disappointed. And why shouldn't he? The man had wasted two full days. He'd been splattered with mud and stuck in the road, and now he would go home with nothing for his trouble.

Or maybe not. Andi waited for the inevitable, "I'll give you a hundred bucks," but Mr. Thomas did not offer one hundred dollars. He didn't speak.

"I'm sorry, sir." Riley turned his back on the muddy colt. "I'll see you to your rig."

Andi threw one last disgusted look at Moonglow then caught her breath in horror. "Riley!"

Moonglow had finished his mud bath and stood up. Instead of shaking off the muddy drips like he normally would, Moonglow took two steps toward Andi and fell through what looked like a solid grassy area into a deep, hidden waterhole. He squealed his terror.

Riley turned at Andi's cry and sprang over the paddock railing. He landed calf-deep in the mucky paddock and made his way through the mud and water until his feet found solid ground. "Easy, Moonglow," he crooned, ever patient. "You'll be fine. Easy now."

Moonglow flailed his front legs, desperately seeking a way out of the sinkhole. He pinned his ears back, screaming his fear.

Mr. Thomas's mouth dropped open. "What's that young fella think he's doing? He's going to get himself killed."

Andi couldn't answer. She buried her head in Jared's warm body and prayed for her husband's safety. Moonglow had transformed into a wild, terrified beast.

"Hey!" Mr. Thomas shouted.

Andi lifted her gaze in time to watch Riley attempt the unthinkable. He jumped into the deep, churning sinkhole next to Moonglow and put his arms around his neck.

"No, Riley!" Andi pleaded, but he appeared committed to rescuing Moonglow at any price.

Muddy water rose to his chest, but Riley didn't seem to care. He focused his full attention on Moonglow. "Take it easy, fella. It's just mud and water." Riley stroked the colt's muzzle and held him firmly. "We'll get you out of here. Just settle down before we turn into mud pies."

At Riley's calm voice and steady touch, Moonglow stopped flailing. He stood with mud and water up to his withers and gave a long, tired shudder.

"That's right, boy. Stand still." Riley turned to Mr. Thomas and Andi. "I need his halter and a lead rope. Could you get them for me, please?"

"Of course." It was too muddy to set Jared down, so Andi held him out to Mr. Thomas. "I hope you like babies." She thrust her small son into the man's arms before he could say yes or no.

Andi made her way to the tack room and pulled the colt's halter and lead rope off their hooks. When she returned to the paddock, Mr. Thomas was bouncing Jared up and down to keep him from crying.

Mr. Thomas need not have worried about that. Jared took to strangers like he'd known them all his life. He and his cousins were passed around from one uncle and aunt to the other every Sunday afternoon. Jared slept in Mitch's arms or Melinda's or even Chad's as readily as he fell asleep with his mama and daddy.

Halter and lead rope in hand, Andi started climbing over the railing to help Riley with the frightened colt.

"Hey now, missy! What are you doing?" Mr. Thomas's eyebrows shot up. "None of that. Don't you have ranch hands for this sort of work?"

Sure they did, but the hands were off on various jobs around the ranch. They weren't standing by waiting for Riley's beck and call. Andi bit down on her tongue to keep the rude words inside.

When she straddled the top railing, Mr. Thomas called her back. "Give me that rope and halter. I'll help the young fella."

Andi climbed down and traded Mr. Thomas the horse tack for Jared. What was the man up to? Why would he go into a muddy paddock to help with a horse he had no intention of buying? She shot Riley a startled look, but he was too intent on keeping Moonglow calm to notice.

Andi's silent questions went unanswered. She held Jared and watched the men work. Between the two of them, Riley and Mr. Thomas lured, cajoled, and pulled Moonglow from the dangerous hole of mud and water.

How this sinkhole had formed was anybody's guess. Andi had seen the paddock dry, grassy, or wet over the past two years. Who could have known that danger lurked just below the innocent-looking surface? Without warning, something had caused the water to settle and erode the firm ground.

A few minutes later, Mr. Thomas and Riley led Moonglow into his stall. Riley repaired the damage to the boards and nailed them firmly back into place. Mr. Thomas pitched in to help remove the worst of the mud from the shivering colt.

While the two men worked on Moonglow, Andi noticed a softening in Mr. Thomas. His irritated features smoothed out. Before returning to the house with Jared, she heard him and Riley sharing horse stories. She even heard a chuckle.

An hour later, Mr. Thomas came to the front porch and spoke to Andi from the foot of the steps. "You've got yourself a winner with that young man of yours, Mrs. Prescott," he said. "Reminds me of my boy, Joseph. He could calm the wildest bronco with a word or two."

Andi didn't reply. This citified man knew about broncos?

When Riley rounded the corner to say good-bye, Andi's surprise turned to disbelief. Riley was leading Moonglow! He tied the colt to the back of the buggy and clasped Mr. Thomas's hand. "Thank you, sir. It's been a pleasure meeting you. Are you sure you won't stay for supper and a clean-up?"

Mr. Thomas shook his head. "No, thank you. They've got a tub and hot water at the hotel in town." He slapped Moonglow's neck. "The livery will clean this fella up spick-and-span before I board the train tomorrow."

He looked Riley in the eye. "The pleasure has been all mine, young fella. I've grown soft in San Jose, forgetting my roots. Sharing in Moonglow's rescue reminded me why I wanted him. He's got heart, and he's spirited like you said." He chuckled. "I'll have to trust that he's as handsome as you boast under all that mud."

"You can trust me on that account, sir," Riley assured him.

Mr. Thomas's face broke into a wide smile. He didn't look grumpy any longer. "Best of all, I've had an adventure." He peered at his suit, which was muddied beyond recognition. "It's an experience I'll enjoy relating over and over again."

He headed for his buggy then turned for a final word. "If I still had my hat, I'd tip it to you, ma'am, young fella. Since I don't, I'll say my farewells. I won't be forgetting this day. You've brought hope and humor back into my life. If you ever pass through San Jose, please look me up."

"We will," Andi promised. "Good-bye, Mr. Thomas."

He climbed into the buggy, waved, and flicked the reins. The horse and buggy headed down the driveway, with Moonglow prancing along behind.

Just before Mr. Thomas rounded the bend, Riley bellowed, "Watch out for that muddy sinkhole in the road!"

PONY MEMORIES

Memory Creek Ranch, July 1889

How can Riley's birthday gift for Jared dredge up so many memories?

CHAPTER 1

"I could sit here for hours and watch the yearlings run and play." Andi slowed her busy fingers. Shelling peas was one garden activity she enjoyed, mostly because she could sit on the shady porch and watch the horses, at least the ones close by.

Riley had moved the yearlings to the paddock nearest the house, and Andi smiled at their play. Four big, healthy colts frisked and leaped and acted like weanlings.

She giggled at their antics then sobered. "I won't have this pleasure for long," she told little Jared. "Daddy's taking the whole kit and caboodle to the yearling sale next week."

Jared dug into another pea pod and stuffed the raw, crunchy peas into his mouth. He turned his round, hazel gaze toward the paddock. "Horseys!" he shouted in glee. Bits of green flew from his mouth. "*My* horseys."

"Yes, sweetie. They're yours and mine and Daddy's." *For now*, she added silently.

Andi had long ago resigned herself to the unhappy fact that Memory Creek raised horses to sell. Thankfully, new foals came along every year, and she wasn't thankful merely for her own sake.

It was no secret that Jared loved horses. He'd quickly lost interest in the toy rocking horse Riley made him last year for his first birthday. He knew the difference between a real horse and a wooden horse. Jared was happiest when plopped in the saddle with Riley on Dakota or on Shasta with his mama.

Jared Prescott and horses—a match made in heaven. He'd received the double love of horses from both sides of his family.

Lately, however, Jared had grown quite demanding. His eyebrows came together in a scowl worthy of his Uncle Chad if somebody tried to cut short his horsey rides. He pulled on the reins more often too, wanting control. "*My* turn," he insisted. "Not Mama."

Not Mama indeed!

To top it off, just last week Jared tried to push Andi off Shasta. "Me do it all by m'self."

Riley had laughed. Andi had not. Jared might be turning two years old in a week, but he was certainly not ready to ride solo.

"Daddy!"

Andi looked up from her pea shelling and smiled. Riley was home early. Maybe he would be willing to watch Jared so she could take her own solo ride on Shasta. It had been days and days since she'd had a good, fast run.

Her grin quickly turned to confusion. Riley straddled Dakota and was leading a small brown pony. Its little hooves clip-clopped in a funny-looking effort to keep up with the appaloosa's longer gait.

What do we need with a pony? Andi wondered.

The answer was not long in coming.

Riley swung off Dakota, gripped the pony's lead line, and jogged to the bottom of the porch steps.

"Horsey!" Jared squealed. He clapped his hands. Peas fell to the porch and rolled in all directions.

"Howdy, sweetheart." Riley smiled from ear to ear.

The wheels started turning inside Andi's head as soon as she saw Riley's silly grin.

Pony. Jared. Birthday.

"Hey, little man." Riley dropped the rope. "Happy birthday. Come see your new pony." He held out his arms.

Jared sailed off the porch and into Riley's arms. "Pony!" He wriggled with joy.

Andi's heart fluttered in unexpected fear. For all of her growing up around horses, the thought of her two-year-old riding alone on a pony took her breath away. Worse, Riley hadn't even consulted her about this birthday idea. "Riley, what's going on?"

"Isn't he a beauty?" Riley's grin was contagious. "I've been searching for weeks for a pony exactly like this one. Today in town I ran into Mitch. He's been on the lookout for me, and he found just the right pony yesterday in Visalia. He bought him and brought him back."

Andi was too surprised to speak.

Riley kept talking. "Mitch was happy to let me take this fella off his hands. 'Saved me a trip out to your spread,' he said. Mitch got him for a good price. Well? What do you think?"

Andi kept her "why's" inside. Riley seemed so happy to surprise her like this. "He *is* a cute little thing," she managed. "Twelve hands?"

Riley nodded. "Twelve hands exactly."

"Does he have a name?"

Riley winked. "Coco."

Andi's mouth dropped open. "Coco?" She peered closer at the small beast.

Yes. Same brown coat. Same dark-brown mane and tail. Same dark eyes that read, *Try as you might, but I will not go faster than a trot.*

Riley saw Andi's expression and laughed. "I wanted to surprise you with a pony for our son, one that looked and behaved just like your old pony, Coco."

He held Jared in one arm. His other hand stroked Coco's nose. "I remember Coco. You never cared much for that slow-poke pony. You pestered me to ride my Midnight instead, and always faster and faster."

129

Andi's tongue felt tied in knots.

Riley, on the other hand, did not control his flow of words. "You told me that Coco was Justin's pony first, and then he got handed down to the rest of you. The Carter pony was slow and easy from the very first ride. I want a safe pony for Jared too."

"But . . ." Andi shook her head. "Justin was four when Father gave him Coco. Jared's only two. He's a *baby*."

Jared heard his name and scowled. "No baby. Cowboy." He squirmed until Riley gave in and set him on Coco's back. "My pony?" he asked, wide-eyed.

Riley looked at Andi with pleading eyes, and she gave in. "Yes, Jared. Daddy says he's your pony. His name is Coco."

Jared clearly loved his new pony's name. "Cococococo," he said, giggling.

Andi stepped off the porch and let Riley wrap his arms around her. "I can't believe you didn't tell me," she scolded. "You caught me clean off guard."

"I figured you'd recover without too much trouble."

Andi allowed a smile to curve her lips. Riley knew her too well.

"Jared's a born horseman," he said. "Even at two years old he'll have no trouble keeping his seat on Coco."

"Hmm," Andi said. She was not quite ready to embrace this new uncertainty with her baby.

"I'll make sure he never rides alone," Riley promised.

Andi nodded and relaxed in Riley's strong, confident arms. He knew what he was doing. She turned to watch Jared become acquainted with his new pony and stiffened in shock. Her baby boy was standing tall and proud on Coco's back.

Andi knew better than to shout. She dug her fingers into Riley's arm and whispered, "Riley."

Riley slowly turned around. His eyes widened.

Jared spread his arms out wide. "Look, Mama! I wide. I twick wide."

Looking sheepish, Riley plucked Jared from Coco's back. Jared howled.

Trick ride? "Riley Prescott!" Andi whirled on her husband. "Where in the world did Jared learn *that*?"

"Aw, Andi. I showed Jared one time how I used to trick ride on Midnight."

"You *what*?" Andi's heart raced nearly out of control. "Oh, Riley, how could you?"

"I'm sorry, sweetheart," he said over his son's protests. "Really, I am. I never dreamed Jared would remember that one time." He shrugged. "I reckon he got the urge to trick ride from you."

He plopped Jared down on Coco's back. "Hush and stay put, little man."

Jared settled down.

"B-but how can you say that?" Andi stammered. "*You* were the trick rider on the Circle C."

"True, but who was always nagging me to let you trick ride on Midnight?"

Long-forgotten memories bubbled up. Riley was right. Andi remembered being obsessed with wanting to trick ride, just like her best friend, as in . . . *Anything Riley can do I can do too.*

"Did you ever listen to Chad or Uncle Sid or to anybody?" Riley asked, arms folded across his chest.

"Of course, I did," Andi protested quickly. *Too* quickly.

Riley laughed. "Sure, you did. Who broke whose arm trying to trick ride on Taffy?"

Andi blew out a breath. "I never should have told you about that."

"Whose backside got paddled by a big brother when—"

"Riley!" Andi gasped. "Who told you that?"

"Oh, someone who will remain unnamed."

Andi furrowed her brow, puzzled. "Chad can't be right about that." Who else but Chad would make up such a whopper to entertain Riley? "He's never paddled me."

She paused, recalling her horror the day she'd seen her friend Macy's stripes at the hands of her brothers. Andi was certain her own brothers had never touched her. Not Justin, not Mitch, and certainly not Chad. Not even when she deserved it, which was often.

"Long, dull days of checking miles of fence line got pretty old," Riley was saying. "Sometimes, certain family members liked to talk. Just to pass the time, you understand."

Oh, yes. Andi understood all too well. Her cheeks flamed at the thought of Chad and Riley gossiping about her like two old biddies.

"I think your brother wanted me to know what I was getting myself into, wanting to marry you and all." His hazel eyes twinkled. "To give me a chance to change my mind, I reckon." He laughed. "But you see? I didn't change my mind."

Andi didn't laugh. A sudden memory tickled the very edge of her mind, a memory she hadn't dredged up for over ten years. A memory that did not raise its head even when she'd seen Macy's bruises. Now, this sneaky memory settled into her thoughts like a stubborn child who refused to be ignored.

Oh, that's right, she thought. *I was that stubborn child.*

"I have supper to prepare," she told her husband primly. "You and Jared have a good time with that pony." She twisted her lips into an expression Riley had better not mistake. "And please make it clear to our son that trick riding is a big, fat no-no!"

"Yes, ma'am." Riley kissed her, tipped his hat, and scooped Jared from Coco's back. "Come on, little man, let's go saddle your pony."

A quick glance showed Andi that Coco wasn't the only birthday surprise Riley had brought home. A small saddle was tied to Dakota's back just behind the appaloosa's saddle. She couldn't help but grin.

Then a sobering thought wiped away her happy expression. *I wonder how much Riley paid for this pony and saddle.*

CHAPTER 2

No matter how hard she tried, Andi could not get a certain memory out of her head. It wrapped its sticky threads around her thoughts tighter than a spider wrapping up a fly. Whenever she saw Jared on Coco, the memory stuck tighter.

Thankfully, Riley had given their son *the word*. After that one time standing up on Coco's back all proud and cocky, Jared sat in the small saddle and held the reins like he knew what he was doing.

Andi's heart slowed down. She didn't worry that Jared would gallop around on Coco and stand up to "twick wide."

But that Coco! Every time Andi laid eyes on him, it was as if God had resurrected the Carter pony. He looked and behaved like the original pony in every way she remembered.

As much as Andi had always disliked riding a hand-me-down pony, she'd carved a soft spot in her heart for that sweet, old pony as she grew older. When he finally died at a ripe old age and in peace, Andi missed him terribly.

Now, Coco had galloped back into her life. She smiled. *No, not galloped. Never that. More like he plodded back into my life.*

She sat in the rocking chair on the back porch and watched Jared ride Coco. A patient Riley walked alongside the little boy, gently guiding the chubby fists that gripped the reins.

A lump crept into Andi's throat. It was as if she was looking through a window into the past. Instead of seeing her sweet boy with a floppy hat and round cheeks, she saw a reflection of herself in her mind's eye—a small girl with dark braids and red ribbons in her hair. A spunky little girl who was acting too big for her britches one long-ago day.

Andi sighed and gave in to the memory.

Once and for all.

Eight-year-old Andi Carter wriggled with delight. "Only one more month 'til I'm nine. Then Taffy and I will be horse and rider at last!"

She sat on the top railing of her filly's paddock just outside the horse barn. Her golden palomino trotted around and around inside the enclosure. After every few circles, Taffy stopped, shook her mane, and stomped a hoof. After yet another circle of the paddock, she stopped beside Andi and whinnied, a very impatient whinny.

Andi stroked Taffy's white blaze and sighed. "Soon, Taffy," she crooned. "He'll come. Then we can work on your ground manners."

She scowled. *Or maybe not.* She'd said "soon" to Taffy four or five times already. Now "soon" had become "later." *Much* later. Andi looked up. The sun shone high overhead. It was nearly noon.

Chad had promised Andi that he wouldn't take long today. Only a few remaining late calves needed to be branded. "Sit tight, little sister," he'd shouted when he galloped away early this morning. "I'll be back in a jiffy for a training session with you and Taffy."

Andi sucked in a disappointed breath. Where was that ol' big brother? He was always getting sidetracked. She let out her breath in a loud whoosh. "Dumb ol' brother."

Andi sat up quickly and looked around to see if anyone had heard those forbidden words. Just yesterday, Mother had taken a switch from the peach tree and landed a few sharp whacks to Andi's backside.

"Your tongue is a fire lately, Andrea," she reminded her daughter. "Learn to control it, or I will have to control it for you."

"Yes, Mother," Andi had fervently replied, sniffing back her tears.

Andi wanted to be good. Maybe not as good as her big sister Melinda, but good like her big brothers Mitch and Justin. That ugly term for her brother had slipped out of her mouth just now, like it had a mind of its own.

No one was hanging around Taffy's paddock, so Andi felt safe from spies for the time being. She swung her legs back and forth, counted to one hundred, and pressed her lips tightly together to prove that she could control her tongue.

A few minutes later, Chad's big buckskin horse, Sky, galloped into the yard.

Yippee! Andi nearly fell from the railing in her haste to greet her brother. "What took you so long?" She ran up to Sky, who danced and sidestepped, trying to avoid her.

Chad hauled back on the reins. "Good grief, Andi. Stay back. You want to get trampled?" His blue eyes snapped in irritation.

Andi stepped back at Chad's sharp tone. She clasped her sweaty hands together and scowled. "You said you'd be back hours ago to help Taffy and me."

"I got tied up," he grouched, dismounting. When his boot heel touched the ground, he winced in pain.

"Who tied you up?" Andi couldn't resist a teasing grin.

"I was *delayed*," Chad said through gritted teeth. He was clearly in no mood for Andi's silly banter.

She slumped then brightened. "Well, you're home now. C'mon!" She grabbed his shirt sleeve. "Taffy and I have been waiting all morning. She wants out of her paddock."

"I can't. Not today." Chad flashed her an apologetic look and peeled her fingers from his sleeve. "I twisted my ankle trying to lasso the peskiest calf on the Circle C. Then the branding iron slipped and landed on the calf's soft belly. Boy, did that critter ever kick! His hooves grazed my shin and jabbed my thigh. I'm headed for a long soak in the tub."

He tossed the reins to a cowhand. "Take care of Sky."

"Sure thing, boss."

Andi stood stock-still. Being kicked by a calf might hurt a lot, but Chad had promised. He needed a reminder, and right now. "But you *promised* to help me train Taffy today."

"I know I did, and I'm sorry. But you and Taffy will have to wait another day."

"That's what you said yesterday!"

Chad turned to go. "Yep, and now I'm saying it again. Put her away and give her some grain."

Andi stood her ground. "Can't I ride Taffy by myself? I don't need a saddle. You let me ride her bareback last week when we worked with her. I can do it myself."

"No." Chad took a few cautious steps across the yard then turned back to his sister. "Listen, Andi. I'm not going to stand here and argue with you. I can't help you with Taffy when I'm tired and beat up."

"But—"

Chad held up his finger for silence. "And for sure you aren't going to climb onto a half-trained filly by yourself and gallop away."

Dumb ol' brother was on the tip of Andi's tongue, but she bit her lip and kept those forbidden words inside. Instead, she huffed. "You *never* keep your promises."

For the briefest moment, a flash of regret crossed Chad's face. "I'm sorry, but it's not my fault I got beat up today."

"You don't care about Taffy," Andi burst out, blinking back stinging tears. "I bet you don't ever want me to learn to ride her, either. Because you don't want me to ever ride good enough to trick ride. But that's not fair. Riley said trick riding is easy as pie and—"

She broke off at the look on her brother's face. *Oops.* "Trick ride" were two other forbidden words on the Circle C ranch. Andi didn't know why she let those words slip out of her mouth. They always made Chad extra irritated.

Why did I get so mad? Andi always said things she didn't mean when she was angry. Like now.

Chad turned around and started hobbling toward the back porch. "Go and play," he said wearily. "Put your filly away and get that 'trick riding' notion clean out of your head. We have gone back and forth over this, and the answer is still no. Do you hear me, little sister?" He shouted these last words over his shoulder.

Andi nodded.

"I've told you before, and I'm telling you again. If I *ever* catch you trying to trick ride on Taffy—before or after her training—I will tan your hide until you can't sit down."

No, you won't, Andi thought. Chad was just talking. He had never touched her.

Only Mother used the peach switch on Andi, but it wasn't very often. Mother's peach switch stung, and Andi tried with all her might to be good and keep that switch away.

But it was hard to be good when big brothers did not keep their promises.

Andi scuffed the dust with her boot toe and let out a long, disappointed sigh. She watched Chad stiffly climb the porch steps and disappear inside the house. The screen door slammed shut behind him.

Andi kicked a rock and headed to the barn. It didn't take long to call her filly back inside her stall and dump grain in her feeder.

A soft, lonely whicker pulled Andi's attention from her golden filly. In the stall next to Taffy, her old hand-me-down pony Coco stood patiently. He thrust his small head through the railings and whickered again. *How about some of that grain?* he seemed to be saying.

A small smile replaced Andi's frown. Ever since Chad and she had begun Taffy's serious training, Andi had pretty much ignored Coco. It wouldn't be long before she would ride Taffy—and only Taffy—every day. She would never mount Coco again.

Somehow, that idea made Andi sad. She grabbed a handful of grain and let Coco nuzzle her palm. He gave little grunts of pleasure, and Andi's heart went out to her pony.

"Want to go for a ride?" Andi could take Coco for a ride whenever she wanted, so long as she didn't go too far without telling someone. Best of all, she could saddle Coco by herself.

Andi had become quite experienced at saddling Coco. She could get it done in less than ten minutes. First, the old, worn-out saddle blanket went on. It was so old that even Justin had used it. But it was soft and comfortable for a great-grandpa pony's back.

Then came the saddle, the one Chad had carved his name and age into: *Chad Carter. Age 6. Keep off.*

Leave it to Chad to claim ownership of the Carter family's saddle. *It's just like him,* she thought. For the barest whisper of a moment, Andi wondered if Father had tanned big brother's hide over carving his name into something that didn't belong to him. *Probably.*

She smiled and wished she'd been born back then to see it.

Coco looked eager to escape his stall and paddock. He let Andi slip the bridle into his mouth and adjust the headstall. He followed her willingly out of the barn and into the sunshine.

Andi blinked at the bright light and mounted Coco in one quick motion. At eight years old, it took no effort to climb aboard a small pony like Coco. She looked down from her seat and giggled. If thirteen-year-old Melinda rode Coco, her boots would drag.

It was not a long way to the ground from the top of a twelve-hand pony. "I bet if I fell off, I wouldn't even feel it," she told Coco. Her pony began to slowly plod across the yard.

Andi felt Coco's slow and steady gait. She watched the ground crawl by slower than a snail.

Then she got an idea. What if she practiced—just for a few seconds—standing up in Coco's saddle? It wasn't actually trick riding to *stand up* in a saddle. It was more like getting taller to see farther. After all, Coco was so short.

Andi let Coco's reins drop. He kept walking, head down and looking tired. She pulled her feet out of the stirrups, pushed herself up, and let her legs curl under the rest of her body.

Nothing happened. Coco kept walking. Andi stayed in one place. She didn't slide one way or the other. So she went higher, onto her knees.

Coco didn't stop. He didn't even twitch an ear.

Andi stood up. Her booted feet found solid places to keep from sliding off. She held out her arms to steady herself. Coco continued to walk as slow as a turtle. *Good ol' Coco!*

For the first time in her life, Andi was glad Coco was a slow-poke pony. She was not worried that he would break into a trot or a gallop and throw her off his back.

This is fun! Andi said to herself. It wasn't dangerous or scary at all. Not from Coco's small back. She could jump off any time she wanted.

Just then, a jerk yanked Andi off Coco. She felt the air squeezed out of her body and gasped. Someone had wedged her under his arm and was lugging her toward the barn.

"Let me go!" she hollered, enraged. A second ago, she'd been standing on Coco's back. The next moment she was being carried like a sack of grain.

Who was this rude ranch hand? Sid? Diego? "You let me go or I'll tell my mother—"

Oof! The cowhand dropped her to the ground under the barn's eaves. Then he sat down on a worn, wooden bench and looked at her.

Andi sat in the dust and stared, mouth agape. It was not a rude ranch hand. It was Chad. Her heart leaped to her throat and stuck there. What was Chad doing here? Wasn't he supposed to be having a long, hot soak in the tub for his aching muscles?

"Didn't I tell you there was to be no trick riding on this ranch?"

Instead of agreeing with her brother and whispering a quick "I'm sorry," Andi leaped to her feet and jammed her hands on her hips. "You said I couldn't trick ride on *Taffy*," she hollered. "This isn't Taffy. It's *Coco*." She wanted to add *so there*, but she didn't.

Chad looked stunned, but not for long. "That does it." Before Andi could blink, he turned her over his knee and landed five quick smacks to her backside.

Never in her life had Andi been so surprised. Chad's whacks through her overalls didn't sting like Mother's peach switch. In fact, they hardly hurt at all, but the humiliation was ten times worse.

Mother always took Andi to a quiet place to discipline her. Chad was doing it right outside in the middle of the yard, where every cowhand who walked by could see what was happening.

From the corner of her eye, Andi counted three ranch hands. Each man looked the other way as he passed by. She felt her cheeks explode in hot shame.

Chad stood her up in front of him. "That should teach you to mind what I say. No trick riding. Do you hear me?"

Andi was too shocked and angry to answer. Her whole body shook. How dare her brother hit her! Who did he think he was? Father? Mother?

She wanted to shout those exact words, but she didn't. His fingers still gripped her arm, as if he was waiting to turn her over his knee again if she spoke even one sassy word. In fact, it looked like Chad expected her to spew angry words in his face, maybe even forbidden words.

Andi would not give him a reason to whack her another time. She would control her tongue rather than feel his hand on her backside. Instead, she would stay mad at him forever. Wait 'til Mother heard what Chad did!

Just then, the full realization of how naughty Andi had been, and what Mother might *really* say about her behavior, brought unexpected tears to her eyes. She hadn't cried when Chad was tanning her. She was too surprised.

But now, with her arm held in Chad's tight grip, she started crying. She couldn't hold back her frightened sobs. Her anger and mean thoughts dissolved, leaving Andi shaky, weak, and ashamed of herself.

New words spilled, words Andi never thought she would say to this mean brother. "I'm sorry for not minding." She gulped and cried some more. "I'm sorry."

Chad rose to his feet, scooped Andi up in his arms, and gave her a warm, cozy hug. Justin was usually the "king" of warm hugs, but today Chad was acting just like Andi's oldest and favorite brother.

Then Chad did something even stranger. He whispered in her ear, and his voice sounded choked up. "All I wanted was a quiet afternoon and a hot soak in the tub. But I'd forgotten to leave Sid instructions, so I had to haul myself back outside."

He hugged Andi tighter. "When I saw you on Coco, I was angry that you had disobeyed me. But I was also scared to death that you might get hurt. I love you so much, little sister. I gave you a firm reminder never to do that again. This ranch is a dangerous place for a little girl who doesn't follow the rules. I never want to lose you"—he took a deep breath—"like we lost Father."

Andi didn't say anything. She was too worn out from shock, anger, and then from crying.

It appeared the licking had worn Chad out even more. He set Andi down and took her hand. "Help me across the yard, will you? I reckon we'd better tell Mother what happened." He looked worried. "What do you think she'll say?"

Andi smiled up at her brother and squeezed his hand. "Mother will say, 'You did good, Chad. You can tan her whenever you think she needs it.'" She harbored a hopeful, secret thought. Maybe Mother would put away her peach switch and let Chad take care of things from now on. His whacks didn't hurt at all.

Chad burst out laughing. "Don't worry, Andi. This is the first and last time I'll ever give it to you like that. It hurt me a lot worse than it hurt you. I'll let Mother have all that kind of pain from now on."

———

Andi brushed a tear from her cheek as the long-ago memory wore itself out . . . at last. Looking at it from the grown-up side of life, she wondered how in the world her family had been so patient with her. It had taken a broken arm to finally convince Andi that Mother and Chad were right. Trick riding was too dangerous for little girls.

Just then, Jared yelled, "Mama, Mama! Look. I wide all by m'self."

Coco moved along at a fast walk, and Jared held the reins like a real cowboy. Riley had rigged the stirrups to fit his short legs.

"I see you, darling," Andi called back. "You be careful."

Andi hadn't understood what Chad meant all those years ago when he said the licking had hurt worse for him than for her. But she understood now. There were times when Jared looked at her with those big, hazel eyes, stomped his foot, and yelled, "No!"

It was Andi's turn to hold the peach switch, and it really did hurt her heart to tap her little boy on his backside. But he had to learn to obey.

Just then, a new thought crossed Andi's mind. *Chad's little Susie is a firecracker. I wonder if he gives her what she needs. I should ask him sometime.*

She shook her head. Maybe not. It might bring back too many memories.

Circle C Ranch, September 1889

My instincts are telling me not to leave my husband and baby for a whole weekend. I'm quite sure this is not one of my sisters' best ideas.

CHAPTER 1

"Psst . . . Andi!"

Andi looked up from where she was dressing Jared in a fresh change of clothes. Five-and-a-half-year-old Sammy had accidentally tripped them both. The two boys fell face-first into the mud puddle the cousins had created with buckets of water from the horse trough.

"Just a second, Kate." Andi buttoned the short, white gown and sent Jared on his way. Kate's oldest girl, Betsy, had promised to read the children a story and keep them out of mischief for a few minutes this Sunday afternoon.

Andi grinned. *Good luck with that.* Keeping four cousins under the age of six contented with a book seemed a task too hard to handle, even for a capable fifteen-year-old.

"Hurry," Kate whispered. "We don't want Mother to find out we're meeting." She snagged Andi's sleeve and hurried her down the hall and into Chad and Ellie's room.

"We?" Andi asked, puzzled.

"All of us," Ellie piped up. She was sitting on the bed next to Lucy.

Melinda reclined on a large, overstuffed chair next to the fireplace. One hand rested on her rounded belly. She looked tired.

Kate shut the bedroom door with a quiet *click* and turned around to address her sisters and sisters-in-law. "We have only a few minutes before Mother wonders where we've all gone, so I'll get right to it. Mother's birthday is coming up fast."

"Not that fast," Andi said. October third was a long way from the first week of September. "What's all the hush-hush, and why talk about it a month ahead of time?"

"We want Melinda to join us," Ellie said. "She can't very well run around in October, not with a baby due the same month."

Andi paused. Run around where? It was on the tip of her tongue to ask, but Kate spoke up first. "We're going to take Mother on a birthday weekend getaway."

Andi's eyebrows rose. "We are? Where?"

"To Madera," Lucy said. "The Yosemite Hotel is a fine establishment. We'll eat out, stay up late, tell stories, and have a lovely time."

The Yosemite was a grand hotel. She and Riley had spent part of their wedding trip there. Madera was only an hour's train ride north. But . . . "A weekend getaway? You mean like overnight?"

"Of course," Kate laughed. "That's part of Mother's surprise. Three days and two nights with her girls."

"But-but," Andi stammered. "That means we have to leave the children behind." She plopped down on the bed beside Ellie. "Jared's only two years old. I can't leave him home all weekend. Riley has a ranch to run."

Ellie patted Andi's arm. "Nonsense. You left Jared for longer than a weekend last winter during the ice harvest, remember?"

Andi remembered. "That was different. Mother watched him."

"Are you saying your child's father isn't capable of taking care of his own son?" Kate accused.

"I didn't say that." To be honest, though, it was exactly what Andi was thinking. Caring for Jared was a full-time job. Riley could not watch an energetic two-year-old if he had to run the ranch too. Besides, caring for Jared was Andi's job. She told Kate so.

Kate laughed. "For goodness' sake, Andi. Jared loves his daddy. Riley is perfectly capable of letting his hired hands take care of the big ranch duties for a few days."

Andi wasn't so sure about that.

"We've already talked to the menfolk," Lucy joined in. "Justin is fine staying home with Sammy and Gracie."

"Chad agreed to keep an eye on Susie," Ellie added.

Melinda giggled. "I'm the only one of us with permission to bring little William or Margaret along on this adventure." She patted her stomach and eyed her sister. "Chad talked to Riley too. He agreed it was a splendid idea. He'll watch Jared for the weekend."

Andi's head swam. They had talked to Riley behind her back! This was too much information too fast. "I'm not sure I want to leave Jared all weekend."

"It's for Mother," Melinda reminded her.

"Easy for *you* to say," Andi argued. "You're bringing your baby along. And the rest of you?" She eyed each lady in turn. "Your children are older. Jared's just a toddler."

"We had an inkling you might say that," Kate said. "Levi, Betsy, and Hannah will stay at Memory Creek and help Riley look after one small boy. What could possibly go wrong with so many caretakers?"

Andi balled her fists and crammed them in her lap. The injustice of her sisters planning Andi's entire weekend without her say-so warred with her desire to do something special for Mother.

"Please come along, Andi," Melinda implored. "It wouldn't be the same without you."

Although five years separated the two youngest Carters, Melinda and Andi had always been close. They'd played together, argued with each other, and shared childhood secrets.

Andi melted at her sister's heartfelt appeal. "All right," she gave in, trying to sound gracious. "After all, it's for Mother."

———

"Let's run through the list one more time while we're waiting," Andi urged Riley. They sat on the high wagon seat in front of the Southern Pacific railroad depot with a few minutes to spare. Mother and the other ladies were due anytime.

Riley groaned. "We've gone over that list a dozen times. I've seen it in my sleep the last three nights. I have it memorized down to the last jot and tittle." He put a tender arm around Andi's waist. "Please stop worrying. Jared and I will be fine."

Andi slumped. This last week had been a whirlwind of preparations . . . and anxiety. Had she left enough clean gowns? Diapers? Jared was not quite ready to use the privy every time. Would Riley remember to take him? What about her little boy's naptime?

"Make sure you never let Jared out of your sight," Andi blurted, hugging her son. "Betsy is good with him, but Hannah is always flitting here and there. She loves Jared but she's careless, and the creek filled up during that big rainstorm last night and—"

"Andi!" Riley admonished. "Enough is enough. Your mother is so excited. Go along and have a good time." He hopped down from the wagon, took Jared, and gave Andi a hand to the ground. He dropped her carpetbag next to her feet. Andi pulled Jared from his daddy for a final, heartfelt hug.

"There they are now." Riley waved. "Levi! Girls! Over here!"

Giggling, Betsy and Hannah ran to the rig and climbed up on the high seat. Levi tossed their baggage in the back of the wagon then squeezed up next to his sisters.

"Bye, Mama!" Hannah yelled.

"Scoot over, Levi," Betsy snapped. "You're squishing me."

"Scoot over yourself."

"That's enough," Riley ordered.

The kids hushed. Riley wrapped Andi in a tight hug and pressed a kiss to her cheek. "Love you. Have a good time."

"Love you too." She lavished her final hugs and kisses on Jared and handed him up to Betsy. "Be good for Daddy, sweetie."

Jared nodded, his hazel eyes serious. "Bye-bye, Mama."

"I'll see you Sunday evening," Riley promised. "The six-ten train."

Andi nodded, sucking in a deep breath. When she'd left Jared with Mother last winter, no separation anxiety had lifted its ugly head for longer than a few minutes. But now?

Her heart pounded, and she felt lightheaded. What-if's flooded her thoughts. Everything inside her screamed to not let Riley leave.

"Andi?" Kate touched her lightly on her arm. "It's time to board."

Andi reluctantly turned away from Riley and acknowledged her sister. Tears stung her eyes, but she would not cry. Not in front of her oldest sister. Without looking back, she picked up her carpetbag and followed Kate to find their seats on the railroad cars.

Please, God, keep my baby safe.

CHAPTER 2

Memory Creek Ranch, September 1889

Riley watched his wife board the train then turned to his charges. One, two, three kids—four if he counted his son on Betsy's lap—took up the wagon seat, leaving no room for the driver.

He planted his hands on his hips and looked at Levi. "All right. Who volunteers to ride in the back?" At eighteen years old, Levi was nearly as big as Riley. He was the perfect candidate to hop over the seat and ride in the wagon bed. Levi didn't answer. Neither did anyone else. The Swanson girls were too busy arguing with each other to hear their uncle.

"Stop that!" Hannah screeched. "Uncle Riley, Betsy pinched me."

"I did not." Betsy's tone suggested that she was above pinching a younger sister.

"Did too!"

"Did *not*."

Riley sighed. Betsy was not above sniping at her sister.

A rough shove nearly threw Hannah off the seat. She shrieked louder and gripped the narrow, metal side railing.

Levi let out an annoyed breath. "Why don't you dump the girls into the wagon box? Then we two fellows and the baby can have peace and quiet."

Riley indicated the wagon box with his thumb. "Thank you for volunteering, Levi. You too, Hannah. Get in the back. Betsy will sit up with me and hold Jared."

"But Uncle Riley," Hannah protested, "it's dirty back there."

Levi scowled and didn't move.

"Now!" Riley bellowed.

Levi scrambled over the seat and into the back of the rig. Hannah was only a little slower joining him.

Riley swung himself up onto the wagon seat, took the reins, and released the brake. "If any of you so much as twitches, you can walk the rest of the way."

Hannah gasped but didn't argue. She found a corner and drew her knees up under her dress. Holding Jared, Betsy stared straight ahead. Levi looked disgusted but made himself comfortable in the opposite corner from his youngest sister.

"That's better."

Riley's confidence as a nanny rose nearly to the moon after the handling of his first dispute. The rest of the lengthy trip home passed in silence. Jared fell asleep in Betsy's arms. To Riley's surprise, Hannah had crawled next to Levi and was dozing against his shoulder.

Leaving on the ten o'clock train had meant an early morning for everyone.

Even Riley was yawning and rubbing his eyes by the time they rounded the rolling, oak-covered hills and Memory Creek ranch came into view.

"We're here." He brought the wagon around to the backyard and stopped near the barn. "Everybody out."

Jared woke up fussy. Worse, a familiar dampness had leaked through his gown and onto Betsy's skirt. She wasted no time complaining about it.

"I'm sorry," Riley apologized. "It's been a long morning for Jared. Could you please take him into his room and find a new gown?" He paused. With Andi gone, Jared's trips to the privy would not be consistent. "Maybe find him a clean diaper for now?" He helped Betsy and Jared down from the wagon seat.

Betsy puffed up with grown-up importance. "Sure, Uncle Riley."

Jared protested, but Betsy held him firm. She lugged him into the house. His cries rose.

Levi jumped down, leaving Hannah asleep in the wagon bed. "I'll put up the horse and wagon," he offered.

"That would be great, thanks." Riley reached over the sideboard and shook Hannah. "Hey, there. Time to get up."

Hannah woke and let Riley drag her out of the wagon. She yawned. "I'm hungry."

"We all are," Levi said. "Mama rushed us out of the house before Nila or Luisa could fix us anything to eat." He glanced up at the sky. "It's nearly noon."

"I'll fix something to eat in a jiffy," Riley promised. He took the back porch steps in one giant leap and pushed through the screen door.

Andi had left the kitchen neat as a pin, and Riley looked around in expectation. He found a frying pan and grabbed eggs from the basket sitting on the countertop. "Yes sirree, this will be easy as pie," he said. "I can't botch a meal any worse than Andi. Eggs and toast coming up."

His stomach grumbled. It had been hours since his own sunrise breakfast. He cracked a dozen eggs into the skillet, whistling his rendition of "Oh, Dem Golden Slippers."

Hannah wandered into the kitchen and peered into the frying pan. "How are you gonna cook those eggs?"

How do you think? Riley wanted to retort. He smiled instead. "In this pan, of course."

"On a cold stove?"

Riley felt heat creep up his neck. How could he have forgotten about the stove? The fire had burned itself out while he was gone. He cracked the firebox door open and peeked inside. "I see a few coals." He stuffed the opening full of small pieces of wood, adjusted the draft, and shut the door. "It won't be long now."

Hannah stared at him. "I'm hungry."

"Be patient," Riley said.

A loud wailing cut through the silent kitchen.

"Jared!" Riley had left his son with Betsy and completely forgotten about him. He dropped what he was doing and rushed from the kitchen. He opened the door to Jared's small bedroom. "What's going on, Betsy? Why is he crying?"

"He won't let me change his clothes." Betsy wrinkled her nose. "And he doesn't smell very nice. I'm sorry, but I think the father should take care of his son's dirty, stinky diaper." Without waiting for a reply, Betsy fled the room.

"Sure. All right," Riley mumbled. His cheerful attitude was slowly draining away.

Betsy was right. Jared did not smell very nice at all. "Your timing is lousy, little man," he said, getting to work on cleaning up his son. "Couldn't you have asked Betsy or me to take you to the privy?"

Jared looked at Riley with round, hazel eyes and shook his head. "No Betsy. No Daddy. Mama take me."

Uh-oh. This was going to be a long weekend. He found a clean diaper and began to wrap it around his son. Andi could deal with this when she came home.

Jared pushed Riley's hands away. "No diaper. Big boy."

Riley sucked in a breath. "Not today, little man. If you won't let me or Betsy take you to the privy, then you'll have to wear a diaper until Mama gets home."

"No diaper." Jared pushed and shoved until his clean wrapping fell to his feet. His white gown covered him from neck to knees.

"Jared," Riley said firmly, "you're going to wear that diaper until—"

"Uncle Riley, come quick!"

Riley spun around. "Now what?"

"Hurry!" Betsy yelled. "Something's burning."

Riley left Jared in his room and ran to the kitchen. "Oh, no!"

Acrid black smoke rose from the cast-iron frying pan. The smell of scorched eggs assaulted his nostrils. He snatched up a dishtowel and pulled the burning mess away from the overheated stovetop. "What's going on? Who did this?"

Tears filled Hannah's cornflower blue eyes. "I wanted to help because I'm hungry. So, I cooked the eggs."

"Have you or Betsy ever cooked eggs before?" Riley glanced into the pan. These were not eggs. They were blackened circles with brown, scorched middles.

"Well, no," Hannah admitted. "But I've always wanted to. Our cook in the city makes it look easy."

Just then Levi slammed through the back door. "You better get out here, Uncle Riley."

"Why?"

"It looks like a coyote dug a hole into your chicken coop."

Riley abandoned the scorched eggs and flew out the door. "Hey!" he shouted, waving his arms. "Get outta here! Go on!" He didn't have time to grab his rifle. He whistled for Tucker.

Riley's dog shot out from behind the barn. As soon as Tucker saw the coyote, he took off after it like a gunshot.

Levi disappeared inside the coop and returned with a casualty. He held the chicken up by its legs. "I think it's dead."

Riley clenched his fists. Andi's favorite setting hen. Could this day get any worse?

Sure, it could. It worsened within minutes.

"I'm hungry!" Hannah hollered from the back porch. The entire ranch could hear her shout. That twelve-year-old girl had a powerful set of lungs.

"I'm hungry too," Betsy added quietly. She was holding Jared, who was sobbing.

"What's the matter with him now?" Riley demanded, hurrying up the porch steps.

"I think he's hungry," Betsy replied.

"Not hungry," Jared wailed. "I want Mama."

"You forgot to put his diaper on," Betsy added.

"Could you please take care of that for me?" Riley asked.

When Betsy nodded and returned inside, Riley sucked in a frustrated breath. *Take it easy*, he warned himself. He exhaled, told Levi to bury the hen, and went back inside.

Twenty minutes later, he had the kids seated around the table. Thankfully, Andi had baked four loaves of bread yesterday. She'd churned the butter, and one of the hired hands had milked the cow this morning while Riley was gone.

Bread, butter, and milk. An excellent lunch.

With their bellies full, Kate's kids settled down. Levi disappeared into the barn, Hannah made her way toward the creek, and Jared followed Betsy toward the horses' paddock.

"Hold his hand the whole time," Riley instructed. "I promised Andi I'd keep him safe and sound."

"I'll hold his hand," Betsy assured him. "If he doesn't like it, I'll bring him back. And we won't go near the horses without you."

Riley sighed. "Thank you."

Finally, something was going right. It gave him time to turn his attention on the kitchen. It was a disaster. Bread crumbs, greasy butter, and spilled milk covered the table.

A dozen flies hovered over the leftovers. Riley grimaced. If only the kids would keep the screen door shut!

The dishpan overflowed with tin cups and plates. By now, the egg mess had hardened into a crust Riley could not scrape off, not even with the metal spatula. He was tempted to throw the frying pan away, but he refrained, knowing Andi would have a fit. She loved that skillet.

He dumped the pan into the sink beside the dishpan and pumped it full of water. Maybe soaking it would loosen the hard-as-rocks egg mess. He squeezed out a rag and headed for the fly-covered table.

Knock, knock, knock.

Riley froze. He glanced around at the crumb-littered table and floor, the dirty dishes, and the cloud of flies that was growing thicker by the minute. Who could that be?

Another hard knocking resounded through the house. Riley knew he had no choice but to find out who was banging on his front door. Sighing, he threw down the dishrag and headed for the door.

CHAPTER 3

Riley curled his fingers around the doorknob and paused. He wasn't quite ready to open the door. He took a few breaths to loosen the knot in his stomach. Then he pasted a smile on his face. He didn't know who was visiting Memory Creek this time of day, but nobody would accuse Riley Prescott of looking frazzled.

Knock, knock, knock. "Hey, Riley! Are you in there?"

Chad! What in the world? He was supposed to be home tending his little girl. Had something happened?

Riley yanked the door open. "What are you doing here? Is everything all right?"

"Everything's fine." Chad shifted little Susie to his other hip and demanded, "What took you so long to answer the door?"

"I was busy," Riley muttered. He stepped outside, closing the door behind him. "What brings you all the way out here to Memory Creek?"

Chad gave Riley a friendly smile. "A favor."

Riley looked from Chad to Susie. The little girl had her chubby arms wrapped around her father's neck. Shiny auburn curls stuck out every which way, clear evidence of a fast ride on Sky. "What kind of favor?" he asked warily.

"I'd planned to take the weekend off," Chad explained. "I really did. But something's come up. Something I need to handle myself. I can't leave it to your Uncle Sid or the hands."

Riley felt himself pale. "What are you saying?"

Chad sighed. "If Ellie learns about this, she'll surely hang me out to dry, but I need to get back to the ranch as soon as possible. Could you watch Susie for me? She's a real sweet kid and would love to play with Jared for a couple of hours. It shouldn't take longer than that to straighten everything out."

Riley hesitated. He was tempted to ask his brother-in-law what in the world needed his personal attention, but the look on Chad's face showed it was something close to an emergency. But another small child? His recent experience with lunch had given Riley a taste of reality.

"I don't know, Chad." He crossed his arms over his chest. "I've got my hands full. Couldn't Nila or Luisa watch her?"

"I already asked. Nila took off to visit Rosa for the rest of the day, and Luisa respectfully declined in her most gracious Spanish." He cringed. "C'mon, Riley. Give me a hand here. Just for a couple of hours?"

Riley chewed his lip. He didn't like turning Chad down when he was in a tight fix. On the other hand, he did not want to add a two-and-a-half-year-old to the mix this afternoon.

"I'd gladly do the same for you," Chad said.

How true this was! Chad always came to Riley's aid when he was asked. Cattle problems, free stud service from any of the Circle C stallions or bulls, offering Riley extra work when money was tight.

He sighed inwardly. How could he turn his brother-in-law down?

"Aren't Kate's kids here with you?" Chad asked, sounding desperate. "If you don't want to watch Susie, lend me Betsy. I'll take her back to the ranch and—"

Riley waved Chad's words away. There was no chance he would let Betsy go. Except for not wanting to change a soiled diaper, she was good with Jared. "No, no, it's all right." He reached for Susie, who fell into his arms. "I'll do it."

Chad slapped Riley on the back and headed for his horse. "Thanks. You're a lifesaver."

Uh-huh. He shifted Susie to his other arm.

"I owe you one!" Chad called as he galloped away.

Riley slammed the door shut, crossed through the front room and kitchen, and hurried to the back door. "Betsy!" he hollered toward the barn.

When Betsy appeared, he delivered Susie into her capable hands and hurried back to the kitchen to finish cleaning up the remains of their disastrous noon meal.

Sighing deeply, Riley collapsed onto the dry, golden grass near the creek. *I can rest at last.* He sprawled out on his back and stared up at the spreading branches of his favorite valley oak.

His eyes drifted shut. He heard laughter and splashing in the distance. His five charges were all in one place and appeared to be having a good time. Even Levi, who had started out the day unwilling to mingle with the younger children, had thawed.

As he lay stretched out in the shade, Riley's confidence began to reassert itself. The dishes were washed and put away, and the skillet had been scraped clean as a whistle. Levi had repaired the chicken coop, and nobody had seen hide nor hair of that pesky coyote.

Jared, thank goodness, had given in and let Betsy wrap a diaper on him. The soiled diaper was out of sight, and he didn't worry about Susie. Betsy took the little girl to the privy whenever it looked like she needed to use it.

Too bad Jared refused to let Betsy take him too.

Maybe I can do this, after all. Riley propped his hands behind his head and envisioned a hot, nutritious supper for himself and the kids. *Let's see. What can I fix?*

"Boss?"

Riley sat up. "What do you want?"

Matt grinned down at him. "Me and the boys need more supplies, if you want that new outbuilding finished. More nails for starters."

Riley fell back to the ground. "So? Run into town and fetch what you need. Just put it on the Memory Creek tab."

"We ain't got time to run to town," came the cowhand's hasty reply. "We got too much to get done here, 'specially with you takin' a couple days off."

True. Riley plopped his hat over his eyes and let out a breath. "Fine. I'll take care of it. You get back to work."

"Thanks, boss."

When his hired hand left, Riley pulled off his hat, opened one eye, and called, "Hey, Levi!"

"Yeah?"

"How would you like to do a man's job this afternoon?"

Levi raced to Riley's side, nearly tripping over him. "What do you need?"

"I want you to go to town. I'll make a list."

"Which horse should I saddle? Can I—" He paused. "Can I take Dakota?"

Riley sat up and wrapped his arms around his knees. "Sure." He peered through the branches to check the time. "It's early afternoon, but town's quite a ride. You can give Dakota a good workout, there and back again."

He stood and stretched. "If I didn't think you knew your way around horses, I wouldn't trust you with Dakota. Come on, young man. I'll write up that list."

Levi flushed with pleasure at his uncle's praise. "You can count on me."

———

Late afternoon was settling over the ranch when Riley realized Levi had not returned from Fresno. He hadn't given much thought to his nephew's whereabouts before now. Eighteen was plenty old. Why, at eighteen, Riley was on his own, working a man's job for a man's pay.

Maybe city kids grow up slower, he mused idly. He sat on the creek bank tossing pebbles into the water and watching the kids.

The afternoon had passed quickly and pleasantly. Riley made it his life's goal to keep the kids away from the house. It was clean right now, and he intended to keep it that way.

A haunch of beef roasted in the oven. Beef and bread were a good, filling supper for his busy young charges. And when Carlos milked the cow, there would be plenty of milk to go along with the meal. Best of all, Riley had noticed the ranch cook slip into the house earlier with a plate of what Riley suspected were cookies.

Yes sirree, this nanny business wasn't too hard. His worries had smoothed out over the last couple of hours, and Riley was glad he had not turned Chad down. Susie was having the time of her life with Jared and the girls.

Every child, from toddler to fifteen-year-old Betsy, was coated in water and mud from the roots of their hair to the bottoms of their feet. A thorough washing under the pump would be in order before Riley let any of them step foot inside the house.

Chad had not left a change of clothes for Susie, but that was not a problem. Little boys and little girls wore the same item of clothing most days—the ever-dingy white gown. Although Susie was older than Jared by six months, she was petite and could easily borrow one of Jared's gowns. When Chad claimed his daughter later this afternoon, the little girl would be clean and dry.

Riley had just decided it was time to haul everyone to the pump when he heard his name being called.

"Uncle Riley!" Levi shouted. "I'm back. I got your nails, the cornmeal for Carlos, the new saw blades, and something else."

Riley spun around and waved. He opened his mouth to direct Levi where to take the supplies, but no words came out. Instead, he felt his chest tighten.

Levi trotted up on Dakota. A large burlap sack of supplies hung down from the saddle. A small girl sat in front of Levi. She raised her hand and flapped it for all she was worth. "Hi, Unca Riley. Hi, Susie!"

"Gracie!" Susie screeched, jumping up and down.

When Levi pulled back on Dakota's reins, Riley's mouth dropped open. A small paint pony trotted around Dakota and stopped beside him. "Howdy, Uncle Riley," the dark-haired little boy greeted him. "Gracie and I get to stay with you for the rest of the day. Daddy says thanks for watching us."

Riley managed a welcoming smile for Sammy Carter then marched over to Dakota. "I want to know," he barked up at Levi, "and I want to know *right now*. Why do you have Justin's two children with you?"

Levi passed Gracie to Riley and swung down from the saddle. "I didn't exactly know how to say no to Uncle Justin." He rubbed the back of his neck and gave Riley an apologetic look. "You know what a good lawyer he is. Andi used to tell me that Justin could talk a fence post out of the ground."

He winced. "And boy, do I ever believe it. One minute I was explaining why you could not watch another kid. The next minute, Sammy's on his pony and Gracie's in my lap."

"What's Justin's big emergency?" Riley sputtered.

Levi shrugged. "I never figured that out. When Uncle Justin talks, you listen, and then you end up agreeing with him. I think it has to do with a big trial he's tied up with. Some new evidence." Levi took off his hat, brushed it off, and replaced it. "Or something like that. He sure looked happy to catch me in town."

"When is he coming to get his kids?" Riley cut in.

"He told me he'd be back before sundown."

Riley relaxed. "Well, that's good news. I've got plenty of roast beef, and Carlos baked cookies."

Levi smacked his lips. "Good thing. I'm near starved to death. When's supper?"

CHAPTER 4

Madera, California, September 1889

I can't stop thinking of horrifying what-ifs. What if Jared burns himself on the stove? What if Riley turns his back and Jared wanders off? What if? What if? What if?

Andi threw herself down on the four-poster mahogany bed and flopped back against the pillows. The coverlet was cool and satiny, a nice change after the stiff, hot atmosphere of the railroad cars. With a deep sigh, she closed her eyes. *This is heavenly.*

Just as quickly, her heart turned over. *I wonder how Riley is doing.*

The mattress bounced and squeaked. Andi opened her eyes to find Kate sitting beside her. Her sister smiled. "Napping already?"

"No, just resting." She propped herself up on one elbow. "And thinking," she confessed.

"I'm sure you are," Lucy called from the corner of their hotel room, where she stood fixing the lace on her Sunday bonnet. "You are thinking too much and worrying too much. Riley and Jared are fine. I promise."

Lucy's words did not make Andi feel better.

"I agree." Mother stepped through the doorway that connected their two hotel rooms. "Stop fussing and enjoy yourself."

"I'm sorry, Mother." Andi sighed. "I don't want to ruin this special getaway but—"

"But *nothing*, little sister," Kate scolded. "Now, it's been a long time since breakfast, and we're all hungry. Let's head downstairs to the hotel dining room. I hear the cuisine is excellent. The smells drifting up the stairs are making my stomach turn somersaults."

She snatched Andi's hat and plopped it on her sister's head. "Come on."

For her mother's sake, Andi pasted a smile on her face and rose from the bed. The six ladies left their two hotel rooms and started for the wide staircase.

Andi didn't follow right away. She bit her lip and looked around. How far from home she was! What if Jared missed her and was sobbing his little heart out? What if he'd hurt himself and cried for Mama? He wasn't used to Riley caring for him all day . . . and all night too.

Her breath caught. What if—

"Andrea?"

Mother's quiet voice sliced into her what-if thoughts, and Andi twisted around. "Coming." She shut the door and inserted the key into the keyhole. *Click.*

If only she could lock away her worries so easily.

———

"Thank you, my dears," Mother said with a satisfied sigh. "This has been a delicious noon dinner. And that peach pie was heavenly." She sighed. "I'm still reeling from this delightful surprise."

Melinda smiled. "We appreciate you, Mother. It was our turn to do something special for you." She winked at Andi. "I bet this was an especially tasty meal for you, since you didn't have to worry about cooking it."

For a moment, Andi's worries scuttled into a corner of her mind. She giggled. "You know me too well." It had indeed been a feast fit for a queen. Best of all, she didn't have to wash up one dish. "Mother, this is *your* time. What would you like to do this afternoon?"

"I'd love an afternoon nap," Mother replied. "It's hot and dusty in this town, and that train ride sapped my energy."

"That sounds lovely," Melinda said. She rubbed a hand over her belly. "Between the trip, the filling meal, and a baby who never rests, I'm all too ready to lie down for an hour or so."

"Madera has an evening exhibition scheduled for tonight at eight o'clock," Kate announced. "It features an up-and-coming young woman performer. I hear she recites poetry so well that she can move even the most hardened listener."

She shot a well-aimed glance at Andi. "And we are *all* going."

Andi kept her mouth shut, but she was thinking a lot. *This is for Mother. This is for Mother.* She could already feel herself yawning. The only thing duller than a poetry exhibition was a school exhibition or an opera singer.

Mother's eyes lit up. "That sounds wonderful."

With their afternoon plans made, they all rose. Lucy motioned the waitress over and paid their bill. "After our rest, perhaps we can sightsee around town before supper."

They filed out of the dining room and were halfway up the stairs when Andi exclaimed, "Oh, for pity's sake. I forgot that pesky reticule, and it has the key to our room."

Melinda shook her head. "Why am I not surprised?"

Andi turned and headed back down the stairs. "Go on up. This won't take but a minute. I'm sure I left it on the table."

Making a beeline across the dining room, Andi passed a solitary woman. It looked as if she had just sat down. There was no menu, no water pitcher, and no food. "Good afternoon," she greeted Andi.

Andi's mind was on her missing reticule, not on polite conversation. However, she could not pass the woman without acknowledging her greeting. "Good afternoon." She flashed her a quick smile and glanced around for the drawstring bag.

"I'm Martha Williams."

Andi paused in her search and turned her attention to this strange woman.

Martha gave Andi a vacant smile. "Have you met my family?"

Andi swallowed her uneasiness. There was something not quite right with Martha Williams, something Andi could not put her finger on. As if she was not . . . all there.

One card short of a full deck, Chad would say, but that was not polite.

Mother would be horrified at Andi's first impression. She smiled warmly to make up for her uncharitable thoughts. "No, ma'am, I haven't met them."

Mrs. Williams tilted her head at the chair to her left. "Frank, greet this young woman." She turned back to Andi. "What is your name, my dear?"

"A-Andrea Prescott," she stammered. Who was Frank? Worse, *where* was Frank?

"We are delighted to meet you," Mrs. Williams said. "And this is our little son, Jonathan. Isn't he adorable?" She smiled at the other empty chair.

Andi's stomach turned over. Was this a joke? If so, it was not funny. It was terrifying.

Just then, the waitress hurried over. "Now, Martha, you know you are not to be bothering our guests. You should return to the kitchen and work on those pots and pans."

"Oh, pish-posh." Mrs. Williams giggled, a frightening sound. "They'll keep. I'll get to them when Frank returns to work and I put Jonathan down for his nap." With that, she rose. "Come along, my dears."

Andi watched, tongue-tied, as the woman walked across the dining room and disappeared down a hallway toward the back of the hotel.

An eerie silence fell.

"I *am* sorry, miss," the waitress apologized. "Martha doesn't usually come into the dining room until well past the noon hour, after the diners have left. I don't know what got into her to wander around so early today."

"I need to get back to my room," Andi whispered. But she couldn't move. What on earth was wrong with that woman?

She kept her rude question to herself, but the waitress seemed to sense her curiosity. "Martha Williams is harmless, miss. She wouldn't hurt a fly."

"She was talking about her family."

"Oh, don't give it another thought. We've grown used to Martha's odd ways." The waitress clucked her tongue. "Captain Mace, the Yosemite's proprietor, felt pity on the poor thing and gave her a job washing up and other odd jobs around the place."

Andi swallowed. "What happened? Why does the captain feel badly for her?"

A sad expression came over the girl's face. "'Tis a sorrowful story indeed. She and her husband used to run a ranch a little east of here. Martha came to town on a lark one day, to get away for a few hours, you understand. When she returned home, she discovered a freak fire had burned down the house, killing her husband and little boy."

She shook her head. "The poor woman has never been the same since. Her mind snapped. She still believes her husband and son are alive."

Icy fingers curled around Andi's heart. Her throat tightened until she couldn't speak. Without even a polite "good day," she snatched her reticule from the table, lifted her skirts, and bolted up the stairs two at a time. In her mind's eye she saw her home a pile of ashes. Riley and her baby . . . gone. Burned to a crisp.

No! She choked back a sob. *I was wrong to leave them. I have to go home, birthday surprise or no birthday surprise.*

Andi dashed down the hall and stopped. It was deserted. Clearly, somebody else had a key to their rooms. Kate stepped out of the nearest room and closed the door. "Where have you been?"

Andi burst into tears. Kate grabbed her by the arm and guided her down the hall. "For pity's sake, Andi, don't wake the others. What's gotten into you?"

She poured out her story. It sounded even more horrifying at the retelling. "Oh, Kate! I want to go home."

Kate's blue eyes had widened at the tale. She drew Andi into a warm embrace. "I've heard such stories before. Some poor souls can't take the shock. They go inside themselves and never come out. But it won't happen to you, Andi. Everything's fine at home."

"My mind agrees with you, but my heart doesn't," Andi insisted. "I can't enjoy this trip. I know I sound like a scaredy-cat, but Mrs. Williams frightened me. I'm sorry to disappoint Mother, but I'm taking the next train home."

Kate pulled Andi from her embrace and held her at arm's length. "I understand how unsettling meeting Mrs. Williams must have been, and I apologize for talking you into this trip in the first place. But we're not letting you go home alone. Promise to stay the night so Mother can see the exhibition. We'll all go home in the morning if you still feel anxious."

It took all of Andi's determination, but she nodded. "All right, Kate. I'll stay this one night."

CHAPTER 5

Morning sunlight trickled through the lacy curtains of the Yosemite Hotel's second-story windows, casting playful rays across Andi's sleeping form. She opened her eyes. *Where am I?*

Yesterday's meeting with that poor soul hit her like a charging bull. She shot up, thrusting the bedcovers aside. Next to her, Kate groaned and rolled over. "It's too early," she mumbled. "Go back to sleep."

Andi glanced at the room's wall clock. It was early, especially after the long evening at the exhibition. She had neither yawned nor nodded off during Mrs. Angelo's long recital of the "Wreck of the Hesperus."

On the contrary, Kate's previous comment about the presenter was spot-on. Mrs. Angelo's vivid description of the frozen little girl caused Andi to see nothing but a burned little boy in her mind's eye. "He wrapped her warm in his seaman's coat against the stinging blast; He cut a rope from a broken spar and bound her to the mast."

What a horrible poem!

The entire audience burst into applause at the end. Some women were openly weeping. Andi wanted to scream and run back to the hotel, but Mother was determined to meet this international celebrity. Andi had no choice but to stay until well past ten o'clock.

The salt sea was frozen on her breast, the salt tears in her eyes . . .

It had taken Andi another two hours to fall asleep trying to rid herself of her own imagined version of Longfellow's poem. He had penned a ballad about the wreck of the schooner *Hesperus* off the icy coast of Massachusetts in 1839.

This morning, Andi's mind was spinning a ballad ten times worse about her little boy. *The flaming rafters fell to his breast, the ashes stung his eyes.*

Enough! She sprang from the bed and began to dress.

Kate stirred enough to ask, "What time is it?"

"Seven thirty." Andi shook Lucy, who looked fast asleep in the other bed. "C'mon, let's get a move on."

Without waiting for a reply, Andi knocked once then barged into Mother, Ellie, and Melinda's connecting room. To her surprise, they were already up.

"Good morning, Andrea," Mother greeted her. "You're up early."

"I didn't sleep well," Andi said. "I kept seeing that poor little girl and her father freezing to death on his sailing ship."

Mother looked sympathetic. "It was a tragic affair, and Mrs. Angelo's recitation was quite graphically portrayed." She crossed the room and hugged her youngest daughter. "I agree we should return home. I had a lovely time last evening and I'm not sure you girls could top it. Staying another day and a night seems a bit much, don't you think?"

Andi nodded, relaxing to the tips of her toes. "I hope we can catch the nine-oh-five."

"Oh, we shall," Mother replied with a laugh. "We'll hustle those two sleepyheads in your room right out of bed."

———

Andi stepped from the railroad car onto the station platform and strained to see past the throng pressing in around her. Saturday morning had brought a good many people from Madera to Fresno, although Andi couldn't imagine why.

She looked around. Same old Fresno. No one was waiting for them. Nobody knew the ladies had returned more than a day and a half ahead of schedule.

Mother, as usual, took charge. "We'll head for the livery and rent a buggy."

"Walk me home first," Melinda suggested. "I don't need a buggy, and my cottage is right on the way."

"Could we stop by my place too?" Lucy asked. "It's only a few blocks past Melinda's. I'd love to see what Justin thinks of my surprise return." She smiled. "I hope the house is still in one piece."

Andi held back a laugh. Of course, the house would be in one piece. Justin did just about everything right. The kids were probably dressed and fed, with their hair combed, and busy doing chores around the house. She wondered if Lucy wished she were still in Madera.

Oh, well, Andi told herself. *The others didn't have to come home with me. They could have stayed.*

Mother agreed that they should accompany Melinda and Lucy home. After all, now that they were in Fresno, there was no reason to rush out to the ranch like their tails were on fire.

The little group continued down Front Street. It wasn't long before they reached Melinda's house. She thanked them, bid them good-bye, and stepped inside.

Maybe Mother and the rest of the family were not in a hurry, but Andi could barely contain her impatience. Lucy's house was only a few more blocks. They would then have to backtrack to Blake's livery stable to rent a surrey.

"Say, Lucy, isn't that Justin coming our way?"

Ellie's eager question brought Andi back to the here and now. Sure enough, big brother had just turned the corner and was heading straight for them.

"It is." Lucy frowned. "But why is he driving the buggy alone? Where could he be going without the children?"

"I guess we're about to find out," Kate said.

Justin pulled the shiny black buggy to a stop beside them. "Lucy!" His voice betrayed his surprise. "I wasn't expecting to see you until tomorrow evening. Is everything all right?" His gaze took in the rest of his family. "Mother, why are you and the girls back so—"

"Everything is *not* all right," Lucy cut in. She made her way to the two-seated rig and looked up at her husband. "Please tell me where our children are."

Justin smiled. "They're fine, sweetheart. Nothing to worry about. I'm on my way to pick them up now."

"Pick them up?" Lucy's mouth dropped open. "Pick them up from where?"

Justin shrugged. "From Memory Creek."

"Memory Creek?" Andi gasped and hurried to join Lucy. Her thoughts spun faster than a carousel. Sammy and Gracie were out at the ranch?

"Now, ladies," Justin said in a conciliatory tone, "it's not what you might think."

"No lawyer tricks!" Andi burst out. "Just tell us straight."

"All right." He lowered the reins and sighed. "An unexpected complication with my current court case popped up yesterday afternoon. It required all my attention, and it couldn't be put off. I was scrambling for a solution when I saw Levi in town. He seemed like a godsend, so I sent the kids with him to Riley."

"You sent the kids to *Riley*?" Andi's breath whooshed from her lungs.

"What?" Now Kate got into the act. "Levi rode all the way out to Memory Creek with two small children? That's an hour and a half. What were you thinking, big brother?"

Andi was thinking Justin would rather be anyplace else right now, but his calm attorney's face betrayed nothing out of the ordinary. "For goodness' sake, Kate. Levi is not a child. He's a young man. He's perfectly capable of taking Samuel and Grace out to spend a couple of hours with their cousin."

"Who are *you* to say what my son is capable of?" Kate snapped.

"What do you mean a *couple of hours*?" Lucy demanded at the same moment, hands on her slim hips. "It looks like they spent all night there too."

Justin winced, clearly caught. "I'm sorry, sweetheart. Honestly, it was not my intention to leave them with Riley all night. But by the time I sorted out the court issues, it was well past sundown. I didn't want to ride out in the dark and I figured they were probably already down for the night."

"You didn't ask Riley?" Andi put in. "Instead, Levi just showed up with two little kids?"

Suddenly, perfect big brother didn't seem so perfect as before.

The only calm ladies were Mother and Ellie. Chad was home with Susie, so why *wouldn't* she look calm? Andi envied her.

"Let's head out to the ranch and see for ourselves how Riley and my grandchildren are doing," Mother put in smoothly. "I'm sure everything is fine."

Justin smiled gratefully. "Like I said, I'm on my way out there right now."

"Yes, I think we'd better." Lucy waved away her husband's offer of help and pulled herself into the buggy. "Would you all like to squeeze in?"

Andi wanted to holler yes, but Mother said, "You go on ahead. We'll rent a rig and meet you at Memory Creek."

Andi opened her mouth to protest. After all, this was *her* ranch Justin and Lucy were heading to. "But Mother, I—"

Too late. Justin slapped the reins across the bay's back. The horse jumped into a fast trot before Andi could say another word. Instead, she simmered all the way to Blake's Livery.

The next hour passed in miserable silence, at least for Andi. No one spoke. The tension in the air felt thick enough to cut with a knife.

Mother, no doubt sensing her youngest daughter's anxiety, drove the rented carriage faster than she ought. A good thing too. If she'd gone any slower, Andi would have gotten out and pushed. Her thoughts seesawed between seething fury at her brother and desperate worry about Jared.

As they made their way past the turnoff to the Circle C, Mother brought the surrey to a stop. She turned to Andi and Kate. "Are you all right with dropping Ellie and me off before heading out to Memory Creek?"

No, Andi was not all right with that idea. She didn't want to take the time to follow the long driveway to the Circle C ranch house and then backtrack. But she sighed and said, "Yes, that's fine."

Before they had trotted even a hundred yards, Ellie leaned forward. "Is that Chad on Sky?" She squinted against the mid-morning sun. "Is he alone?"

Chad's dark silhouette drew closer, confirming Ellie's suspicions. "Where's Susie?"

Andi stiffened. She took a good guess where Susie was—on Memory Creek ranch.

CHAPTER 6

Memory Creek Ranch, September 1889

Sighing deeply, Riley stood just inside the kitchen door and surveyed the current state of his home. It wasn't a pretty sight.

Cups and plates from supper lay soaking in the dishpan. Cookie crumbs and spilled hot chocolate stuck to the table and floor, evidence of a late night trying to settle seven restless kids. Thick, black coffee dregs covered the bottom of the coffeepot.

Riley had used the coffee to keep himself awake long past sunset, hoping Chad and Justin would make good on their promises to come for their kids. But once full dark settled over the ranch, Riley had given up.

Finding sleeping places for seven kids had been no easy task, but he'd made do. The four girls squeezed into Andi and Riley's bed, Sammy shared Jared's small bed, and Levi escaped as fast as he could to sleep in the barn.

Traitor! Levi was the only person who passed a peaceful night. Even Jared, who slept in his own bed, had wrestled with Sammy for his share of the covers. The dispute had continued late into the night, with loud wails and Riley's multiple interventions.

The girls jostled for the best positions. Susie and Gracie had to be separated before they scratched out each other's eyes. When they finally fell asleep, Kate's girls smashed the two little ones in the middle of the bed and lay like guards to keep them from falling out or escaping.

By midnight, Riley wanted nothing more than to join Levi in the barn for a little peace and quiet. The sweet smell of alfalfa, the soft, sleepy neighs of Dakota, Shasta, and the other horses. Pure heaven.

But he could not in good conscience leave Betsy and Hannah with the full care of the little ones. What if something happened? So instead, Riley found an extra blanket in the cedar chest, punched a stiff pillow into a shapeless mass, and bedded down on the settee for what remained of the long, wearying night.

He spent a restless night on the sofa, which was too short for his long legs. Grumpy and still half asleep, he rose before dawn and hurried outside to snag Levi to help with the chores. Carlos had just milked and passed a frothing pailful to Riley as he passed by.

"Is everything all right, Uncle Riley?"

Levi's question brought Riley back to the present dismal situation. His gaze swept the kitchen for an empty counter spot. "I'll live. Start a fire, would you?" He set the pail of milk between a stack of dirty dishes and a pile of wet dish towels.

Levi nodded and went to work on the cookstove. "Maybe the others will sleep late," he whispered.

"After their late night, I'm sure they'll sleep a couple more hours," Riley hoped.

A howling from one of the bedrooms sent Riley out of the kitchen at a run.

He stopped in dismay at the state of the sitting room. A quick glance at the windowpanes showed greasy streaks from too many sticky fingers. Discarded nightclothes and underclothes lay strewn over the rocking chair, littered the braided throw rug, and lay scattered in a trail to both bedrooms. A couple of wet but clean diapers hung on a rack near the cold, dead ashes of the fireplace.

He groaned. All this wreckage from one afternoon and night?

"Mama!" Susie burst out of the bedroom clutching Andi's pearl-handled hairbrush. The expensive one Riley had given her for Christmas last year.

Gracie followed close behind hollering, "Gimme that!" They chased each other around Riley, around the dirty clothes, and then into Jared's room.

"I'm sorry, Uncle Riley," Betsy apologized from the door frame. "Susie's awfully quick."

Riley opened his mouth to respond but screaming and crying spewed from Jared's tiny room just then. Samuel appeared, holding the hairbrush high over his head. "I got it for you, Uncle Riley," he yelled over the din.

The little girls jumped and grabbed for the brush then cried when they couldn't reach it.

"Quiet!" Riley roared. He took the brush from Sammy and faced the girls. "You can't have this."

Susie and Gracie gulped back their tears. "I want my mama," Gracie said.

You're not the only one who wants your mama, Riley wanted to say, but he held his tongue.

Jared appeared just then looking wet and miserable. He sniffed back tears. Sammy wrinkled his nose. "Jared wet the bed. I guess his diaper wasn't on good enough."

Riley picked up his son. "It's all right, little man. We'll get you changed and ready for the day."

"I'll dress him," Betsy offered, stepping forward.

"Thanks." He gave Jared to Betsy and turned to Hannah. "You make sure the two little girls are dressed."

Hannah yawned. She looked in no mood to give her uncle a helping hand. "Do I have to?"

"Yes, you have to." Scowling, Riley pointed to the bedroom. "Now."

Hannah gulped and herded Susie and Gracie back into the room. The door clicked shut.

Riley returned to the kitchen. The room felt stifling, and no wonder. The cookstove was burning like a runaway locomotive engine. "What in the world?" He closed both dampers and threw open the back door.

"I hope it's hot enough," Levi said. "I haven't had a lot of practice with cookstoves." He nodded at a pan on the stovetop. "Leastways, I got the water boiling."

"It's fine," Riley assured the youth. He forced a smile. "Andi had all kinds of trouble with this black beast at first too." He dumped a big scoop of oats into the boiling water, cleared the table, and wished he had a cup of strong, hot coffee.

A few minutes later, a hoard of hungry children crowded around the table. When Riley set bowls of steaming oatmeal in front of them, gloomy silence fell. They looked at the thick, lumpy cereal and didn't say a word.

Except Jared. "No mush, Daddy." He pushed it away.

Taking their cues from their cousin, the other little children refused breakfast too.

Gracie whimpered. "Don' like mush."

"Me neither," Sammy said.

Susie burst into tears. "Mama!"

"I think it tastes great." Levi lifted an overflowing spoonful of oatmeal. "See?" He plunged it into his mouth. "Mmm . . ." His cheeks bulged.

Hannah gagged. Betsy made choking sounds. The little ones cried louder. Jared upturned his bowl. Mush and milk streamed across the table and onto the dirty floor.

Riley's temper boiled over. "Then you can all go hungry." He turned and stomped out of the kitchen.

CHAPTER 7

When Riley returned to the kitchen, the mush was gone . . . and so were the kids. All except Jared, who sat beside a puddle of milk under the table, petting Tucker. Tucker lapped up the milk with the ease of much practice.

Riley set the coffeepot brewing and surveyed the mess. Why hadn't Justin returned for his kids last night? Why hadn't Chad?

"Just for a couple of hours," Chad had promised.

Those "couple of hours" had added up to more trouble than Riley could handle. He'd rather break a dozen broncs than repeat this experience. He squatted next to Jared and ruffled his hair. "What are you doing in here by yourself?"

Jared didn't answer. Instead, he found a piece of toast from yesterday and offered it to the dog. Tucker gulped it down and went back to lapping milk.

"Come on, little man." Riley heaved his son out from under the table and opened the back door. Levi and Hannah were nowhere in sight, but Betsy and the three little cousins were sitting on the porch steps. They stared unhappily out at the yard.

Betsy turned her head at Riley's approach. "Are you mad at us, Uncle Riley?"

"No. Just a bad morning. Sorry I snapped at you." He held out Jared. "I'll grab a cup of coffee and then we'll head for the creek."

Shouts of *yippee* were music to Riley's ears. It was only mid-morning, but already the sun was blistering. Fishing and splashing in the creek would keep everybody out of the house for the rest of the morning. He would attack the kitchen mess later . . . much later.

Peace at last, Riley hoped. Happy children splashing in the creek; older kids fishing or catching frogs. He and Levi could discuss manly subjects and maybe even catch a few minutes of sleep after last night's commotion.

Riley's peace lasted less than an hour. Susie, the "sweet kid" Chad had boasted about yesterday, was as stubborn as her father. And that auburn hair she got from Ellie? Riley had experienced Susie's temper this morning, but now she displayed it in full bloom.

When Sammy accidentally conked her on the head with his makeshift fishing pole, Riley thought the Civil War was about to be replayed. For a small, not-yet three-year-old, Susie was a fighter. She went after her cousin with a vengeance. In the process, she plowed over Gracie, who was sitting quietly on the creek bank pretending to fish.

Gracie howled and fell headfirst into the water. *Splash!* "Mammmaaa!" she screeched.

Betsy came to her rescue, but Gracie did not stop crying. Creek water mixed with tears dripped down her face. Her sobs grew louder.

Gracie's cries set Jared wailing. Riley had his hands full trying to calm his son, round up Susie, and pull Sammy away.

Levi finally yanked the two children apart. "How did you get yourself into this mess, Uncle Riley? I wish Mama had left the girls and me at the Circle C. I could've watched out for them rather than be lassoed into this circus."

Oh, how right Levi was!

Riley did a quick head count. Jared in his arms, check. Sammy and

Susie being held at arm's length by Levi, check. Gracie bawling her head off and standing up to her waist in the creek, check. Thankfully, she finally let Betsy lift her onto the creek bank, where she shivered. But at least she stopped bawling.

Four little people under the age of six, plus—

Riley glanced around. Where was Hannah? At age twelve, she was certainly capable of taking care of herself. Now, she was nowhere in sight.

"Levi!" Riley snapped. He instantly regretted his impatient tone.

"What?" Levi hollered back, clearly in just as much of an ill temper as his uncle.

"Where's Hannah?"

"How should I know?"

"Find her!"

Levi dropped Susie's and Sammy's arms and hit the dirt path running.

"I fell for it." Riley simmered. "I bet Chad laughed all the way to town after his *urgent* ranch business, what with a couple of free hours on his hands."

By now, Gracie's tears had been wiped away. Betsy set her down on the creek bank with her fishing pole. Betsy caught a frog and passed it to Sammy, who forgot his feud with Susie and turned all smiles. Betsy found another frog for Susie, and the cousins happily set off to have frog-swimming races.

Riley let out a sigh of relief. Betsy was worth two of himself. "Thanks, honey." He smiled.

Betsy grinned back.

When Levi dragged Hannah back from wherever she'd been exploring, Riley set the young man to another task, one of high importance. "I want you to ride over to the Circle C. Find Chad, and don't come back without him."

"I will!" Levi took off running for a horse. He sounded relieved to be given an errand far away from a bunch of grumpy children.

Riley wished for a fleeting moment that Betsy was the confident rider Andi had been at age fifteen. At Betsy's age, Andi had taken charge of an entire *remuda* on a long and dangerous cattle drive. Riley had heard the story countless times.

Betsy, on the other hand, although sweet and helpful, had not spent a lot of time on horses. Besides, as much as he would have liked to send the girl into town for Justin, Riley needed her here to help ride herd on the four youngsters.

Riley pulled his gaze away from Levi's retreating form and back to his present troubles. His house was in shambles, and the children were damp, filthy, and short-tempered. What would Andi say when she found out that instead of Riley and three older kids watching one toddler, he was watching four little kids—five if he counted the dreamy Hannah, who tended to forget whatever task she was set to.

Riley shook his head. "I won't think about that now."

He jostled Jared until his son was giggling and happy again. Then he held the boy's hand and let him splash in the creek. Pretty soon, Riley felt relaxed enough to splash Sammy in a mock water fight.

Little by little, Riley settled down. He drained the rest of his now-cold coffee and relaxed. Chad and Justin would eventually return. They were probably on their way out to the ranch right now. After they picked up their kids and left, Riley had the rest of the weekend—and Kate's kids— to help him put the house in order. Why clean anything now, only to have it messed up in no time? Andi wouldn't be home until tomorrow evening, which seemed an eon from now.

Yes, Riley had all the time in the world.

———

The sound of hooves tearing up the summer-dead grass, along with Levi's frantic "Riley!" drew Riley from his drowsy stupor on the creek bank, where he lay on his side watching the kids play. Betsy and Hannah had woven the stiff, golden grass into crowns, and each child sported one, even the little boys.

He leaped to his feet. "What's wrong?" It had only been twenty minutes since Levi galloped out of the yard.

"Did you get Uncle Chad?" Hannah bellowed. "Why are you back so soon?"

Levi dismounted, breathing hard. "You won't believe it," he said, jogging up to Riley.

"Believe what?" Riley demanded. *It had better be no less than a cattle stampede that kept Chad away for so long*, he growled inwardly.

"Uncle Justin is on his way here."

"It's about time. What about Chad?"

Levi shook his head. "I dunno. I never made it to the Circle C. I was halfway there when I saw Uncle Justin and Aunt Lucy in the distance."

"What? Lucy?" Riley caught his breath. "Are you certain?"

Levi nodded. "I can recognize Justin's fancy rig as good as the next fella. I didn't stick around to see 'em up close, but who else would be riding with Uncle Justin?"

Levi had a point.

"I figure they'll be here in less than half an hour." Levi looked troubled.

Riley's stomach lurched. If Lucy was back, then Andi could not be far behind. And if Lucy was with Justin, then Andi must have learned that Sammy and Gracie were with him.

He shook his head. What had happened to bring the ladies home from Madera more than a day and a half early?

"As soon as I recognized the buggy, I hightailed it back here," Levi said. "I thought you'd want to know because . . ." His voice trailed off as he glanced back at the house.

Riley's eyes widened in sudden alarm. A thought worse than injury or illness in his wife or sisters-in-law slammed into his head. They were on their way *here*!

"C'mon, boy." Riley jerked his thumb in the direction of the house.

"Rally the troops. We've got a lot of cleaning to do and not much time to do it." When Levi hesitated, Riley shouted in his father's army-captain's voice. *"Move!"*

Levi took off toward the barn like a shot out of a cannon to put up the horse.

CHAPTER 8
Memory Creek Ranch, September 1889

Running into Chad on his way out to Memory Creek was the last straw to this topsy-turvy day. Andi's eyes were not deceiving her. Chad was indeed riding solo.

Susie must be out at the ranch too, Andi fumed silently.

She wanted to fly into Chad the minute he caught up to the surrey, but she resisted the urge when he waved and called out, "Howdy, ladies. What are you doing here? Why aren't you in Madera?"

"What's going on, Chad?" Ellie demanded, ignoring her husband's query. "Where's our daughter?" Her voice sounded strained.

Mother brought the surrey to a standstill, which raised Andi's anxiety another notch. She listened in simmering silence as her brother explained the ranch problems that had come up. Yes, they did sound serious, but where was Mitch? Couldn't he have pitched in so Chad could watch his own child?

This was too much! Why, oh why, hadn't she jumped into Justin's buggy and squeezed in between him and Lucy? She wasn't very big. Andi could be home already, if only things hadn't progressed as slowly as a turtle race.

And now? The minutes were ticking by. Lucy and Justin appeared to have more than an hour's head start.

"Chad . . ." Andi began.

Chad ignored her, as usual. "I told Riley I'd pick Susie up last night," he finished. He sounded sheepish.

"Clearly, you didn't," Ellie accused. "Why not?"

"I intended to ride out there after I settled things, but Beauty decided to foal early, and she needed help. I couldn't let just anybody take over and—"

"Mitch could have taken over!" Andi burst out before Ellie could say anything. "You left your baby overnight with Riley, knowing he already had his hands full, on account of a birthing mare?"

"I couldn't have said it better myself," Ellie said.

"Now, hold on a minute. What do you mean 'his hands full'? One little girl is not a handful, not with Kate's kids helping out." He glared at Andi. "Besides, I remember a certain night not many years ago when you pulled me from my well-deserved sleep to tend *your* birthing mare."

Andi fell silent. Chad had certainly saved the day when Taffy was foaling.

"The least you could do is understand why I couldn't leave Beauty like that," he went on.

"Maybe Andi can understand, but I can't," Ellie broke in. "Justin's two children were delivered to the ranch later that day, and they spent the night too."

Chad's eyes widened. "No!"

"Yes!" Ellie, Kate, and Andi shouted at the same time.

Chad threw up his hands. "Hey, it's not my fault. How was I supposed to know?"

"Please," Mother said. "Save the squabbling for another day. You are all turning this into something more serious than it is. 'A tempest in a teapot,' as they say."

Leave it to Mother to bring everyone back to reality. She chirped to the horses and urged them into a jaunty trot. Chad nudged Sky to ride alongside the buggy.

Half an hour later, they trotted onto Memory Creek land.

Chad put his heels to Sky, but Andi shouted, "No! You can stay right here with us. Justin and Lucy already shot ahead, and I refuse to be the

last person to find out if I have a husband and child left . . . or a home."
She took a breath. "Please remember that it's *my* house and *my* husband
you and your brother have overwhelmed."

For once, Chad held back. He slowed his buckskin to a walk. "Would
you like a ride, little sister?"

Andi shook her head. "We're nearly there now."

Waves of relief flooded her as they rounded the last oak-covered hill-
ock. The house was still standing. A thin plume of smoke trailed up from
the kitchen chimney. Andi's heart slowed down, and she allowed herself to
relax.

It was her turn to feel sheepish. Maybe she had overreacted yesterday,
just like a first-time mother. She'd worked herself into a dither for no
reason after meeting that poor woman. Yet, Mother and the others had
humored her.

Mother pulled the surrey to a stop in front of the porch. Not far
away, Justin's empty buggy was tied to the hitching rail. There was no
sound. Not a crying child. Not a yelling Riley. Not a passel of fighting
children.

Nothing. It was eerie.

"Riley!" Andi yelled. "Justin! Lucy! Where *is* everybody?"

There was no answer.

Andi didn't wait for Chad to lend her a hand down from the surrey.
She gathered up her traveling skirt and jumped from the rig. She tripped,
caught herself, and regained her footing. She flew up the porch steps.

Lucy met her at the front door. "Shh," she warned.

Kate, Ellie, Mother, and Chad joined Andi on the porch. They entered
the house together.

Andi's breath caught when she stepped inside. Everything looked
exactly the way she'd left it yesterday morning. The windows glistened
and the floor was swept. Every piece of lint and scrap of trash had been
plucked from the braided rug.

A quick peek inside the kitchen made Andi feel silly. Why had she rushed to get home? The kitchen was neat as a pin. A fresh pot of coffee bubbled on the stovetop.

Riley was pulling a sheet of cookies from the oven. "Welcome home, ladies." He lifted the tray. "You're just in time for cookies and coffee, or tea if you prefer." He nodded to Chad. "Howdy, Chad. It's about time you showed up."

Chad didn't answer. Neither did anyone else. They stared at Riley, speechless.

Justin sat at the table, nursing a cup of coffee. Lucy stood behind her husband, calmly watching the reunion.

Something's not right, Andi thought. Riley was too cheerful. Justin was too quiet. Lucy was smiling too widely. She looked from one to the other. "Where are Jared and the other children?"

Lucy plucked Andi's sleeve and led her through the sitting room. At the main bedroom, she put a finger to her lips and cracked the door open a sliver.

Samuel, Grace, Susie, and Jared lay sound asleep, tangled together in a heap of arms and legs. Susie's auburn curls covered Gracie's dark hair. Sammy had an arm around Jared.

Andi's hand flew to her mouth. Never had she seen such tousled, filthy children. Torn crowns graced their heads. Pieces of golden grass sprinkled their clothes and the bed coverings. Jared yawned, rolled over, and stuck a thumb in his mouth. A dirty thumb. It matched his dirt-encrusted blond hair.

The ladies tiptoed backward and clicked the door shut.

"Where are *my* kids?" Kate asked when they returned to the kitchen.

"In the barn tending the horses." Riley piled the cookies onto a plate and offered them all around.

Andi took a cookie but didn't eat it. She studied Riley. Although he put on a cheerful face, there was no mistaking his haggard look. It showed in the dark circles under his hazel eyes. What was he hiding?

Kate declined refreshments and headed out the back door. She returned a minute later, shaking her head in bewilderment. "The girls are asleep in the hay." Her words came out in a whisper. "Levi is brushing Dakota. All he said was, 'Hi, Mama. Did you have a nice trip?'"

Andi fell into a kitchen chair. "Riley, I'd like to know—"

"Hey, Riley," Chad broke in. "I'm sorry I didn't come for Susie last night. I was caught off guard with a foaling emergency. By the time I delivered and tended the foal, it was too dark to make the trip." He shrugged. "I knew Susie would be asleep by then, anyway. I came this morning as soon as I could get away."

Riley's face told Andi that Susie had *not* been asleep late last night, but he waved Chad's apology aside. "Levi, Betsy, and I handled it."

Chad grinned. "I figured you did."

End of the story for the two men.

Justin said nothing. He looked too guilty or too tired to add anything to the waning conversation. Andi's curiosity rose sky high.

Riley didn't ask why Andi had come home early. Lucy had most likely explained. He pulled her into a tight hug. "It's good to see you."

"It's good to see you too, but . . ." Her words trailed away.

How in the world had Riley managed seven young guests and kept the house so clean? How did he have time to bake cookies? Especially if he had not expected the ladies to come home early. Were the cookies for the kids?

Andi rarely had time to bake anything extra, and she only had Jared to tend.

But the biggest question of all? Why did he look so completely done in? What was he *not* telling her?

Riley's high spirits continued during the unplanned visit. Levi and two sleepy-looking girls came indoors and helped themselves to the cookies. Instead of Hannah's incessant chatter and her tendency to "tell all," she was exceptionally quiet. So were Betsy and Levi. They smiled and answered questions, but they did not speak unless spoken to.

When one of the little ones awakened, the rest tumbled from the bed and ran into the kitchen. Shrieks of "mama" echoed from the walls. Andi snatched up Jared and hugged him tight. He didn't smell very good, but he was happy and healthy.

Andi was glad she'd come home. It was worth it to find out everything was fine.

Half an hour later, Kate, Mother, Ellie, and the kids squeezed into the rented surrey. Chad tied Sky to the back of the rig. "I'll drop you off at the ranch and return the rig."

Justin and Lucy pulled their two children into the buggy and left. Gracie cried, "I want Susie!"

Riley rolled his eyes and said nothing.

Hmm . . . I wonder what that look means, Andi wondered.

Alone at last with her husband and baby, blessed silence fell. Andi dropped to the settee beside Riley, with Jared in her lap.

Riley flung his head back and draped one leg over the side of the couch. He closed his eyes and let out a long, weary sigh.

Andi's eyebrows shot up. So, things were not as Riley had made them appear. "All right, what really happened?"

Riley cracked open one eye and held Andi's curious look. "What do you mean 'what happened?' You can see for yourself that nothing 'happened.'" He shrugged and closed his eye. "The evidence speaks for itself."

"Oh, no, you don't." Andi jabbed Riley in the side.

"Ouch!" Riley jerked up, frowning.

"There's something you're not telling me," Andi insisted. "The kids sleeping in the middle of the morning and dirty as pigs? The house spick-and-span? Hannah as quiet as a deaf-mute?"

Riley crossed his arms and settled back down for what looked like a well-deserved nap. "There's absolutely nothing to tell. And now, if you don't mind, I'm going to take a little snooze." He was asleep an instant later.

Andi let out a huffy breath, gathered Jared into her arms, and headed to the kitchen for a cup of coffee. "Oh, Jared, if only you could talk!"

CHAPTER 9

Jared couldn't tell Andi a thing. In the days that followed, Riley was close-mouthed too.

He finally opened up two weeks later while they were picnicking by the creek. Andi found part of a woven grass crown and fingered it, remembering her short-lived getaway. She wondered once again how Riley had managed to do all he had done.

"I feel like a failure," she confessed. "You managed a young man, two chatty girls, and four little children, and you still kept the house clean. You even baked cookies." She sighed and let the crown fall from her fingers. "I can barely manage Jared." She peered into Riley's eyes. "How did you do it? I would really like to know."

Andi's quiet words clearly hit Riley hard. He swallowed, took a deep breath, and then blurted out the entire tale of Friday, Friday night, and Saturday morning. The more words he spilled the wider Andi's smile grew. It was satisfying to learn that he had not managed as well as he'd led her to believe.

"Saturday morning was all Justin's and Lucy's idea," Riley confessed, leaning back in the grass. "They stepped into the middle of an absolute catastrophe. The faster Levi, Betsy, and I worked to clean, the worse the house looked.

"Thankfully, Lucy took charge, and the kids responded. She had Betsy mix up a batch of cookie dough. Hannah was set to washing windows. Levi helped me clean the house, and Lucy took over the kitchen chores. She's a wonder at organizing. She even put Justin to work. He was in charge of keeping the four little ones out of the way."

Andi laughed. No wonder big brother had slumped over his coffee that morning. "Poor Justin."

"Justin was told to get them to take naps at any cost. When I peeked in, he had the kids on the bed and was reciting legal precedents from one of his law books."

That sounded just like Justin. He'd memorized half of those dusty old law books.

"It didn't take long for the kids to drift to sleep listening to all that legal drivel," Riley finished. "Besides, I'd had such a hard time getting them to sleep last night that they were ready for a nap this morning."

He shook his head. "Truly, the house was a disaster. The kids were hungry all the time. They were filthy and fighting like cats and dogs. Oh, the noise!" He grimaced. "Louder than a stampede. Levi, Betsy, and I despaired of ever getting things back in order."

The pictures had no trouble forming in Andi's mind. "I'll bet."

"When Lucy and Justin showed up, it was like the Second Coming," Riley admitted. "They wanted to help me out and make it appear as though I had everything under control, even though I didn't." He gave Andi a lopsided grin. "I don't think I had you completely fooled."

"Well, maybe a little." Smiling, Andi reached out and smothered her husband in a happy embrace. "What a dear you are to want to put our house back in order and show me you could manage the little ones."

"I wanted the house to look nice for you," Riley said. "I knew if you returned and it looked like the Battle of Gettysburg, you would never feel easy in your mind to do things with your Mother and sisters again. And you should."

Andi kissed him then untangled herself from his arms. "I love you. Thanks for everything you do."

Riley returned her kiss. "Sure thing, sweetheart. But next time, it's Chad's turn to watch the kids." A mischievous smile crept over his face. "I can't wait."

Andi giggled. "Neither can I."

COUNT YOUR BLESSINGS

Memory Creek Ranch, November 1889

I sometimes forget how thankful I am for my husband and my family.

CHAPTER 1

"What a wretched way to begin the holidays."

Andi couldn't keep her complaint inside. "One week before Thanksgiving, and it has to dump all this rain?" It was as if the heavens had taken a bucket and tipped it over from on high.

Andi drew back the lace curtain and peered out the front window. She could barely see through the gray haze. She could scarcely hear herself think. The rain rattled against the rooftop like a drummer gone mad.

"That's just swell," she muttered, letting the curtain drop back in place.

She returned to the kitchen and picked up a dish towel. Last night's clean supper dishes were stacked on the counter. She'd been too worn out to put them away. This morning's breakfast dishes soaked in the dishpan.

And the rain was not giving up. A loud boom of thunder told Andi that this late fall storm would probably last all morning, maybe even into the afternoon. Three days ago, the sun had shone down warm and bright. The temperature had soared into the eighties the week before.

She needed to latch on to the memories of those warm autumn days before they disappeared down a deep, dark hole. November days were short, but Riley had taken extra care to stop his ranch work early every afternoon to take Andi and Jared riding before nightfall.

Just last week, Andi's heart bubbled over with joy when she pulled herself onto Shasta's back. She had exciting news she couldn't wait to share. When Riley asked what she was so all-fired excited about, she'd beamed.

"I might take a trip to town sometime to let Doc Weaver confirm my suspicions, but . . ." Her voice trailed off.

Riley's brow wrinkled. "What suspicions?" Then his mouth fell open. "Do you mean . . ."

"I do." Andi grinned and reined in Shasta. "We're having another baby."

Riley thrust his fist in the air and whooped. Then he yanked on Dakota's reins, dropped to the ground, and pulled Andi from the saddle. She giggled when he swung her around. Then she collapsed against his chest, her heart pounding from the thrill of it all.

From Coco's back, Jared clapped. "Mama! Daddy!"

The next few days had passed in a happy blur. Andi was sure that nothing could dim her joy.

She was wrong.

Nausea, lassitude, grumpiness. Andi was suddenly thrust under a wave of something entirely new and unwelcome. Was this what her sister-in-law had experienced four years ago, when they'd been torn away from their families and taken to the Mexican outlaws' hideaway?

No wonder Lucy wanted to sleep all the time, Andi mused. *Anything to escape this wretched feeling.*

Today, with the gloomy weather and the chores piling up at lightning speed, Andi's mood took another plummet toward rock bottom. It didn't help that Jared, who had started out as the sweetest, quietest, sleepiest baby ever born, had transformed into a busy, stubborn two-year-old.

Every time Andi turned around, Jared was into something. Yesterday, she found him on the top shelf of the knickknack cabinet. "How did you get up there?" She needed a footstool to drag him down.

When Andi looked around later that day, Jared had vanished. She'd forgotten to latch the screen door after bringing in the clean laundry. She found Jared in his pony's paddock, sitting high and mighty on Coco's brown back.

A loud wailing wrenched Andi back to this soggy, dismal morning. She wasn't worried that Jared might disappear today. No toddler would wander out in this downpour. Besides, he was miserable with a runny nose and a cough.

Thank you, Susie Carter. Andi flung down her dish towel and headed for the front room. Jared's cousin, six months older than he, had shared her cold at Sunday dinner last week. She'd no doubt shared it with Sammy and Gracie too. Hopefully, Melinda had kept one-month-old William far away from Susie.

Thanksgiving at the Circle C would surely be full of coughs and sniffles.

Andi picked Jared up and tried to comfort him. His nose ran down to his chin. A quick wipe only made him cry louder. He tossed his head, arched his back, and screamed.

Andi plopped down in the rocking chair. Tears welled up. "I am so tired."

Jared had been up half the night. Riley had taken his turn rocking the stuffy boy, but Andi had not been able to sleep.

This sudden, drenching downpour was the last straw.

Andi let an unsuspecting Riley have it with both barrels when he came indoors for the noon meal. He stomped the water from his boots, threw off his poncho, and shook off the raindrops before entering through the kitchen door.

"Hi, sweetie." He grinned. "What's for lunch?"

"Nothing, unless you cook it yourself," Andi hollered over Jared's screeching.

Riley glanced around the kitchen. The breakfast dishes soaked in the dishpan, the table was littered with crumbs, and the fire in the cookstove was out. The coffeepot, usually simmering in readiness for a hasty cup of brew, looked cold.

Riley's grin faded. "Uh-oh."

"Uh-oh is right," Andi agreed. She thrust the fussy child into Riley's arms. "Please, Riley. I need a break."

Before he could reply, Andi flew out the back door. The privy was not far, but she was soaking wet by the time she threw the door open. It didn't take long to empty her stomach.

Weak with fatigue, she huddled in the damp, chilly privy and let the tears come. Why did the weather have to change today of all days? Why did Chad bring Susie to dinner when he knew she had a cold? "Ooh, I'd like to tell big brother a thing or two."

She hugged her knees and shivered with cold. The rain hammered the thin roof. Her stomach turned over.

Andi had the sense not to stay outside for too long. Her throat felt scratchy, and she could not afford to come down with Jared's cold. She felt miserable enough already. Slamming the privy door shut, she dodged raindrops and scurried up the back steps.

When she barged through the door, Jared was asleep on Riley's shoulder. Her husband put a finger to his lips and hustled him into his small bed in the other room.

When Riley returned to the kitchen, he lit the stove, peeked into the coffeepot, and began to tidy up the worst of the dishes. "Are you feeling all right?" he asked softly.

Andi shrugged.

"Are you catching Jared's cold?"

She was, but that was not the reason she was so weary and out of sorts. She sat down at the table, buried her head in her arms, and choked back a sob.

"Andi!" Riley leaped to her side and laid a gentle hand on her shoulder. "What's the matter?"

Riley's question burst the dam that was holding back her feelings. They came out in a flood with her next words. "It's this awful weather, Jared's sick, the house is a mess, and . . ." She paused and took a breath.

"Carrying this baby is nothing like what I remember with Jared. I've felt so sick every day this week. And tired. And groggy. And it won't go away."

Another pause. Another breath. "I don't think I can do this, Riley. It's just too hard."

Her hasty words sounded awful, even to her own ears. She cringed. It was too late to take them back now. *Why do I always speak before I think?*

On the other hand, Andi couldn't keep everything inside for much longer. If her nausea followed what she remembered of Lucy's time, she was in for several more weeks of this.

How would she care for Jared and keep up the house? Lucy had depended on Andi's help during those days when she felt so ill. Andi had no one but Riley, and he was gone most of the day. Who would watch Jared when she napped? Who would fix the meals if she couldn't even look at food?

Fear bubbled up, threatening to choke her. How would she manage?

Riley's silence brought Andi around to the here and now. She looked up into his face.

"I'm sorry," he said simply.

Andi's heart wrenched. He shouldn't be sorry. He should be turning cartwheels with joy. Had it been only one short week since she'd told Riley they were having this baby? So much had happened between then and now.

A wave of pain for hurting Riley enveloped Andi, and fresh tears rose. She reached up to wipe away the few drops that had squeezed from the corners of her eyes. "Oh, Riley, I didn't mean it like that. Maybe it's this miserable weather or Jared's cold."

More silence, except for the battering raindrops.

"Maybe." Riley flashed her a lopsided smile then returned to the stubborn stove. He stuffed in a few more sticks of wood, latched the door, and sighed. "I don't want to make more work for you. I'll eat with the hands." He crossed the small kitchen and gently tugged Andi's sloppy braid. "Why don't you catch a nap while Jared's asleep?"

Without another word, Riley picked up his hat, stepped outside, and quietly shut the door behind him.

CHAPTER 2

Andi lay down and drew the cozy quilt around her shoulders. She was asleep in an instant. It didn't last long, though. Jared woke whimpering and snuffling.

Andi opened one eye and peeked at the small clock on her bedside table. She'd slept for less than an hour. She opened both eyes but could not pull herself out of bed. She knew the instant she rose her stomach would protest.

Jared's whimpers turned into serious sobbing. "Mama!"

Andi groaned. "In here, sweetheart. Come to Mama."

Jared's pattering feet soon made their way into Andi's room, but he didn't want to cuddle with her in bed. "Hungry." He yanked on her fingers. "Up, Mama."

"All right, all right." Andi pushed back the quilt and sat up. She cocked her ear and listened. Had it stopped raining? No. Hard drops continued to pelt the rooftop.

Andi pressed her nose to the bedroom window. She could not see past the drops plastered to the glass pane. "Rain, rain, go away," she chanted. "Come again another day." *Or not at all*, she added silently.

Jared clapped his hands. "Rain!" A watery smile parted his lips. Then he sneezed, and his nose ran afresh. Andi made a face and grabbed a handkerchief.

By the time Andi fixed a late lunch for Jared, the rain had lessened. The kitchen had not, however, transformed itself from a cold, clammy mess into a warm and welcoming haven for her family.

That task was up to her. After all, there was supper to fix. Riley would not want to take another meal with the ranch hands today. "I'll blow the fire into life and put together a hot stew," she decided.

Stew did not sound very appealing to Andi, but Riley would appreciate it. Perhaps she would be able to force a few bites down. And maybe, just maybe, a thick, hot stew would make up for her hasty words to Riley at noon.

Happy to create a bright spot for her family, she set to work. But the stove Riley had so easily blown into life earlier refused to light for her. A sudden gust blew thick, gray smoke down the stovepipe, out the door, and into Andi's face.

"Augh!" She sprang to her feet and slammed the firebox door shut. "No, no, no!"

A breeze meant that starting the stove without a good updraft was practically impossible. Only Riley could coax the black beast into life when the wind acted up. "Why, oh why did I let it go out?" she wailed, falling into a kitchen chair.

A cantankerous black beast of a stove was just one more grievance to add to Andi's growing list. "I wish I was—"

No! She swallowed. *I will not think about that.* She could never be Andi Carter again, free to let Mother and Luisa and Nila mind the stove. Free to run and play with Taffy or Shasta, or to groom them in the barn on a rainy day. Free to curl up next to a warm fire in the library and let the storm rage.

"No," Andi whispered, pushing her foolish thoughts deep into a corner of her mind. She loved her little family, even if caring for them was sometimes a struggle.

Being grown up and married was hard work, even after three and a half years. Having a child, as much as she loved him, was hard work. Cooking and cleaning were the hardest work of all.

"Let's see the horses," she decided suddenly. She rose before she changed her mind. "If the stove won't light, I can't fix supper. We'll have to wait for Daddy to light that beast." Once lit, Andi could fall back on a no-fail meal—sourdough pancakes and eggs.

"Horseys!" Jared ran to the door. He stretched his small fingers toward the knob but couldn't quite reach it.

"Hold *your* horses, little man." She gave him a lopsided smile. "Let's find your coat."

A minute later, Andi and Jared were bundled up against the damp, chilly weather. To her joy, the rain had let up. She stepped outside and gasped. The entire backyard was a lake.

"Well, that's just dandy." She would have to navigate along little peaks of high ground to reach the barn. That is unless she wanted icy water to slosh over the tops of her high-topped shoes and soak her feet.

Andi shivered, but she could not change her mind now, not after promising Jared. He would scream if she took him back inside. Besides, the fresh air was already helping settle her stomach. "Come on. Let's go see the horseys."

She hefted Jared high to spare his shoes and gingerly picked her way from mound to hummock as they crossed the yard. They had just reached the barn when one of the hands came galloping toward them.

Andi set Jared down. "Howdy, Joey."

Joey didn't greet her. He took no notice of the lake that surrounded the barn. His horse splashed through the muck. Rainwater and mud flew in all directions. He reined in his big sorrel a safe distance from Andi and shouted, "Mrs. Prescott! I need the wagon quick!"

Andi did her best not to smile at the cowhand's agitated words. Even after two years on Memory Creek, Joey had stayed a little "green." However, Riley insisted Joey had heart and great potential. He wasn't much older than Levi, but the boy sure knew his way around horses. He had no fear of any creature on four legs.

But the young ranch hand spooked easily over any other little thing, especially after his frightful experience at the hands of Vega and his men a year and a half ago. He'd been knocked out and dumped into a roadside gully to spend the night.

Right now, Joey looked downright terrified.

"What's gotten into you?" Andi asked. "You look like you've seen a ghost. Why do you need the wagon in this weather? Settle down and give your horse a chance to breathe."

"No time, ma'am. I need the wagon for the boss." He slid off his horse.

Andi's eyebrows shot up. "Why does Riley need the wagon?"

"He's hurt," Joey said. "Got thrown pretty hard. Took us by surprise. It happened so fast."

Andi sucked in her breath. Riley? Thrown from his horse? That was impossible. Dakota would no more throw Riley than Shasta would throw Andi.

Joey's words tumbled out, one on top of the other. "Matt went to fetch Doc Weaver. I've come for the wagon. Where should we take him? Back here?"

"Where is he?" Andi demanded, ignoring his question. She felt close to swooning. *Stay on your feet*, she ordered her shaky legs. Blood rushed to her head, chasing any weariness or nausea away.

Joey rattled on. According to the young cowhand, Riley had fallen many miles away from Memory Creek ranch.

Jared pulled on Andi's hand. "Mama. Horseys."

"Hush, Jared." Andi hiked him up in her arms and held him tight.

If Joey's babbling description was accurate, Riley lay much closer to the Circle C than to Memory Creek. Andi chanced a quick glance over her shoulder at the cold, dark, and unwelcoming house. "Not here. Take him to the Circle C."

Mother was there. She would know what to do.

Andi could not tend Riley alone, especially if he were as badly hurt as Joey let on. She couldn't fight the cookstove on this wet, blustery day. The Circle C ranch house was warm, clean, and inviting. Much better for an injured man.

"Yes, ma'am." Joey sloshed through the knee-deep, murky water and disappeared inside the barn. Five minutes later, he led two horses outside and hitched them to the wagon. He tied his horse to the tailgate and paused. "You comin', Mrs. Prescott? Or do you want to go to the Circle C and meet us there?"

"I'm coming with you." Andi wanted to see for herself how badly hurt

Riley was. Maybe Joey was overreacting. Riley might be sitting up, insisting he was fine. Perhaps this whole thing was only a tempest in a teapot.

She handed a fussy Jared to Joey and hauled herself up onto the high wagon seat. Joey plopped the toddler on her lap then swung up beside her. "Hang on, ma'am. I ain't gonna spare these horses none. Every second counts."

It started raining by the time they reached Riley twenty minutes later. Dakota grazed nearby. His tail swished, and he shook his mane. Drops sprayed. He looked like nothing had happened, as if the appaloosa could not have been the cause of Riley's injuries.

Andi passed Jared back to the cowhand and dropped to the ground as soon as the wagon came to a stop. Jared wailed, but Joey held him fast. "Thanks, Joey." She lifted her damp skirt and slogged to Riley's side.

He lay on his side in the deep, sticky mud. His white face and bloody head told part of the story. The large, mud-covered rock told the rest. Andi reached for him, but Carlos held her back.

"Do not touch him, *señora*," the cowhand warned. "We do not yet know how badly he is hurt. Or what is broken. You must wait for the doctor."

Andi fell backward into the mud, unmindful of the freezing dampness that seeped through her skirt. She had seen Riley only a few hours ago, and how had she replied to his cheerful greeting? With selfish whining.

Guilt washed over her in waves. *I complained about Jared, the weather, the house, and my own misery.* She swallowed. *I even complained about the coming baby. Oh, how could I?*

Her complaints now seemed trivial. Who cared if the stove backfired? Or if rain drummed on the rooftop and turned the yard into a sloppy mess? Or if Jared was awake all night?

All that mattered was her precious husband, the kindest, most considerate man in the whole world. Unshed tears stung her eyes. "Oh, Riley! I'm sorry."

He didn't move. He lay in the mud, pale and still.

Andi looked up into the cloud-soaked sky. Raindrops splashed her face and mingled with her tears. "Oh, God, please let him be all right. Don't let him die."

CHAPTER 3

Andi paced back and forth, not caring if the rain splattered her bare head. "Where's Dr. Weaver?" she snapped.

Carlos and Joey shrugged. What could they say? "Perhaps Matt couldn't find him," Joey ventured.

Andi stopped pacing and glared at the two cowhands. "We can't wait any longer for the doctor to give us permission to move Riley. He'll catch pneumonia lying out here in this weather. Put him in the wagon and take him to the Circle C."

"Yes, ma'am." Joey looked relieved that somebody was telling him what to do.

Carlos muttered a few words in Spanish then motioned Joey to give him a hand loading their boss into the wagon.

Andi scurried to help. She glanced at Jared, who sat under the wagon box out of the rain. His hazel eyes were dark with fear and uncertainty. He coughed, shivered, and whimpered. "Mama." He raised his arms. "Up."

"It's all right, honey," Andi told him. "You must stay there a few more minutes. Then we'll go to Grandma's house."

Jared stopped whimpering. "Gra'ma? Susie?"

"Yes, and a cup of warm chocolate if you promise to sit still for a minute more."

Jared put his thumb in his mouth, but it did him no good. His nose was too stuffed up. More whimpers escaped.

Poor little boy, Andi mourned silently.

Unfortunately, Jared would have to stay sad, lonely, and miserable for a few more minutes. She turned back to help lift the unconscious Riley into the wagon.

Joey had done more than hitch up the wagon. He had thrown half a dozen saddle blankets into the wagon bed. They laid Riley on half of them and covered him with the rest of the blankets. He didn't move. He didn't groan.

A stab of fear pierced Andi. This was nothing like the day the cougar slashed him. Riley hurt something fierce, but he'd managed to talk and even joke before passing out. This was different. Scary different. What if Riley didn't wake up?

Don't think about it! Andi made herself comfortable next to Riley in the wagon bed. Joey plopped Jared, wet and shivering, in her lap. Carlos tied Dakota to the back of the wagon, and Joey climbed up on the seat.

"I will tend the ranch, *señora* Andrea," Carlos promised. Then he shouted to Joey, "*Vete, chico. ¡De prisa!*"

Joey didn't need to understand Spanish to know Carlos was telling him to get going and be quick about it. He urged the horses forward, and they were off.

Andi almost lost the contents of her stomach during the bumpy ride. The wagon lurched over rocks. It ground its way through thick mud. It slipped and slid and tilted precariously before leveling off.

Andi bent over Riley and hugged him tight to keep him still. Jared lay squished between his mama and daddy and wailed. Andi closed her eyes and prayed they'd make it to the Circle C in one piece.

The wagon gained speed when they traded the rolling hills for the flat valley road. Dr. Weaver and Matt met them just before the team turned into the ranch driveway.

When Joey pulled into the yard, everyone sprang into action. No words were needed. The Carter family worked together like a well-oiled machine. Ellie took Jared from Andi's arms, and Chad swung his sister out of the wagon.

"You'd best get inside," he told her when her feet touched the ground. "You look cold and wet."

What? No teasing words about Andi playing in the mud? No raised eyebrow or twitching lips? *Chad must really be worried about Riley.*

The next hour passed in a blur. Dr. Weaver would not let Andi see Riley until he'd cleaned the young man up and thoroughly examined him. She passed the long wait by changing into dry clothes and accepting a cup of tea from Nila.

However, her throat was too tight from worry to swallow the hot, sweet-smelling brew. Even if she coaxed the tea into her stomach, it would come right back up.

Leaving her teacup behind, Andi headed for the library, where she sank onto the settee and let her tears come. "Please, God," she begged. "Protect Riley."

Her eyelids fluttered. She was *so* tired, but she couldn't give in to sleep. Not yet. What if Riley woke up and needed her?

No sooner did she resolve to stay awake when Andi's head lolled onto her chest. Her eyelids closed of their own accord, and she drifted into a deep, dreamless sleep.

"Andrea."

Mother's soft whisper penetrated Andi's wooziness. Her eyes flew open, and she sat up. Her stomach turned over at the sudden movement, and she flinched. *I feel sick.*

Before Andi could ask about Riley, Mother said, "Dr. Weaver wants to talk to you. He's in the guest room."

Andi leaped out of the cozy chair, swallowed her queasiness, and took the stairs two at a time. When she burst into the guest room, she stopped short. "Dr. Weaver? Is Riley going to be all right?"

"Shh." The doctor led her to an overstuffed chair next to the bed. "Sit down."

Andi obeyed. She clasped her hands into two tight fists and buried them in her lap to keep from shaking. Her gaze darted from the white, still figure in bed to the doctor's grim expression.

Dr. Weaver sat down and picked up Andi's clammy hands. "I'm not going to pretend everything is all right, Andrea. It's not."

Hot tears sprang to Andi's eyes, but she blinked them back. "Tell me."

The doctor squeezed her hands. "Riley might have a couple of cracked ribs, but I can't be sure until he wakes up to tell me about his various aches and pains." He sighed. "However, his cracked ribs are nothing. The real problem is that he's deeply unconscious."

"Can't you give him something to wake him up?"

"I tried smelling salts, but he didn't even twitch," Dr. Weaver said. "He hit his head pretty hard. Either he has a skull fracture or—at the very least—a serious concussion. Whichever the issue, it means swelling inside his head."

Andi's throat tightened until she could hardly breathe. "When will he wake up?"

"I don't know." He took a deep breath and let it out slowly. "I'll be honest with you. There's a chance he might never wake up."

Andi's world spun. Black spots danced before her eyes. "Oh, please, Dr. Weaver. Can't you do something? I can't lose Riley. I can't."

"There's nothing more I can do. He will either wake up or he won't," the doctor replied. "There is, however, one thing we all can do. We can pray for your young man." He pressed her hands between his own strong hands. "We need to pray for you too. Even if Riley does wake up, it may be a long time before he's fully back to his old self."

Dr. Weaver released Andi's hands and rose. He picked up his black bag. "I'll come every day to check on his progress. Don't give up hope, my dear."

Andi closed her eyes and nodded. "Thank you, doctor." When she opened her eyes, he was gone.

CHAPTER 4

Andi spent every waking minute beside Riley. She watched and waited for a sign, *any* sign that he might regain consciousness. Ugly swelling covered the left side of his head. The bruise turned purple and yellow.

Riley never moved. He didn't notice when Jared patted his arms and whispered, "Wake up, Daddy."

Three days later, Sunday dinner came and went as usual. Andi and Riley were the only family members missing from the table. Mother brought a tray upstairs and watched Andi choke down every bite. Even a roiling stomach dared not defy Elizabeth Carter's stern eat-this-or-else look.

Three more days passed. Mother helped Andi drip broth past Riley's lips, but his swallowing did not encourage Andi. Occasionally, one of Riley's eyelids twitched, and he moaned. Dr. Weaver saw nothing in those signs that meant Riley would be waking up anytime soon.

The family set up a small cot in the guest room so Andi could sleep beside the bed. Riley might wake up in the middle of the night, and Andi intended to be the first person he saw when he did.

Thanksgiving morning dawned dismal and dreary. A full week had passed since Riley's accident, and Andi was not in a thanksgiving mood. Her hands fluttered like a shaky old aunt's as she adjusted the bed coverings.

"Oh, Riley, you have to wake up. You just have to. Please!" Her words poured out like a little child's. "You can't die. Not like—"

A painful childhood memory sprang to the surface in a flash. Father's fatal accident reminded Andi so much of Riley's. She buried her head in her hands and tried to keep the past from creeping to the forefront, but weariness had dropped her mental guard.

"Father!" five-year-old Andi begged. "Let me go too. You promised. You said I could watch when you brought down the herd. You said I could bring my lasso."

Father chuckled from deep inside his throat. "You don't forget a thing, do you, Andrea? Run along and collect your rope and meet me in the barn."

Andi flew upstairs and changed into the overalls Father said she could wear whenever she rode around the ranch. She slid down the banister railing, raced past Luisa, and slammed the kitchen door shut behind her.

"Riley!" she shrieked. "I get to go with Father to round up the horses and bring them back to the ranch. Maybe Uncle Sid will let you go too."

Riley shook his head. "Uncle Sid says Cook needs me today." He frowned. "I sure wish I could go." He scuffed the dirt with his boot toe.

Andi was too happy to feel sorry that her friend couldn't go along. She skipped to the barn, lifted her lasso from its nail hook, and patted her pony on the way out. "You can't come today, Coco. You're too little."

Ten minutes later, Andi sat in the saddle on Father's lap. He loped Caesar out of the yard and toward the range. "Big day today, sweetheart."

"Uh-huh!" Andi wriggled with anticipation.

Father brushed a tickly kiss against the back of Andi's neck and hugged her. "We'll round up the winter horse herd and separate some of the foals for branding. You can try roping one from up here on Caesar's back."

"By myself?" Andi's heart thumped. "I want to rope a golden foal."

Father ruffled her hair. "We'll see what colors there are this spring. Maybe there's a golden filly just your size."

Father kept his promise. Foals of all different colors stayed close to their mothers' flanks. Andi squealed and twirled her lasso. "Over there, Father! The paint."

He guided Caesar closer to the mare and foal.

"Watch me rope that paint colt!" Andi shouted to her three big brothers.

They paused and watched the loop fall onto the spotted foal's head, slide past its ear, and plop on the ground. The foal scurried away and hid behind his mother. Her brothers laughed.

Andi scowled. "It's harder than it looks."

"You can practice on a fence post while the boys and I round up some of the peskier critters," Father said. "They've been out on the range all winter and are mighty skittish." He lifted Andi from the saddle and lowered her to the ground. "Love you."

"Love you more!" Andi sang.

Father nudged Caesar into a lope. "Love you most!" he called over his shoulder.

Andi grinned and waved. Then she coiled her rope just like Chad had shown her dozens of times. She twirled it over her head and let the lasso fly. But that ol' fence post seemed to move whenever her loop got near it. "No fair!"

A tremendous commotion full of whinnying and stamping hooves sent Andi running for the temporary corral's fence. She scrambled between the railings just like she'd been taught to do in case the livestock ever stampeded. Then she climbed to the top and watched everything with wide, scared eyes.

One of the biggest stallions, a huge sorrel, reared and rushed toward a cowhand on the ground. Why had Ben left his horse? He was in terrible danger now.

Father and Andi's big brothers leaped into action. They distracted the stallion and waved him off. It gave Ben the few precious seconds he needed to bolt for safety.

Suddenly, faster than a blinking eye, the stallion turned on Father and charged. Caesar, caught by surprise, rose on his hind legs and turned a complete circle to avoid the attack. The whiplash sent Father flying from Caesar's back in a wide arc.

Flailing his arms, Father tried to land on his feet. But everything happened too fast. He hit the ground with a loud *thunk* and lay still. An instant later, before the Carter brothers or their hands could intervene, the rogue stallion ran right over the top of Father.

Crack! The stallion dropped like a stone.

Sid McCoy lowered his rifle and ran to Father's side.

Everybody forgot about Andi. She clung to the fence post and stared at her father, her brothers, and the ranch hands.

Then she screamed.

Andi lifted her head from her hands and found them wet with tears. Father's best horse, Caesar, had thrown him all those years ago. Not on purpose, of course. But the fall and the stallion's trampling had killed Father instantly.

Dakota had thrown Riley, just as accidentally.

The sticky, slippery mud probably trapped one or more of Dakota's feet, and the horse would have panicked. Perhaps Andi would never know for sure how it happened. That was a good thing. She knew exactly how Father had been killed. She had watched it happen.

It was several weeks before Andi had stopped waking up with nightmares.

Father's death had haunted Chad for much longer than several weeks. He kept Andi on a short leash for many years if it involved anything risky with a horse, like trick riding.

Andi looked around for a handkerchief to wipe her eyes and blow her nose. As usual, she couldn't find one. Too tired and sad to search for one, she did what her two-year-old son did. She wiped her face on her sleeve.

"You never have a handkerchief around when you need one."

Andi's heart flew to her throat. She lowered her arm. "Riley! You're awake!"

Her husband looked terrible. His cheeks were hollow, the bruises had spread, and dark circles showed beneath his eyes. But his eyes were open, and his gaze looked alert.

"Yes." He took a shallow breath. "I feel terrible. What happened?"

Andi sat down on the bed and picked up his hand. "You got thrown."

Riley looked confused. "From a horse?"

"Dakota."

A shudder went through him. "I'll take your word for it, but I don't remember. I don't remember anything after eating lunch with the hands."

His words wore him out. An instant later Riley was asleep.

Bursting with thanksgiving joy, Andi flew out of the room. She raced down the stairs and into the kitchen, where Luisa, Ellie, Mother, and Nila were putting the finishing touches on several pies. The whole room smelled like pumpkin and spices. "Mother! Riley woke up."

Mother nearly dropped the apple pie she was carrying. "Oh, thank God." She set the pan down and wiped her hands on her apron. "Nila, prepare a bowl of turkey broth for Riley, please."

"*Sí, señora*," Nila said with a wide smile.

Mother curled an arm around Andi's waist and led her to the stairs. "This is a blessing, Andrea. I was so worried."

Andi's throat tightened. "Oh, Mother, I love Riley so much. I don't know what I would do if he was taken away. I was simply horrid to him last week. And then he had the accident, and—" She couldn't go on.

"Never mind," Mother said softly. "Riley knows you love him. He understands you didn't mean it, whatever you said or did."

Andi and Mother slipped through the doorway into Riley's room. His eyes opened. "Tell me what's going on. I'm weak as a kitten, and my head is pounding. How long have I been lying here?"

"Too long," Andi said softly. "I've missed you so much."

"You are going to *keep* lying there, young man," Mother said, smiling.

She put her hands on her hips. "It's Thanksgiving Day. Nila is bringing you some hot turkey broth, but that's all the Thanksgiving dinner you'll be eating."

Riley frowned. "But—"

"No buts," Mother cut in. "I'm going to bring Jared up. He's missed his daddy." She crossed the room and turned for a final word. "In the meantime, you and Andrea can take the time to count your blessings. They are innumerable."

Andi closed her fingers around Riley's in a comforting squeeze and sat down on the bed. She didn't speak. Her heart was too full of gratitude.

Riley peered up at her. "What's wrong?"

"Oh, Riley, you had me so scared. I've stayed by your side every minute since the accident, praying that you'd wake up. And you did." She paused, swallowing hard. "I was simply wretched to you last week. I'm so sorry. You're such a blessing to me, and I can't begin to imagine life without you."

Her fingers curled tighter around his hand. "No matter how sick I may feel, I am grateful for all the babies that God chooses to send our way."

"I know, my princess." Riley smiled up at her. "I forgive you, even though I don't remember anything you said. Let's start over, shall we? With God on our side, we can tackle anything life throws us."

Andi nodded, then managed a small chuckle. "I want to throw my arms around you and give you a hug, but since you're trussed up tighter than a calf for branding, I think I'd better wait."

"Yeah," Riley agreed. "You'd better."

Footsteps and a toddler's excited squeal from outside the door told Andi that Jared had arrived.

Riley smiled. "Hey, little man," he greeted his boy.

"Daddy!"

Andi's heart swelled. She was truly blessed beyond measure.

WINNING ISN'T EVERYTHING

Circle C Ranch, February 1890

I really shouldn't boast, not even in my private journal, but I like being the Carter family checkers champion. I feel unbeatable.

CHAPTER 1

Sunday dinner around the Carter family table was the highlight of Andi's week. Especially during cold, rainy February days that appeared with no warning. Like today.

Andi, Riley, and Jared had entered the church service under sunny skies and a crisp breeze. They left dodging raindrops and circling mud puddles. Riley was helping Andi into the buggy when the skies opened up. Rain came down in sheets.

"Mama!" Jared wailed, covering his head. "Wet!"

Riley plopped the two-year-old on Andi's lap and set to work on the buggy. The storm hammered the buildings and turned the already-soft streets into thick, clinging mud.

Andi pulled the lap blanket from around her feet and legs and encircled her little son. She wanted to spread the covering over her own head, but that would not look dignified. Instead, she waited while Riley fought to loosen the buggy's black canvas roof and snap it in place.

Rain pelted the canvas. Jared refused to come out from under this warm tent. Andi held him close and scooted away when Riley swung into the buggy. Water dripped from his wide-brimmed hat. His Sunday-go-to-meeting clothes were drenched.

"I'm glad we're going to the Circle C today," Andi commented to her soaked husband. "The thought of going home to a cold house and a dead fire gives me the shivers."

Riley nodded and slapped the horse. "Giddup." Dakota broke into a fast trot, as anxious as his driver to reach a destination where he could find shelter. "I appreciate Sunday dinner with your family too." He swiped raindrops from his face. "Today more than most. It will be nice to find a warm house and a hot meal waiting." He chuckled. "And conversation around the Carter table is never dull."

This Sunday was no exception. Circle C roast beef sliced thin, whipped potatoes dripping with butter, hot rolls and apple butter, last summer's green beans from jars, and Luisa's famous peach cobbler.

Andi threw decorum to the wind regarding the way a young lady should conduct herself at the table. While Melinda took her usual bird-like helpings, and Lucy and Mother kept their plates only half full, Andi went for seconds.

I'm making up for all those weeks of nausea, she told herself, *when I couldn't eat more than a bite.*

If her family noticed Andi's voracious appetite, nobody teased her. If they did, she would point out Ellie, who had also taken another serving. Women in the family way were exempt from every rule of propriety in *Mrs. Beeton's Manners of Polite Society* handbook.

Pleasantly full and sleepy, Andi joined the rest of the family in the parlor. She watched Nila carry Jared upstairs for his nap and secretly wished she could join him. The conversation about the latest fashions for dress-wear and a new recipe for angel food cake was lulling Andi to sleep.

Baby William cooed and gurgled in Melinda's arms. Sammy sprawled on the rug in front of a roaring fire in the hearth, working one of Mitch's childhood wooden puzzles.

"Peter bought me a newfangled rotary beater," Melinda was saying. "It whips up egg whites in a quarter of the time it takes with a fork and plate. You stick the beaters into the whites and turn the handle."

Andi's ears pricked up. She wouldn't mind seeing a mechanical device that whipped egg whites so quickly. Her lemon meringue pie could use one.

Across the parlor, the men's discussion sounded more interesting. A wild horse had broken out of the corral, and Chad still hadn't gotten it back. Justin shared a hair-raising story about his latest criminal trial. Mitch's herd of black Angus had doubled in size and were worth a pretty penny.

Outside, the storm worsened. Raindrops thrummed against the windowpanes and streaked the glass. The whoosh of an occasional wind gust rattled the shutters. Rain dripped down the chimney, making the fire hiss.

Andi glanced out through the French doors leading to the patio. It would be a long, wet ride back to Memory Creek. She never liked the rare but heavy winter rainstorms. February was the worst. One day it would be sunny and warm. A few hours later, the clouds rolled in from the mountains and dumped their load on an unsuspecting valley.

Andi turned away from the windows, wrapped her fingers around her mug of chocolate, and settled back against the settee. Wisps of steam wafted up, tickling her nose and bringing a smile to her lips. She thoroughly enjoyed these lazy Sunday afternoons, when she could enjoy her family.

Her gaze drifted lazily around the room. Riley and Chad's conversation had turned from the runaway horse to other ranch-related subjects. She frowned. Big brother better not be trying to convince Riley to come work for him again. Chad's temporary jobs always ended up costing Riley more time than he could spare.

Justin and Peter had moved off to no doubt discuss town matters, something Andi found extremely dull. Mother settled into an overstuffed chair and took a turn cradling baby William. He yawned and closed his eyes. Mitch had dropped to the rug in front of the fireplace to help Sammy.

He caught Andi watching him and winked. "How about a game of checkers, Sis? You look lonely with everyone else chitchatting."

Andi was not lonely, but Mitch's bright-blue gaze told her he'd rather play checkers than work a puzzle. "Sure." She set aside her chocolate and sat up. Mitch carried over the board and a box full of checkers, dragged a low table, and set everything up.

"May I watch?" Six-year-old Sammy abandoned his puzzle and hurried over.

"Of course." Mitch drew Sammy beside him. "You can be my partner. I need all the help I can get to beat your Aunt Andi. She's the Carter checkers champion, you know."

Sammy turned dark, admiring eyes on Andi. "Really?"

"I can beat your Uncle Mitch, anyway," Andi answered with a grin.

Ten minutes later, Andi took a black checker and jumped two of Mitch's red ones. Sammy gasped.

Mitch's face showed his surprise. He rubbed his chin and moved one of his few remaining checkers to another square, but it was obvious he was fighting a losing battle.

A minute later it was all over. Sammy looked from Andi to Mitch and back to Andi. "I think I will be Aunt Andi's partner next time."

From across the room, Chad laughed. "Smart move, boy. Learn the game early in life."

As usual, Chad was speaking loud enough for the whole family to hear. All other chatter ceased. Chad's smile grew wider at the attention. "Don't put it off or you'll lose big. Isn't that right, Riley?" He nudged his brother-in-law.

Riley's face reddened, triggering an event in Andi's memory from the long, *long* year they were engaged to be married. It was a miracle her husband had not run away, what with the Carter brothers constantly ragging on him with their teasing ways.

Riley waved the words away. "Leave off, Chad."

Mitch got into the act. "I, for one, will never forget the day when

Mr. Prescott revealed a long-buried secret." He could barely contain his laughter.

"You mean the one about not being able to dance?" Riley bantered back, his face still red.

Mitch shook his head. "That's no secret. We learned of your lack in that skill during Chad and Ellie's engagement party." He furrowed his brow. "Although, you never did tell us how you learned to waltz in time for your wedding."

Chad coughed. Only he, Riley, and Andi knew the truth about Riley's secret dancing lessons. Riley had sworn her to secrecy. Chad would have their hides if the secret ever came out.

It was time to change the subject.

Andi sent her husband a grin. "You and I had been officially courting for one week when you revealed a shocking truth. You did not know how to play checkers."

Sammy's eyes grew wide. "That so, Uncle Riley?"

"True enough. I did not know how to play checkers." Riley crossed to the settee and sat down. He picked up Andi's hand. "But you taught me quickly, remember?"

It was Andi's turn to blush. She ducked her head and suddenly wished Mitch had not brought up the word *checkers*. Like Riley's dancing lessons, only a few members of the family knew the checkers story. "I don't think there's any way I can forget."

"That would be an interesting story for this rainy afternoon," Mother said.

"Yeah, Andi," Chad added. "I haven't had my laugh for the day."

She scowled at Chad and pressed her lips tightly together. But when the rest of the family cajoled and coaxed, Andi had no choice but to give in.

Oh well, she thought. *It was bound to come out sooner or later.*

CHAPTER 2

Five years earlier
Circle C Ranch, April 1885

Seventeen-year-old Andi Carter scooped up her cape from its place on the empty pew, tightened it around her shoulders, and weaved her way through the sanctuary. The long service was over at last. She could head home, change clothes, and go riding with Riley today after Sunday dinner.

A shiver of delight skittered up Andi's spine. Barely a week had passed since she and Lucy fled the Mexican bandit's outlaw camp in the wilderness. Only a week since Riley had announced to their small band of rescuers his intentions to court Miss Andrea Carter.

Andi had been away from the ranch for too long and couldn't wait to ride far and wide. She missed riding almost as much as she'd missed Riley and her family.

She bounded outside, expecting to be embraced by the warm April sunshine. Instead, gray clouds scudded across the sky. A stiff breeze foretold the coming of a late spring shower.

Her joy deflated faster than a balloon. *No fair!*

Riley exited the sanctuary just behind her. He grinned. "You ready?"

Mother had given Riley permission to drive Andi to and from church in his spanking new buggy. He had paid much more than a hired wrangler could afford to spend, in Chad's opinion, but Riley was mighty proud of his sleek, new rig.

"That's all *you* know, big brother," Andi had snapped. It was none of his business what Riley spent his wages on. She would not tell Chad that Riley was a master when it came to haggling.

Andi took another glance at the sky and headed for the buggy. "Ready as I'll ever be."

Riley's grin disappeared and he helped her into the rig. "What's wrong?"

"This horrific weather." Andi slumped back against her seat and crossed her arms. "I had the whole afternoon planned for riding and look at it now." She waved a hand toward the clouds. "They're gonna dump rain any moment." As if to prove her point, a raindrop smacked the palm of her hand. "See?"

Riley nodded his sympathy and raised the buggy cover. Then he swung up beside Andi and flicked the reins. Dakota trotted forward. "It won't last long. After all, it's April. Maybe there's something we can do indoors while we're waiting for the weather to clear."

Andi glanced at the soggy landscape. Orchards blossomed in white and pink. Beehives lined both sides of the road. "I bet the bees don't like this rain either," she grumbled.

"What did you like to do on rainy days when you were younger?" Riley asked.

Andi pondered. Curling up with a cup of hot chocolate and reading one of Mitch's dime novels was high on her list. However, that was not something Riley and she could do together.

Hmm, what else?

"I liked playing checkers with Chad and Mitch," she said. "I remember one stormy night. Mother had gone to the city and Kate's kids stayed with us. Levi and I played checkers over and over." She nudged Riley with her elbow. "Are you any good at checkers?"

Riley cleared his throat and didn't answer.

"What?" Andi asked, puzzled.

"I . . ." His voice trailed away, replaced by a sheepish grin. "I've never played."

"Never played?" Andi sat up so fast that her head spun. "I don't believe it."

"It's true." Riley shrugged. "I never had the time or interest. I don't remember playing when I stayed on the Circle C when I was a boy."

Andi laughed. "That's because we were always too busy riding or playing in the hayloft."

"When I went back to San Francisco, Pa was away a lot," Riley continued. "There weren't many kids at the other forts. Who would I play checkers with?"

Good point, but still . . . Andi didn't know anybody who couldn't play checkers. Even Levi had come to the ranch already knowing the game. "Were you living under a rock?" she asked. "How is that even possible?"

Riley laughed. "You can teach me today, if you'd like."

"I would," she answered. "It might be fun. But you're not funnin' me, right? You truly have never played checkers?"

"I have not, nor do I know the rules."

"Hmm." It would take less than five minutes to show Riley the ins and outs of playing checkers. She might even take it easy on him for the first couple of games, maybe let him win one. Then she would swoop in for the kill.

Andi knew she was the Carter family checkers champion. This would be her chance to prove it to somebody other than her brothers, whom she beat soundly most of the time.

Yes sirree. This rainy afternoon might not prove to be dull, after all.

CHAPTER 3

Andi tore up the wide staircase and burst into her room. She couldn't change clothes fast enough.

She peeled off her Sunday outfit, including the corset and stays that always squeezed the life out of her, and slipped into a comfortable split skirt and blouse. She removed the pins from her stiff bun and let her dark waves cascade down her back in wild tangles. Snatching up a brush, she pulled out the snarls and plaited her hair into a sloppy braid that she flipped behind her shoulder.

Sunday dinner would not be served for another two hours. She had plenty of time to show Riley how to play checkers and beat him once or twice before they sat down to the meal.

Wriggling with anticipation, Andi left her room and headed for the stairs. Her hand brushed the surface of the wide banister and she paused.

A tempting thought sneaked into her mind. A year from now, she would leave home for good. Her own little house would probably not have a stairway, a banister, or even a second floor. What harm was there in enjoying this childhood delight a few more times before she left?

She glanced around. No one was here to scold her, not even their housekeeper, Luisa. Before Andi could talk herself out of it, she hiked herself up on the smooth railing and let go. Her heart picked up speed when the familiar feeling of flying overcame her. Loose strands of hair blew across her face.

Just like the old days, she thought with a giggle, plummeting downward.

Just like the old days, she didn't prepare herself to slow down. A few seconds after mounting the railing, Andi sailed off the end and into midair. *Oh, no!* She closed her eyes and waited for the inevitable crash onto the foyer floor.

Instead of feeling hardwood, Andi collided with something soft and warm. A muffled grunt erupted from her rescuer as they toppled together to the floor. If this was Chad or Justin, she was in deep trouble.

She opened her eyes, scrambled to her knees, and gasped. "Riley!"

Horror of horrors! This was worse than crashing into a brother, worse than a scolding from Mother or Luisa. A hot flush rushed up Andi's neck and exploded in her cheeks. What would Riley think of such behavior? He might not want to marry a girl who sailed down banister railings like a nine-year-old.

Riley sat up, rubbing his wrist. "Andi! What got into you?" He pushed himself to his feet and stared down at her.

"I-I . . ." Andi ducked her head. Her cheeks burned.

Riley chuckled. When Andi looked up, he was reaching out his hand. "You must have been testing my abilities as your knight in shining armor, eh?"

Andi's tongue stuck to the roof of her mouth. In silent humiliation, she accepted Riley's help standing.

He winked. "Don't fret about your tumble, my princess." He lowered his voice to a whisper. "We will keep this between ourselves."

Andi nodded her thanks and smoothed the hair from her face. A strange thrill tickled her insides. His princess? Something told her this pet name would stick. *Shining knight rescues his princess from a fate worse than a dragon—a family scolding.* A giggle bubbled up at such a silly notion and she grinned.

With his brave deed accomplished, Riley smiled back. "Are you ready to teach me checkers?"

Andi's embarrassment fell away. "I am."

She followed Riley into the spacious library, flicking a glance at the tall grandfather clock in the hallway as they went by. She smiled. Plenty of time left to add another player to her list of conquests, and all before Mother's Sunday dinner. Her smile widened when she found the library deserted. The last thing Andi wanted was an audience.

Locating the playing board, Andi spread it out on a table between two comfortable chairs. After her indiscretion with the railing, it might be best not to plop to the floor with a hassock between them.

It didn't take long for Andi to show Riley how to set up the pieces and explain the object of the game. "The one with the most checkers wins."

"Sounds easy enough," Riley admitted.

"Easy to learn," Andi agreed. "A little harder to figure out your strategy for winning." She drew a deep breath and reached for her first checker. *Well, here goes nothing.*

She nudged her checker to the first square. "Your turn. Pick a black square near you and move to it. You want to get close enough to my checkers to jump them, which removes them from the board."

"Hmm," Riley said, as if trying to put all the rules and different moves into a semblance of order. His gaze carefully swept over each piece on the board.

Good grief, Andi thought. *It's checkers, not chess.* At this rate, dinner would be called before Riley made his first move.

Finally, after much deliberating, Riley put a finger on a black checker and slid it to a black square.

Andi nodded. "Yep." She quickly made her move.

The next three moves crawled by like thick molasses. Riley pondered long and hard over each checker. He finally lifted a black checker and jumped one of Andi's. "Right?" he asked.

Andi nodded. "Yes." *Perfect*, she added secretly . . . and pounced.

Two black checkers went flying into the box. "That's called a double jump," she explained.

Riley gaped but only said, "Hmm." He went back to studying the board.

Chad strode into the library just then and joined the players. A wrinkled copy of the *Fresno Daily Expositor* was jammed under one arm. "I've taken it upon myself to chaperone you two."

Andi scowled. It was just like Chad to intrude on her like this. "Thank you, but we are fine by ourselves," she told him with stiff politeness. "Go read your paper."

Chad's grin didn't fade. He settled into an overstuffed chair by the fireplace and sent Riley a last word. "Better watch out, boy. You're playing against the self-proclaimed Carter checkers champion."

Self-proclaimed? That was an outrageous fib. There was no "self-proclaiming" about it. Even Justin bowed to Andi's skill at checkers. An angry flush began to wash over her.

"Never mind," Riley whispered. "Chad just wants to see you riled. Ignore him, and he'll probably go away."

Go away? Not a chance.

Riley was right, though. Nothing good could come from getting into a dither over Chad's teasing. She must not let anything distract her from this all-important first game.

"So, I think I go next?"

Riley's question brought Andi back to the game. She nodded then proceeded to consider how she could "help" Riley during this first game without letting him win. Just a confidence booster.

Andi was working out the details of her strategy, moving and jumping unconsciously, when it dawned on her that there were fewer red checkers on the board than before. Her pieces were crowned double, but she frowned. Riley's checkers had been crowned too.

She snapped out of her mental musing and focused on the game. Her original plan had been to take it easy on Riley for the first half of the game before going in for the win, but something had changed. During the past few moves, Riley had shown surprising and unexpected tactics. If she wasn't careful, he might win without her help.

Andi set her jaw. She simply could not lose now, not with big brother circling like a vulture to crow over her loss. She would never hear the end of it, not even if she pretended that she'd let Riley win.

She saw one last chance to trap Riley's crowned checker into a corner and took it. She relaxed, but not for long.

"No!" A gasp tore from her throat when Riley's arm launched across the board. He jumped two of her three remaining checkers and tossed them in the box. "Did I win?" he asked innocently.

Andi wanted to shout, "Not yet," but one glance at the board told her how impossible it would be to fend off Riley's attacks. One lingering checker sat all by itself in a corner, in the very same trap she had set for her opponent. She nodded. "You win."

The words felt like sour vinegar in her mouth. Why, oh why, had she not paid more attention before she fell for that last move? She answered her own dumb question with scorn. *I was too busy trying to figure out how to let my opponent enjoy a few victories before I tromped him.* She clenched her fists. *Never again.*

Riley sat back and smiled. "That was fun, my princess."

Heat jumped to Andi's cheeks, and not just because of his use of her new pet name. She swallowed. Had she really just lost to a young man who had never played a game of checkers before in his life?

Chad's snicker confirmed it and kindled Andi's fury into a blaze. She met Riley's gaze. "Rematch?"

He shrugged. "Why not?"

"That was quite a game," Chad remarked as Andi and Riley placed their checkers on the board. "Especially against someone who has never played before."

"Where did you hear that?" Andi snapped.

Chad shrugged. "Oh, word gets around. I thought you had him beat."

"As did I." A look of triumph curved Riley's lips.

"Beginner's luck." How Andi wished she had beat him outright rather than play foolish strategy games in her head to let Riley feel good about the game. "It won't happen again."

Chad smirked. "If you say so, little sister."

Andi drew a long breath and started the game, devising a plan for a quick victory. However, Riley's next few moves sent her schemes spinning into oblivion. Though he'd been uncertain as to the rules at the beginning, the young man appeared to know exactly what he was doing now. His hazel eyes twinkled when he jumped yet another checker and dropped it in the box.

Andi bit her lip and plunged on. What was happening here? Riley had never played checkers before today, and yet he seemed to have an extraordinary grasp of the tactics. It was evident that she would not be winning this battle either.

Andi's hands felt clammy. She could already hear Chad's laughter and the retelling sure to take place at Sunday dinner today. Justin's raised eyebrows. Melinda's quiet giggling. Mitch's shocked look. Even Mother would say a few words, something like, "Pride goeth before destruction, and a haughty spirit before a fall."

Andi mentally dug in her heels. *Concentrate! Don't let Riley beat you without a fight.*

The rain pelted the French doors of the library, mirroring the storm raging in Andi's heart. Frustration simmered. She choked back ugly words with difficulty. What had happened to a peaceful afternoon playing checkers with Riley while they waited for the storm to pass?

While the match wound toward a close, likely leading to Andi's ultimate defeat, Chad pulled up a chair and leaned forward. "It looks like you're losing again, little sister." He chuckled. "The Carter checkers champion is being dethroned. Will you ever live it down?"

Andi's face flamed. Unshed tears swam in her eyes. She glanced up to see a muscle twitch in Riley's jaw. Then he moved his checker and sat back. "Your move."

Andi caught her breath. Why had Riley made such a vulnerable move? Was he giving her the advantage? She tried to look into his eyes, but he averted his gaze.

She turned back to the board. Her thoughts whirled. Maybe he'd honestly missed something.

Whatever the reason, Andi did not waste this window of opportunity. One, two, and then three checkers fell into the box, leaving only two blacks and three reds. A couple of swift moves later, Andi destroyed the rest of Riley's playing pieces.

She won. But how? And why?

Riley smiled. Not a trace of disappointment showed on his face. "Good game, Andi. Your championship status is secure. Thanks for teaching me how to play."

Chad looked thoughtful. "That was quite a turn of events." He rose and headed out of the library. "Got some ranch chores to see to."

Andi and Riley were left alone. She fiddled with a checker in her hand and burst out, "Why did you let me win?"

Riley gave her a puzzled look. "What are you talking about?"

"I saw what you did. Chad made a teasing remark to me. Then you put your checker in the most vulnerable spot on the whole board." She paused. "Why did you do it?"

At her words, Riley's confused mask slipped away. "I didn't like the way your brother was teasing you," he confessed. "Along with catching you when you sail off a banister, part of my being your knight in shining armor means warding off Chad's attacks whenever I can. Besides, it's just a game. You mean so much more to me than winning a checkers match."

A glow enveloped Andi, as warm and bright as the sun beginning to shine through the windows. Being the Carter family checkers champion suddenly didn't mean a lot. Riley did. What had she done to deserve such a sweet, caring man?

Nothing. Yet, God had given Riley to her. "Thank you, Riley. One more question. Do you know anything about the game of chess?"

"Not a thing."

"Good!" Andi giggled. "Neither do I. Maybe someday we can learn together."

"Someday," Riley repeated, "but not today." He pointed toward the French doors. "I believe the storm is over. Would you like to take a quick ride before dinner?"

Andi's face broke into a beaming smile. "I'd love to!"

A NIGHT TO REMEMBER

Memory Creek Ranch, April 1890

Some nights are best forgotten.

Sunday dinners at the Circle C usually lasted until long past nightfall. Not the meal itself, but the conversation, the laughing, and being together. Nobody wanted to go home, but sleepy babies and fussy children were eventually bundled up, packed into buggies, and hauled back to town or to Memory Creek.

All except Chad's little girl, Susie. Her sleep was never disturbed. Nor was her brother's. Newborn baby Thomas didn't have to be wrapped up for the chilly spring night and bounced around for half an hour or more. He slept untroubled in his cradle upstairs next to Chad and Ellie's bed.

The children were not the only ones who didn't like to be packed into a buggy. Andi didn't like it either, especially on this particular later-than-usual evening. It was only early April, but Andi felt like she had been in the "family way" for years. This new baby did somersaults day and night.

Thankfully, Riley took care of Jared tonight. He scooped the fussy little boy up in his arms and wrapped him in a quilt for the frosty ride back to the ranch. Sierra foothills days might be toasty but the nights often plunged to near freezing temperatures. Andi shivered all the way home.

By the time Riley pulled into the yard and hopped down to help his wife and son out of the rig, Andi was wide awake. So was Baby Prescott. "I'm never going to fall asleep with the baby rolling around and kicking like a skittish foal," she complained, stifling a yawn as they headed indoors.

Riley closed the door to Jared's small room and joined Andi in the kitchen. He poked the cookstove fire to life, added a few sticks of wood, and shut the firebox door. "Want me to stay up with you after I put the horse and buggy away?"

Andi shook her head. "You'll be up at the crack of dawn tomorrow to oversee your own chores before heading out to work with Chad. You need all the sleep you can get. I'll brew some tea. Maybe that will settle the baby down and we can both get some sleep."

Riley nodded and headed outside. A few minutes later, he returned, gave Andi a kiss, and muttered a sleepy, "G'night." Then he vanished into the other part of the house. Within five minutes, Andi knew he'd be out cold.

"I should be so lucky." She rubbed her expanding belly and smiled. "I didn't mean it, sweetheart," she whispered. "An active baby is a healthy, growing baby."

A growing baby often told his mama he wanted another snack, like right now. Since her nausea had subsided several months ago, Andi was making up for not eating much during that horrible time. Today, Nila's fried chicken had been too tempting to simply take a few ladylike bites. No sirree!

Right now, though, Baby Prescott was begging for more. *Sourdough biscuits with butter and honey dripping over the sides. Please.*

Andi's mouth watered. Biscuits and honey at ten o'clock at night for the baby's snack. Biscuits and gravy at six o'clock in the morning for Riley's breakfast. Perfect.

Biscuits were easy to mix up. She combined the flour, some sugar, and a little baking powder, then cut in a dab of shortening. The cup of sourdough starter fell into the mixture in a lumpy glob.

This sourdough never failed her. She floured her hands and got to work. By the time she slid the pan of biscuits into the black beast, Andi's long day had caught up to her. It must have caught up to the baby too, for he'd settled down during the past ten minutes.

Instead of washing up the doughy bowl and mixing spoon, Andi headed for the sitting room to cozy up with the Jules Verne novel she'd talked Mitch into letting her borrow.

"I haven't finished it yet, Sis," he'd protested last Sunday. But one look at Andi's pleading face softened big brother, and *Twenty Thousand Leagues Under the Sea* found its way into Andi's eager hands. "I'll have it back to you in a week," she'd promised.

When Andi didn't return it at Sunday dinner today, Mitch gave her an understanding smile and told her to keep the book another week.

The biscuits would take about twenty minutes to bake, just enough time to read the crew's next adventure aboard the *Nautilus*, Captain Nemo's underwater submarine. Andi drew the lamp closer and opened to her bookmarked place. Then she traveled to far-off Antarctica and forgot about everything else, especially the time.

An overpowering stench brought Andi up for air and out of the imaginary submarine. She wrinkled her nose. "Oh, no! My biscuits!"

Andi leaped from the settee and hurried into the kitchen. The baby protested with a hard kick. She grabbed a potholder and opened the cookstove's heavy door. Thick, black smoke poured out of the oven and into her face.

Andi coughed, sputtered, and waved the smoke away. No use. It was like the whole stove was on fire, but no flames. Blinking back stinging tears, she pulled out the biscuit pan and dropped it on a towel in the middle of the table.

Her vision of fluffy-white biscuits smothered in butter and golden honey disintegrated before her very eyes. It was replaced with the reality of nine scorched and blackened lumps that resembled pieces of coal.

Andi's no-fail biscuits had failed her just when she wanted them most.

The smoke continued to rise from the pan. She threw another dish towel over the mess to smother the stink, but by now the entire kitchen was filled with acrid smoke.

There was nothing to do but open the kitchen window and let the chilly night air cleanse the room before Riley woke up and discovered what she'd done.

After cleaning up the doughy mess from earlier, Andi dropped into a kitchen chair. She lifted the towel, picked up a biscuit, and tapped it on the tabletop. Hard as a rock. Not even the chickens would be able to peck these lumps apart. She scraped them into the garbage can and sighed.

Another baking disaster. Riley would laugh . . . again.

Tired and disappointed, Andi left the window open and headed to bed. Hopefully, the smoky, smelly evidence of her carelessness this evening would blow away during the night.

Just when Andi was dozing off, the baby decided he'd had enough rest and began his nightly exercise routine. She groaned and rolled over, trying to find a comfortable spot.

Riley slept on, just like a rock.

Just like a rock-hard biscuit. Andi muffled a giggle. *I'm never going to fall asleep.*

Tea might help, a soothing cup of brew that even Andi could not mess up. Yawning, she rolled out of bed, tied her housecoat around her bulging middle, and lit a lamp. Carrying the light, she shuffled back to the kitchen to boil some water, but only if the fire had not gone out.

"Please, just enough hot water for one cup of tea," she pleaded.

By now, the entire house stank like a charred forest. There was no chance Riley would not notice his wife's latest cooking failure. Andi shook her head, stepped into the kitchen, and stopped short.

A dark, furry animal perched on the kitchen windowsill. Andi peered closer, trying to make it out. A possum? A raccoon? One of the barn cats? The glare from her lamp made it hard to see into the shadows.

"Shoo!" Andi set the lamp on the tabletop and flapped the hem of her housecoat at the creature. She should never have left the window open like that. "Get out of here!"

The animal didn't move.

She took two steps closer. "Get out, I say!"

Hiss! A low growl followed the hissing.

Andi froze mid-step and caught her breath. It was not a cat. But why didn't the wild creature turn tail and run away?

The animal growled again. Then it sprang.

Andi shrieked, stumbled backward, and banged into the kitchen table. The animal's identity was shockingly clear now. It was a raccoon. A mean one, and a bold one. What raccoon would be bold enough to attack a person inside a building?

The raccoon began to dash around the kitchen. It jumped on the counters then scurried across the stove. She'd seen raccoons before, but never one that ran around so crazy and wild.

There was only one answer, a horrible answer—hydrophobia.

A rabid raccoon, right here in her kitchen. Scared half out of her wits, Andi did the most natural thing in the world. She screamed. "Riley!"

Riley tore into the kitchen at a run, clad only in his long johns. "What's wrong?" He sniffed. "Is there another fire?"

"N-no," Andi said through chattering teeth. "I left the window open, and a raccoon got in." She pointed. "It's acting crazy-wild."

Just then, the creature leaped and landed on the table. The lamp went sailing. Riley caught it just before it toppled to the floor and broke. With his other hand, he grabbed Andi's arm and yanked her away. "Stay back!"

Andi was only too happy to get out of the way. She stood shaking in the kitchen doorway, with her gaze fixed on the dangerous animal sitting in the middle of the table. At this distance she saw the foam around its mouth. The raccoon stood on its hind legs and growled. Razor-sharp teeth glinted in the lamplight.

Quick as a rifle shot, Riley grabbed the broom. With one swipe, he sent the raccoon flying. It thudded against the back door and dropped to the ground, temporarily stunned.

Andi's mouth dropped open. A broom? Riley was going to kill a mad raccoon with a *broom*?

An instant later, Riley flung open the back door. Using the broom, he whacked the dazed raccoon over and over then swept it outside and onto the porch. He ran back inside, grabbed the rifle from above the door, and hurried outside.

One shot rang out, and it was over.

"Did you get rid of it?" Andi blurted when Riley returned several minutes later. The baby turned somersaults, clearly shaken.

"Matt said he'd bury it," Riley replied quietly. "My shot woke the hands, and they all came running." He leaned the rifle against the counter and drew Andi into his arms.

She burst into tears. "I'm sorry. It's my fault. I burned the biscuits, so I left the window open to clear out the smoke. The raccoon would never have gotten inside if I—"

"Shh." Riley held her close. "It's all right. I got him. The raccoon didn't bite you, did it?"

Andi shook her head.

"Like your mother is fond of saying, 'All's well that ends well,'" Riley said. "It smells like there was a good reason for keeping the windows open." He chuckled.

Andi didn't join her husband's laugher. She was too busy thinking about how close they had come to life-threatening danger. A bite from a rabid animal was nearly always fatal. There was no cure. No medicine. Just a slow, lingering death.

"What were you doing up so late?" Riley wanted to know. "You said you were going to brew some tea. I assumed you would come to bed after that."

"I forgot about the tea and made biscuits instead," Andi whispered, burying her head in Riley's warm chest.

He gently lifted Andi's chin to look into her eyes. "After that big meal at your Mother's?"

Andi grinned. "The baby insisted."

Riley choked back a laugh.

Andi lost her smile and sighed. She felt like a fool. "But I burned them."

"Your no-fail biscuits?"

"Yes," Andi said. "Imagine that. Sometimes, I can't do anything right."

"That's not true, sweetheart." He pulled her into another hug. "You're great with horses, and you're a wonderful mother to Jared."

Andi didn't reply.

"Most importantly," Riley finished, "you're great at being a wife. *My* wife." He squeezed her, being careful of the baby that was wedged between them. "I love you."

"I love you too," Andi murmured, relaxing. Riley's words felt like a warm, cozy blanket.

So what if I can't cook? Andi thought, deliciously sleepy and at peace. So what if the house stank? It would air out tomorrow. So what if she'd rather ride and rope than clean the house?

Riley loves me anyway.

For sure, God loved Andi too. After all, hadn't He given her the best husband in the whole world?

Memory Creek Ranch, June 1890

I wish this baby would make an appearance soon.
I'm tired and ungainly.

CHAPTER 1

Andi Prescott settled herself onto the settee and let out a long, exhausted sigh. "Just for one minute." An hour later, she jerked awake and sat up on her makeshift napping couch.

Oh, no! Not again. "Jared!" she called in a frantic voice.

There was no answer. Andi's heart skipped. Her little boy could be anywhere. "Jared! Answer me this instant!"

Andi wanted to leap off the couch and find Jared, but this newest baby refused to cooperate. He or she sapped every bit of energy Andi might feel first thing in the morning. By noon, she was drooping and counting the minutes until Jared's nap.

Worse, she often fell asleep when she shouldn't. Like this afternoon, when she'd promised herself that she would sit and rest for only a minute. And now? Where was Jared?

Andi carefully pushed herself up from the settee and took two steps across the sitting room. "Jared!" Fingers of fear clutched her throat.

Picking up her pace, Andi made her way into the kitchen. The back door stood wide open. So did the screen door. Flies buzzed in and out of the house. Some landed on the dirty dishes that lay scattered on the table, the counter, and in the sink.

Ignoring the noon-dinner mess, Andi walked to the barn. She wanted to run but she felt clumsy and off-balance. "Jared!" she called into the dusty, dimly-lit structure.

No little boy answered. No horses, either. They were all out on the range or in their spacious paddocks.

"Hi, Mama."

Andi whirled. Weak with relief, she sank to the ground and held out her arms to her son. "Where have you been?"

"Catchin' fwogs." He ran to Andi and wrapped his muddy arms around her neck. "Why you sittin' in the dirt?"

"Mama's tired." She squeezed her almost-three-year-old's warm body. "You know you mustn't play in the creek alone," she scolded.

Jared stepped back and gave Andi a serious look. "Not alone. Fwogs there." He pointed to the sky. "An' God too."

Andi was too grateful to argue. "Yes, He is."

Jared tugged on her hand. "C'mon, Mama. Get up."

Andi could not get up. This baby was too big. How dumb could she be to sit down in the middle of the yard? "And I still have nearly a month to go," she muttered.

A new thought cheered her but didn't help her climb to her feet. Perhaps she had miscalculated. Maybe the baby would come today. *Oh, happy thought!*

Riley loped into the yard just then. When he saw Andi, he yanked Dakota to an abrupt halt and flew from the saddle. "Andi! What's wrong?" he asked, crouching beside her. Fear filled his hazel eyes.

"Mama's tired," Jared said in a sad voice. "Won't get up."

Riley's face paled under his tan. "Is the baby—"

Andi burst out laughing. "No, the baby is fine right where he is." She shared her story, confessing how scared she'd been to wake up and find Jared missing. "I should not have sat down, not even for a minute."

Without a word, Riley helped Andi to her feet. He looked deep in thought.

Andi watched him. What was he up to now? Sometimes, her husband got wild, silly ideas, but sometimes his ideas were full of fun—like trick riding or finding a secret glade.

Stiff and sore, she let Riley help her across the yard and settle her into the rocking chair on the back porch. "I feel eighty years old."

Riley sat down in the rocking chair beside her and pulled Jared onto his lap. "We can practice rocking for the day when we actually *are* eighty years old."

Squeak, squeak. Back and forth Riley rocked.

"Faster!" Jared crowed.

"You're going to wreck it," Andi said, giggling. "It's not a wild bronco that needs breaking."

Riley smiled, happy to see his wife back in good spirits. He cleared his throat. "I've decided that we are going to take a little holiday."

"Are you crazy?" Andi rocked faster. "Look at me." She pointed to her belly. "I don't even go to town these days. I'm not going anywhere until this baby is born."

"Oh, yes, you are." Riley smirked. "Your birthday sneaked by me a couple of weeks ago because you were too tired to enjoy it. I'm not waiting a day longer. What you need is a nice rest at your Aunt Rebecca's house before the baby comes. I've already arranged it with Kate. She would love to have us come for a week, maybe two. You won't have to do a thing, not with all the servants your sister kept on after your aunt passed."

Andi paused in her rocking. San Francisco? Kate's big, rambling house? Betsy and Hannah to play with Jared? Tea, sugar cookies, servants, and—

Her lips curved into a lazy smile. *No cooking.*

Then reality hit her like a bucket of creek water. "It's too close to my time." She *hoped* it was too close to her time.

"I suppose you would know more about that than I," Riley admitted, "but I thought you told me the baby would be coming around Jared's birthday."

Andi sighed. Riley's memory was sharp, as always. "I'm hoping I figured wrong, and the baby will come before then. I feel like he could come any day."

"Wishful thinking, darling. Remember, Jared ended up arriving later than we thought he would."

Andi scowled.

"Even so," he went on, "one or two weeks at Kate's gives us plenty of time to come back to Memory Creek before he's born." Riley reached out and gave Andi's belly a light rub. "Hear that, baby boy? Hold off until your mama and I have a nice little vacation."

The response was a hard kick, and Andi laughed. "Oh, all right," she said, giving in. "I suppose an eight-hour train trip is worth a week of lavish living in the city."

Riley shot out of the rocking chair and threw his Stetson high in the air. "Yee haw!"

"Yee haw!" Jared echoed, clinging to his father's neck.

CHAPTER 2

San Francisco, June 1890

When Mother heard how Riley had talked Andi into taking a holiday in San Francisco, her eyebrows rose. Everyone else at Sunday dinner paused in their chewing and conversing.

"You're going to the city willingly?" Chad asked.

"I am." Andi lifted her chin, daring her brother to make even one more teasing remark.

"Will surprises never cease?"

"It's an excellent idea," Mother broke in. "And a lovely gesture, Riley." She smiled at Andi. "I don't want to intrude, but would you and Riley like another traveler?"

Andi sucked in a delighted breath. "Oh, Mother, I would love it if you came along."

So, it was settled.

The next two days flew by faster than a galloping horse. Riley arranged with Matt, Carlos, and Joey to take over full management of Memory Creek while he took the week off. Chad promised to ride over a couple of times during Riley's absence to check on the ranch hands.

Andi hummed and packed her carpet bag. She packed a small valise for Jared, and Riley packed his own duds. For a wonder, she didn't feel tired. Not one bit. The thought of a short holiday, even if it was in a city for which Andi had no love, energized her.

"Could we take Jared to Lands End?" she asked Riley as he loaded up the buggy. She smiled, remembering her childhood visit to the popular seashore attraction just west of the city.

He shook his head. "No. We're staying at Kate's, where you are going to rest and visit, not run every which way and wear yourself out even more."

Andi lost her smile and sighed her acceptance.

"Troy and I will take the kids to the beach," Riley said. "I wouldn't mind getting to know that scoundrel better than what I observed at our previous meeting."

Andi laughed. Riley's first encounter with Kate's husband had not left a good impression. Being held up at gunpoint on your honeymoon was not a good way to be introduced to your new sister-in-law's husband.

However, after that unfortunate event, Troy had agreed with Andi that it was time to turn himself in. True to his word, when the passenger he shot recovered, the outlaw had followed through. Troy was tried, convicted, and sent to San Quentin. He could thank his lawyer brother-in-law, Justin, for wrangling a short, three-year prison term.

Troy had been released in January and hightailed it to San Francisco to patch things up with his wife. All the news Andi heard from Kate was that things were going well since Troy rejoined the family.

Not quite a happily ever after, she thought while Riley settled her in the buggy, *but moving in the right direction.*

The trip into Fresno to catch the train was a bumpy blur. Andi wondered how she would survive the upcoming eight hours on the railroad car.

To her joy and relief, the plush, velvet seats immediately eased her concern. Riley minded Jared for the entire eight hours. Andi dozed, read, and ate the refreshments Mother had packed in a wicker basket.

Even the short ferry trip across San Francisco Bay felt refreshing. The boat churned its way through the dark waves, throwing up spray. Andi welcomed the salty taste and cool drops against her face. June in the city was not usually so pleasant.

For once in her life, Andi looked at the City by the Bay with grown-up eyes. Maybe it wasn't such a bad place after all. The tall buildings kissed the cloudless, blue sky. Cable cars clanged their way up and down California and Market Streets.

Jared's hazel eyes grew huge. "Daddy!" He pointed. "Wide!"

Riley ruffled Jared's sandy hair and promised him a ride on the streetcar later. "He and I can take the Cliff House Railway all the way to Lands End," he explained to Andi. "The new line opened two years ago."

Andi gave her husband a puzzled look. How did a small-time foothills rancher know so much about the streetcar system of the largest city on the West coast?

He caught Andi's look and winked. "I did my homework before bringing my family here. Justin is a fountain of knowledge about San Francisco."

Yes, Justin would know all about the city he admired so much.

The rest of the ride up to Pacific Heights passed exactly as Andi hoped. The view of the city, the bay, and even faraway Lands End put a lump in

Andi's throat. "Everything looks just as I remember it from my younger days," she said softly when the rig stopped in front of the Victorian mansion.

Andi shivered. She had not visited the city since Aunt Rebecca's funeral four years ago. San Francisco was not sunny and warm that sad day in January. The skies did nothing but pour rain the entire week, as if the heavens also mourned the old woman's passing.

"Andi!" Hannah's squeal broke into Andi's thoughts. "Where's Jared?"

"Right here. Take him." Andi lowered Jared into Hannah's outstretched arms.

Grinning, Hannah carried her cousin around the house and into the backyard, chattering about a new sandbox and a swing, and other fine toys a little boy would love.

Andi smiled. She probably wouldn't see Jared until suppertime. She squeezed Riley's hand when he reached up to help her down. "Thank you," she whispered. "Coming to the city is your best idea ever."

CHAPTER 3

Andi was awakened the next morning by a quiet tapping on her bedroom door. Yawning, she rolled over and opened her eyes. Riley was gone. Jared was gone. Her eyes opened wider.

The large bedroom window had been raised halfway. A balmy morning breeze ruffled the curtains, sending a tangy salt-sea aroma drifting across Andi's face.

She sat up, startled. How late was it? "Come in."

The door opened, and Sylvia appeared. "Breakfast, Miss Andi," the maid said cheerfully. "Your favorites. Your mother saw to that."

Breakfast in bed? What a lovely holiday this was turning out to be! "Thank you, Sylvia. Please set it on the bedside stand for now."

The maid nodded, lowered Andi's tray to the small table, and left, clicking the door shut.

Andi glanced at the clock and nearly gasped. Ten o'clock! How was it possible that she had slept so late? The baby had been still the entire night. A flash of fear prompted her to lay her hand against her belly. "Are you all right?"

When a slight movement fluttered against her hand, she felt foolish. "I complain if you kick and roll too much," she told the baby. "The next minute I worry if you don't kick and roll enough." Andi sighed. Would she ever get used to being a wife and mother? "Maybe when I'm old and gray," she answered herself.

Laughing at her silly worries, Andi dug into her meal. Mother had overseen a breakfast fit for a queen. Waffles smothered in butter and thick syrup, which Andi usually only ate on her birthday, a serving of fluffy scrambled eggs, hot chocolate, and a tall glass of freshly squeezed orange juice.

"You and I are feasting today, little one," she said between mouthfuls.

Andi took her time enjoying every bite. She lingered over her toilette, brushing her long, dark hair one hundred strokes before braiding it. She never had time at the ranch for more than a quick combing, so today she made up for it.

By the time Andi was dressed and ready for the day, the baby had jumped into high gear. No worries there. She didn't have to care for an active little boy, or manage the laundry, or bake bread, or tend the garden. Not today. Not all week.

"Thank You, God, for giving Riley this wonderful idea," she prayed. Then a new idea crept into her mind. Perhaps Riley would let her stay the entire month. Maybe she could have the baby here in San Francisco.

No, that was silly. Andi wanted this baby to be born in her own home, like Jared had been. But still, the temptation lingered.

Picking up the breakfast tray, Andi left her room and headed downstairs. Mother and Kate sat at the dining room table, visiting over what looked like a second or third cup of coffee.

"It's so quiet." Andi set the tray down on the table and found an empty chair. "Where is everybody?"

"Riley and Troy packed up the kids right after breakfast and headed for the beach," Kate answered. "It's an all-day outing."

"Even Levi?"

"Oh, yes," Kate said, smiling. "He wouldn't miss it. I think he's trying to make up for all the time he lost when his father was not part of his life."

Andi nodded. She winced mentally, remembering Levi's childish but honest words the last time he'd seen his father. *Kinfolk don't treat each other that way. If you want to be an outlaw, you go ahead. But do it by yourself. Now go away and leave us alone.*

Now, God was giving Levi a chance to turn his bitterness into healing.

"Levi likes being around Riley too," Kate added. "He still talks about the time he and Riley watched the little children. He thought it was the funniest thing he'd ever seen."

"It wasn't very funny at the time," Andi remembered.

"I suppose not," Kate agreed, "but—"

A sudden, slight trembling cut off Kate's words. The chandelier hanging over the dining room table clinked. Then everything stilled . . . just like that.

"Oh, dear," Mother said.

Kate rolled her eyes. "Not again."

Andi didn't ask what was going on. She knew. Years ago, she'd been sitting in an apple tree in Aunt Rebecca's backyard when an earthquake shook the branches like a giant's fist. She never forgot her feeling of terror and helplessness.

"A month doesn't go by when something isn't trembling under this city," Kate said in disgust. She reached across the table and patted Andi's arm. "Don't worry about it. We're used to these little hiccups." She rose and picked up Andi's tray. "Let's drop this off in the kitchen and—"

Rumble, rattle, creak, clink.

Andi's heart leaped to her throat. This was more than a hiccup. *Much* more.

"Come on," Mother ordered. "Let's head outside."

Kate dropped the tray. "I agree." She led them through the dining room and into the kitchen.

Sylvia was wringing her hands. "Miss Kate, what shall—"

"This way!" Kate ordered.

The four women ran for the back door, ducking when dishes flew from the cabinets. Andi threw her hands over her head just as the ceiling plaster loosened and crashed onto the cookstove. She stifled a shriek and hurried to catch up with her mother and sister.

The small "hiccup" turned into a full-fledged earthquake that would not stop. The walls groaned and heaved. The hanging lamp in the kitchen dislodged and crashed to the floor in a tinkle of glass and metal.

"Oh, ma'am, oh, ma'am!"

Sylvia's terrified wails sent shivers up and down Andi's back. The back door and safety seemed miles away.

More dishes broke. More plaster fell. The kitchen floor rolled and twisted. *Crack!* The floorboards snapped. The whole house shifted, tilting at an odd, eerie angle.

The shifting floor sent Andi sprawling. She scrabbled for a handhold, but her fingers found only debris. Then the floorboards parted, and she was rolling down toward the cellar. Pain lanced her back as the floorboards followed her into the hole and landed on top of her.

She heard Sylvia scream just before everything went black.

CHAPTER 4

With a frightened yelp, Andi jerked awake. Her head pounded. Her back throbbed. She tried to sit up, but something heavy kept her wedged between the dirty cellar floor and freedom.

At least the earthquake is over, she thought.

Wrong. More rattling sent dirt and small pieces of wood down on Andi. She blinked dust from her eyes and looked around. She couldn't see a thing. Except for a few cracks of light streaming in from high overhead, it was black as a dark night.

Two more aftershocks, and then an eerie stillness fell.

"Andrea?"

Mother's frightened voice penetrated Andi's pain-filled, groggy thoughts. "I'm here but trapped under some boards."

"The baby?" Mother made her way to her daughter's side and began pulling off the floorboards.

Andi's breath caught. She rubbed a hand over her belly. "I think he's all right. I remember rolling more than falling. I curled up in a ball." Unshed tears clogged her throat. She hurt all over. *Please, God, let my baby be all right.*

Mother soon cleared away the debris and Andi sat up. She winced. Something hurt deep inside, but she didn't want to worry Mother. "Where's Kate?"

"I'm here," her sister answered. "I had to dig myself out, but I found a lantern. I'll have it lit in a moment." Her words were accompanied by a scratching sound. A match flared. "Let there be light!" she called cheerfully.

Kate held the lantern high and joined her mother and sister. Blood seeped through Kate's blouse sleeve. Her face looked battered. It wouldn't be long before large, dark bruises appeared.

"I think we're stuck down here for now." She waved a hand toward the far corner. "Those are where the cellar steps should be. We won't be getting out of here that way, though. It's choked with plaster, bricks, and other wreckage."

Andi's stomach turned over. She felt her breakfast close to coming back up. "Stuck down here? For how long?"

Kate set the lantern on a crate and settled to the ground beside Andi. "Until somebody figures out we're down here and clears away the debris."

"That could be quite some time from now," Mother said softly, brushing off her hands. Her blond hair had turned dirty gray, and her face was smudged, but she looked whole and unharmed.

However, the cellar looked as if a giant had used it as a garbage dump. Rubble from the upper floor had tumbled into the cellar and filled any possible openings for escaping. The storage shelves had fallen over. Broken jars of canned goods were mixed in with the dirt. Bins had cracked. Sawdust and stored apples spilled out.

"What a mess," Kate murmured. "All my hard work last summer spoiled in thirty seconds."

Andi licked her dry lips. "Thirty seconds? That temblor felt more like thirty minutes to me." She shuddered. Then she remembered Sylvia's scream. "Is Sylvia all right? Is she down here too?"

Mother shook her head. "I don't know. She might have been buried under the debris just across from us."

"No!" Andi gaped at the pile of rubble and sucked in a breath. "How awful! You have to find her, Kate."

Her sister hurried over. "I got a glimpse of Sylvia slipping out the back door just as we fell into this hole." She patted Andi's hand. "Don't worry. I believe she made it outside in time. She's safe."

"That's good news." Andi relaxed. More than ever, she was grateful that God had spared her life. A small kick told her that He had spared her baby too.

Just then a wave of unexpected nausea flooded her. She leaned against Mother. "I don't feel very well."

"You need to rest," Mother encouraged. "Once the emotional shock wears off, you'll feel better."

Andi wasn't sure about that. Between the nausea and a throbbing pain deep inside, she didn't want to move. She wanted to sit here until Riley rescued her and found her a warm, safe place to sleep. When she awoke, she could pretend this earthquake had only been a bad dream.

Another temblor rippled through the wreckage. Dust and plaster particles drifted down. Andi stiffened.

Mother wrapped an arm around Andi and drew her close. "It's all right, sweetheart. The aftershocks will subside soon, and they're never as damaging as the initial earthquake."

A sudden, terrifying thought crowded out Mother's words. "What if nobody knows we're down here?"

Kate laughed. "Where else would we be, little sister? Riley knows we wouldn't take you visiting. Don't fuss."

She was right. Andi only had to wait until Riley and Troy brought the kids home from the beach. Surely, the earthquake had not affected them. Lands End was clear across the peninsula.

I'm being silly. She calmed down, counting the hours before she could leave this dark, gloomy place. Until then, Mother and Kate were right here. She laid a protective hand over the baby and prayed everything would soon be back to normal.

Ouch! Andi winced. The dull pain deep inside suddenly spread its tendrils up and around her belly. Anxiety washed over her. Had her fall banged up her insides? What if her injuries hurt the baby? She shifted away from her mother and sat up.

"What's wrong?" Mother asked in a worried voice.

"I'm not sure. I have a lot of pain in my gut, and my lower back is stabbing me. I must have fallen harder than I thought." She sucked in a breath. "*Ohh,* it hurts."

Mother and Kate exchanged knowing looks. Without a word, Kate rose and started rummaging around the cellar.

"Where are you off to?" Andi asked.

Kate replied with a sisterly smile. "Oh, I'm just looking for things we might need during the next few hours."

The next pain exploded through Andi like fire. *No, no, no!* It couldn't be. The baby couldn't be coming. This pain was much different, nothing like the first time. "Mother?"

She nodded. "Yes, dear. I believe the baby is on his way."

CHAPTER 5

A wave of panic washed over Andi from head to toe. "It's too early."

As often as she wished this baby would be born before the end of the month, she had never been serious. She groused because she felt tired, ungainly, and impatient. *I didn't mean it, Lord*, she wailed silently.

When another pain ripped through her belly, Andi tried to hold it back. "The baby can't come now. Not here in this filthy place." She looked at her mother. "Can't you make it stop?"

"No, sweetheart," Mother said softly. "I'm afraid not. If the pains do not stop on their own, there is no turning back. The tumble you took during the earthquake must have set things in motion early. You must face what is coming with courage."

Andi shook her head. "I can't. The baby is too small."

Mother stroked Andi's filthy, tangled hair. "None of that. You were born three weeks early and look how you turned out. Besides, I'm right here. We'll deliver a healthy baby for Riley, or my name is not Elizabeth Carter."

Andi's panic receded. *A healthy baby for Riley*. Yes. She must focus on that, and on the glorious blessing that Mother was beside Andi this time, not an hour or more away, like on the day of Jared's birth.

She squeezed Mother's hand. "Maybe the pains will subside."

"Perhaps."

Another gripping stab mocked Andi's hope. Like it or not, her tiny baby was coming.

Kate returned from her explorations with an armload of clean woolen blankets. "Look what I found." She held her prizes up and grinned her satisfaction. "I had to poke around, but I knew they were here somewhere. I also found a paring knife to cut the baby's cord."

Andi gaped at her sister. "Are you *loco*? How are you going to get that old thing clean?"

Kate winked. "You'll see." She tore a strip from her clean, white petticoat and wiped the knife blade free of dirt and dust. Then she laid it across the top of the lantern's glass chimney. "There. Now the knife can burn clean."

She and Mother unfolded the blankets and spread them out on the cellar's dirt floor. Andi settled herself onto the blankets just as another pain ran her over. She closed her eyes and determined to get through each pain one at a time. Perhaps after an hour or two, they would recede.

Oh, please, God, make it so, she pleaded silently.

The alternative was indeed dark. Her poor baby, born in a dim, dirty cellar. His first breath would be full of plaster dust.

A ripping sound pulled Andi's attention away from her own misery. She opened her eyes and watched, fascinated, as Kate and Mother pulled their undergarments off. "What are you doing?"

"A couple of clean petticoats will make excellent swaddling clothes," Kate said cheerfully. She folded them up and set them aside to use later.

Andi let her mother and Kate take over. The pains didn't allow for any argument or discussion. They came hard and fast, much faster than when Jared was born. That day she'd had brief moments of rest during her long hours of labor. Riley had brought her tea and rubbed her back, and never let her out of his sight.

Oh, Riley, she moaned. *Where are you?*

The day wore on. Andi had no idea if one hour or two had passed. Kate sat beside Andi and held her hand. She rambled on about Troy, the kids, baby names . . . anything to keep her sister's mind off the current predicament.

What seemed like hours later, Mother shushed Kate's chatter. "Listen."

The faraway sounds of shouts mixed with the distinct, thudding *clunk* of rubble being cleared shot Andi's hopes to the sky. "Somebody's looking for us!" she cried out in relief.

"Thank God," Kate whispered. She brushed a kiss across Andi's forehead. "It won't be long now. What a surprise they'll have when they see the baby."

Andi hoped they broke through the wreckage long before this baby came. *Please, God. Make them hurry!*

Andi's throat turned dry as sawdust. She could barely swallow. The constant pain with no rest sapped her energy.

"Here, Andi, drink this."

A drink? Andi forced herself to sit up. Kate had found an unbroken jar of peaches and loosened the seal. Andi gratefully guzzled the sugar water and felt her strength returning.

Not long after she'd swallowed the entire jar of peach water, Andi felt a familiar change deep inside. Soon, she was birthing the baby into the world. To her surprise, this part of her labor hardly hurt at all. The tiny infant slipped easily into Mother's waiting hands.

When Andi heard the shrill wail, she relaxed. The baby was alive and healthy. "Thank you, God." She sighed in relief and gratefulness. "This baby was much easier to birth than Jared," she remarked, closing her eyes. Sleep would soon overtake her. When she awoke, maybe Riley would be here.

"It's the first baby that is hard," Mother comforted her. "This baby is much smaller too, given that you brought him into the world before his time." Then she laughed. "I beg your pardon, little one. I mean *her*."

Andi opened her eyes. "Her?"

"You have a baby girl," Kate told her. "She's beautiful! Bright blue eyes, just like yours."

"Let me hold her," Andi demanded, rousing herself from her lassitude.

A sudden, agonizing pain made her bear down. "What's happening, Mother? Something's wrong."

The baby was born. The pain should not come back. Was she too badly injured from tumbling into the cellar? Had her insides been torn apart? Would she *die*?

Andi caught her breath as terrifying images crept into her mind. "I'm scared, Mother. What's wrong with me?"

"Andrea," Mother said in her no-nonsense voice. "Calm yourself." She handed the crying newborn to Kate. "Nothing's wrong."

Kate wrapped the baby in the clean petticoat and held her close. "Shh, little one." She peeked over the bundle and grinned at her sister. "Mother's right, Andi. Nothing is wrong. Everything is marvelously all right." She leaned closer. "You're birthing a second baby."

"Yes," Mother confirmed. "I see another one. Push hard, daughter. You have twins."

Andi was too surprised to do anything but obey. When the next awful pain gripped her, she pushed the second baby into the world. Then she collapsed and lay back, totally spent.

"It's another girl," Mother announced. She took care of the cord and wiped the baby down with clean strips of cloth. Then she handed her to Kate to wrap up.

"Blue eyes too," Kate said, cuddling both babies. "And that Carter black hair. They look as alike as two peas in a pod." She giggled. "How will you ever tell them apart?"

Andi didn't respond to Kate's giddy chatter. Telling two babies apart was the least of her worries. She wanted out of here before the dirt and the gloom pulled her into a dark place. She wanted her babies bathed and fed and brought into the light.

Most of all, she wanted to see Riley.

Mother took over and made sure Andi was all right after such an unusual birth. "See if you can find more canned fruit," she ordered Kate. "Andrea looks peaked. She needs something to eat." She helped Andi sit up against a crate and settled the two babies in her lap.

Andi did whatever her mother told her. She forced down a portion of canned applesauce, slurped more juice from another jar of peaches, and fed her newborns. Gazing down at the two tiny bundles, she blinked back sudden tears. "They're so tiny, Mother. Will they live?"

"They're small but strong," Mother assured her. "These little girls are having no difficulty filling their bellies. They will do well." She smiled. "I promised you we would deliver a healthy baby for Riley. I never dreamed we would deliver two."

"Listen!" Kate urged.

Andi strained her ears. The shouting and clanging were getting closer. "Hallo!" Somebody shouted down through a newly created hole in the rubble. "Is anyone down there? Are you all right?"

Kate shot to her feet. "We're here! We're all fine!"

Shouts of joy and relief came from several voices. "Hang on. We'll have you out in a jiffy."

A fresh wave of hope made Andi's heart leap. Soon, very soon, she would be out of here.

Soon, very soon, Riley would meet his new daughters.

Unable to fight the overwhelming exhaustion any longer, Andi's eyelids fluttered, and she yawned. She felt Mother settling her more comfortably on the thick, woolen blankets. The next moment Andi gave in to the blessed relief of deep, dreamless sleep.

RILEY TO THE RESCUE

San Francisco, California, June 1890

Riley will always be my knight in shining armor.

CHAPTER 1

"What was that?"

Riley squinted up at Levi and kept brushing sand and sticky seaweed off his son. "What was what?"

"An odd rolling feeling," Levi replied. "Made me dizzy."

"I don't feel anything." Just then, the sandy beach under Riley rolled. It felt like how he imagined the deck of a sailing ship might pitch and roll. "Oh!"

Troy pointed to the water. "Look at the waves."

Instead of gently lapping at their feet, the waves churned and crashed against the shore. Breakers whooshed toward Riley, collapsed in a big splash, and then slid back out to sea.

Riley grabbed Jared and backed away. He frowned. "That's strange."

"We usually see breakers like this during a storm," Troy said. "But it's calm and sunny today."

Ten minutes later, the Pacific Ocean had settled down to the usual small waves breaking on the seashore. Seagulls called, mud crabs scuttled under rocks, and all seemed as before. Hannah and Betsy took Jared's hands and led him across the sand to wade in the salty water. He giggled and kicked the waves.

Riley thought no more of the seashore's strange behavior. He laid back against a large piece of driftwood, clasped his hands behind his head, and watched Jared play in the surf. Guilt washed over him for slipping away this morning while Andi slept. She'd wanted to come to the beach, but he'd talked her into resting at home with Kate and their mother.

Riley's eyes drifted shut. This was about as restful as it could get. "We should have waited for the ladies," he said, opening his eyes and squinting at Troy. "I didn't realize how relaxing this place is."

"We can make it up to them tomorrow." Troy waved at his two daughters and Jared. "They'll be happy to come back every day this week."

"Very true," Riley agreed and settled back down to enjoy the warm, late-morning sun.

An hour later, Levi, who had wandered off to explore farther down the beach, pounded his bare feet through the sand dunes and skidded to a stop next to the log. Sand sprayed the men.

"Pa! Uncle Riley!"

Troy sat up. "What is it, Son?"

Levi gasped. "A rider galloped past, a regular Paul Revere." He drew a shaky breath. "He says the city was hit by a big temblor."

"What?" Riley and Troy shouted together.

"Where?" Riley demanded. "Which part of the city?" He exchanged worried glances with Troy. An earthquake would explain the rolling beach and crashing waves from earlier today.

"He says 'most everybody in the city must've felt it, but Golden Gate Park and Pacific Heights are the worst hit." Levi's eyes grew dark with anxiety. "Do you think Mama, Grandmother, and Andi are all right?"

"I'm not waiting around for another rider to spread more bad news." Riley leaped to his feet and called to the girls to bring Jared back. "I'm heading back to the city."

"I'm coming with you," Troy agreed. "Let's get home as fast as we can."

———

"End of the line, folks." The conductor brought the streetcar to a screeching halt. "Everyone must get off."

Riley bit back his frustration before a scathing remark slipped between his teeth. It wasn't the streetcar company's fault the tracks were covered with debris just below Pacific Heights. But it would be a long hike uphill before he could find out if Andi and the others were safe.

Please keep her safe, God, he prayed. He jogged behind Troy and started up Pacific Heights. With Jared perched on his shoulders, Riley made short work of the first block, but the steep climb had him breathing hard after two more blocks.

The higher Riley climbed, the more destruction he saw. Troy whistled his shock. Toppled telegraph poles, their lines tangled up in tall trees. Cobblestone streets full of holes and cracks. Roofs partly crumbled.

Most houses still stood, although many tilted at cockeyed angles. Windows had burst and chimneys lay in scattered heaps of bricks, but for the most part the dwellings were in one piece. Some homes looked as if a giant had stepped right over the top of them and then used his fist to crush the neighbor's roof instead.

Riley shook his head to dispel the gruesome image. Every fiber of his being wanted Kate's home to be one of the lucky few left standing, whole and undamaged.

When Riley's steps slowed, Troy plucked Jared from his perch and swung him up on his own shoulders. Jared crowed his delight. "Giddup, Unca Troy!"

"Don't worry." Troy laid a comforting hand on Riley's shoulder and squeezed. "The Lord is watching over our wives. They're safe, and I'm sure your baby is too."

At that moment, Troy Swanson—former rogue, thief, outlaw, and all-around scoundrel—became a true member of the family in Riley's eyes.

"Thanks, Troy. I appreciate your words." Newly energized, Riley pressed onward.

The time dragged. Block after endless block, Troy and Riley picked their way around the debris. *Hurry, hurry!* Riley pushed himself harder, but the girls were falling behind. They could not keep up with the men and Levi.

"Wait, Pa!" Hannah yelled.

Riley turned around. Half a block away, Betsy was tugging on her sister's hand, urging her to go faster. Hannah ran a few steps, tripped, and fell.

The men waited for the girls to catch up, but Riley was itching to get going.

"I'll stay with the girls," Levi offered. "There's no hurry for them to get there."

"Good idea." Troy swung Jared down from his shoulders. "You need to leave Jared with Levi too," he told Riley. "When we arrive at the house, it might show extensive damage. We'll need to pitch in. It's no place for a young child."

Troy was right. Riley engulfed Jared in a tight embrace, prayed that God would keep him safe, and left his little boy with Levi and the girls.

"Don't worry, Uncle Riley." Betsy's voice shook only a little. "I'll take good care of him." She gave her uncle a confident smile.

"Thanks, Betsy."

Riley's stomach churned at the idea of leaving his son in the middle of this devastation. However, Betsy was nearly sixteen years old. He knew from experience how good she was with Jared, and this was her neighborhood. She and Levi would make sure Jared was cared for and brought safely home.

"Bye, Daddy!" Jared hollered. "I be good."

"I know you will, Son," Riley called over his shoulder. His words caught in his throat. He turned and hurried after Troy.

Without the children slowing them down, the men made good

progress. They crested Pacific Heights and stopped short. The Swanson mansion had fared just as poorly as the rest of the houses on this street.

Maybe even worse, Riley thought as his horrified gaze swept over the ruined homes.

To darken matters further, Andi, Elizabeth, and Kate were nowhere in sight. Were they trapped under the wreckage? Wherever Riley turned, men dug at the rubble, looking for lost friends and relatives.

Riley and Troy broke into a run. Panting and sweating, they arrived at the damaged house. The front yard of the once-stately Victorian home appeared to have less garbage piled up, but the structure titled at a crazy angle. Riley's head spun when he saw it.

Troy shook his head. "How in the world—"

"C'mon," Riley cut in. "Let's check around back."

When the men rounded the corner of the house, they found the Swanson household help digging through wreckage near the back door.

A shout went up when they saw Troy and Riley.

"Oh, Mister Troy!" Sylvia wailed. "They're trapped. All three ladies. Nobody knows if they're dead or alive. I barely escaped." She dabbed her eyes with the hem of her apron. "I slipped through the back door just as the kitchen floor gave way. We've been digging for hours, but we need more help."

Riley rolled up his sleeves. "Where do we start?"

CHAPTER 2

The afternoon wore on. Heat from the June sun scorched Riley's back. He worked feverishly to lift bricks, old plaster, and heavy beams away from what had once been the cellar stairs.

Others cleaned away the kitchen debris. The cookstove and stovepipe were in good shape. The chimney also appeared to have escaped damage.

Troy ordered the kitchen staff to find something to feed the hungry crew. "And be quick about it!" he barked.

They jumped to obey.

When Levi, the girls, and Jared finally arrived, Riley sighed his relief. He didn't, however, spare even a moment to greet his son. Thankfully, the little boy was fast asleep on Levi's shoulder.

"We have a quiet place for him," their neighbor offered. "He can sleep in the shade in our backyard. The girls can watch him." Betsy and Hannah nodded their agreement. They looked too tired and upset to speak.

Levi turned the sleeping child over to the kind woman. Then he joined his father and uncle to continue unburying the steps.

The late afternoon sun was dipping behind the rooftops when Thomas, one of the servants, turned to Riley and said, "I can see inside the cellar." He thrust his head close to the hole and yelled, "Hallo! Is anyone down there? Are you all right?"

A high, clear voice echoed from the darkness. "We're here! We're all fine!"

"That's Katie," Troy said, slumping to the ground.

Levi touched his father's shoulder. "She's fine, Pa. So is everyone else."

"Thank God." He pulled his son down next to him and they embraced.

The rest of the rescuers shouted their joy and relief. "Hang on. We'll have you out in a jiffy," Thomas called down through the opening.

The steps were soon cleared wide enough to allow a man to squeeze past the rubble and descend into the cellar. Before anyone could hold him back, Riley shoved the remaining loose bricks and boards aside and slid inside, feet first.

Troy held his arms until Riley could drop safely into the cellar.

Thud. Riley landed with a grunt on more rubble. He groped and crawled the rest of the way to the floor and stood up. Peering over his shoulder, he spared a quick glance at the lower half of the steps.

The rest of the debris could be cleared away from down here. It wouldn't take long if enough helping hands pitched in.

"Riley, is that you?" Kate called. "We're over here."

He whirled. Just across the dark, dingy cellar, a lantern sat on an over-turned crate. An orange glow illuminated the women. Elizabeth Carter and Kate sat quietly on the edge of a blanket. Both wore wide smiles.

Then Riley saw his wife. She lay pale and unmoving next to her mother and sister. "Andi!" She didn't respond. He rushed over and knelt by her side.

"She's asleep," Elizabeth warned. "Shh."

Riley swallowed. Andi looked completely done in. But his mother-in-law would not be smiling if her youngest daughter was at death's door. "What happened to her? Is she hurt?" he finally asked. "What about the baby?"

A high, shrill wailing caught Riley by surprise. A small cloth bundle wriggled under the blanket. His eyebrows shot up. "Andi had the baby?" His voice cracked. "Down here?"

"She did indeed," Elizabeth said.

Heart pounding, Riley gently lifted the blanket away. A small head covered with dark hair made his breath catch. "He's so . . . so tiny."

"She," Kate corrected him, chuckling.

"A girl." Riley sat back on his heels, stunned.

A thumping noise interrupted them. "Katie!"

Kate immediately rose and ran into Troy's arms.

Riley turned back to Andi. He leaned close and kissed her forehead. "I'm so sorry I wasn't here for you." Remorse flooded him. He should not have left her for a moment today. He should have been here when she needed him most.

Andi's eyes fluttered open. "Riley, you came." Tears gushed.

"Hey, don't cry." He pulled a bandana from his pocket and wiped the worst of the dirt and tears from her face. He couldn't help the smile that curved his lips. Didn't Andi *ever* carry a handkerchief? "I'm here now."

"I'm j-just so happy to s-see you," she stammered between tears. "It's been a long, horrid day."

"I bet." Riley pocketed the bandana and glanced around. Andi's mother had joined Kate and Troy. The three of them were engaged in deep conversation, leaving Andi and Riley alone.

He bent over Andi. "I'm so proud of you," he whispered, stroking her hair. "Even an earthquake couldn't stop you from giving me the most precious little girl." He gave her a silly grin. "A girl, with dark hair just like yours. Are her eyes blue?"

Andi nodded. Color returned to her cheeks. "It's *girls*, Riley." She lifted the blanket on her other side. Another baby lay wrapped in an identical white bundle.

Riley's eyes widened, and he gasped. No words came. He simply stared, startled into silence.

"Aren't you going to say anything?" Andi gave him a soft, happy smile. "We have twins. Quite a lovely San Francisco surprise, don't you think?"

Riley nodded wordlessly. His gaze darted back and forth between the two tiny babies wrapped in what appeared to be lengths of white, lacy petticoats. His eyes stung. Never in his life had he imagined he could be so blessed.

Gently, he lifted one of the girls and held her close. "This explains the reason you felt the way you did these past couple of months."

"Yes, and probably why I felt so sick in the beginning." Her smile widened. "I wasn't carrying one big baby boy, but two little girls. Who could have guessed? They're so tiny, but Mother says they're strong and will do fine, even though they came a few weeks early."

Riley chuckled. "This complicates things, you know. We already settled on a girl's name. Lillian Joy."

"Charlotte was next on our list," Andi reminded him. Her eyes closed, and she let out a long, deep sigh. Was she falling asleep? Then her eyes opened. "What about Charlotte Faith? It took a lot of faith to endure this day and not give up."

When Riley nodded his approval, Andi nestled Charlotte closer. "I was so scared that I'd hurt them when I fell down here. Then when Mother said the babies were on the way, I just wanted to—"

"Shh," Riley said, returning baby Lillian to her warm spot next to Andi. "Like your mother is fond of saying, 'All's well that ends well.'"

Andi choked back the rest of her words and rubbed her watery eyes. "You're right." She smiled up at him. "Now that you're here, everything will be all right."

Elizabeth and Kate returned, along with Troy.

"Congratulations, Riley." Troy was grinning. "Twins, and quite unexpected. I wonder what the rest of the Carter clan will say about this."

Andi carefully pushed herself to a sitting position against the overturned crate and looked at her family. "I know exactly what one Carter will say when we bring Lilly and Lottie home."

"Oh?" Riley asked, curious. "Who?"

"Chad, of course. He'll say that it wasn't good enough that Taffy had twins. I had to go and do it one step better."

The cellar rang with laughter.

Riley couldn't wait to clear away the rest of the rubble and carry his wife and babies out to meet their big brother. He would give his mother-in-law and Kate exactly one week to fuss and spoil the new mother, and to make sure the babies stayed strong and healthy.

But not a day more. He couldn't wait to head back to the ranch to show off his two charming little girls to everybody he met.

———

Historical Note

For story purposes, this earthquake has been depicted as more severe than history would record. San Francisco experienced hundreds of earthquakes in the decades leading up to the devastating earthquake of 1906. There were four earthquakes in 1890. They all occurred around the time of this story's setting. So, while not accurate in representing the earthquake's intensity, this story is entirely possible.

I can scarcely believe it, but over the past couple of years, I have turned a corner regarding cooking and baking. With a lot of practice, careful consideration of a recipe's instructions, and finally learning to manage the black beast—our cookstove—I'm beginning to conquer the I-can't-cook monster. Needless to say, Riley takes fewer meals with the ranch hands.

Cook's Sourdough Starter

To make recipes with sourdough, one needs a good starter. Cook has his favorite, and Mother has hers. Mother's starter came all the way from Pittsburgh, Pennsylvania. Her mother, my grandmother, kept it safe and warm on their trip to the gold fields in 1849. Mother says Grandma Johnson's original starter was in the family for two generations!

When Grandfather died of influenza in the gold camps during the winter of 1850, Grandmother packed up her three younger children and went home to Pennsylvania. My mother, Elizabeth, was twenty-one and decided to dig in her heels and stay in California.

Grandmother left some sourdough starter with Mother, and through the years, she passed it down to Kate, Melinda, and me. Since nobody really knows the original recipe to create Mother's starter, Cook was kind enough to give me his recipe. I can't tell the difference.

2 cups lukewarm potato water (boil two peeled potatoes, cubed. You don't need the potatoes for your starter, but you can save them for another meal.)

2 cups white flour

1 tablespoon sugar

1 shy teaspoon active dry yeast (Optional: to give the starter a quick boost)

In a large glass bowl, mix the potato water, flour, sugar, and optional yeast into a smooth paste. Cover and set in a warm spot until mixture doubles in size, which may take several hours. Stir. Repeat the rise and stir procedure two times a day during the next few days. Store in a cool place to use often or keep in the refrigerator for longer storage. Warm to room temperature before using. To "feed" the starter, remove one or two cups. (Make biscuits or pancakes. Recipes follow.) Replace what was used with ½ cup flour, ⅓ cup water, and 1 teaspoon of sugar. Stir and return to cool storage. This keeps the starter fresh.

Did you know? San Francisco sourdough bread tastes different than other sourdough breads. Why? Because of a specific kind of yeast that hangs out only in the San Francisco Bay area. The Boudin Bakery in San Francisco has kept their sourdough starter alive since 1849 by refreshing it regularly.

Cook's Sourdough Biscuits

The Circle C cook insists that the only right way to bake biscuits is in a heavy Dutch oven over a campfire. A cookstove oven works fine, but it took me awhile to perfect these biscuits. Mostly because I couldn't figure out how to keep a constant temperature in that black beast of a cookstove. More than once, the bottoms of my biscuits burned black. Riley is a fine example of patience and understanding. "You'll figure it out next time," he says while scraping off the blackened bottoms. After two years, the cookstove and I have come to an understanding. I rarely burn the biscuit bottoms any longer.

Preheat oven to 375°.

1 or more cups flour
1 tablespoon sugar
1 teaspoon baking soda
3 tablespoons shortening
2 cups sourdough starter (stir down before measuring)

In a medium-sized bowl, combine flour, sugar, and baking soda. Cut in the shortening until it resembles small pieces. Make a well and add the sourdough starter. Mix until dough forms a ball. Add more flour if needed. Knead a few minutes. Pat or roll out about ½ inch think. Cut into biscuits using a floured biscuit cutter or the floured rim of a glass. Bake at 375° for about 20 minutes or until golden. Makes six to nine biscuits.

Sourdough Pancakes

These are the best pancakes in California, and they turn out every time. They are so easy to whip up that I am often tempted to double the mixture and save the leftover batter from breakfast for supper pancakes. Freshly churned butter and maple syrup add to the spongy texture and slight sourdough flavor. Crushed strawberries or peaches taste good on the pancakes too.

Preheat griddle to medium heat.

2 cups white flour
2 tablespoons sugar
2 cups whole milk
1 cup sourdough starter (Stir it down before measuring.
   You can feed the leftover starter after you remove the

cup you need. Feed by adding ½ cup flour, ⅓ cup water, and 1 teaspoon of sugar.)

Combine the four ingredients above in a large glass mixing bowl. Cover and let rest all night (about 10 hours) or all day (for supper pancakes). Stir down the spongy batter and add:

> 2 large eggs
> ¼ cup melted butter (or vegetable oil)
> ½ teaspoon salt
> 1 teaspoon baking soda

Mix well and pour a shy ¼ cup batter onto a lightly greased griddle pre-heated to medium. Cook until bubbles form and pop. Watch carefully to keep the underside from scorching. Flip the pancakes and cook until done. (Approximate cook time: 1–2 minutes per side.) Serve with butter, syrup, or your favorite fruit topping.

Strawberry or Peach Syrup

Crush strawberries or skinned and pitted peaches in a saucepan over medium heat. Mix equal parts of corn-starch and water (start with 2 tablespoons of each and increase depending on the amount of fruit). Cook until thickened as desired. Sweeten to taste.

Cook's Trail Beans

I learned to cook this delicious concoction during the cattle drive to Los Angeles years ago. Cook didn't teach me. He had no time for such niceties. Instead, I watched how he dumped everything together in a large, covered pot and hang it over the fire. Ellie threw store-bought tins of beans together during our first night up at Mirror Lake. Best of all, this recipe carried me through Riley's and my first year of marriage, when the cookstove and I were learning to get along. I use dried beans, but Ellie's use of canned beans works well and takes much less time.

1 16-ounce can of each of the following (If you want to create it just like I would, you need 2 cups cooked of each):

> pinto beans
> pork and beans
> red kidney beans
> black beans
> white beans

> 1 pound bacon, chopped
> 1 onion, chopped
> ½ garlic bulb, peeled and pressed (or use garlic powder)

Combine all the above ingredients in a large crock pot.

Mix together, simmer until sugar is dissolved, and then pour over the bean concoction:

> ½ teaspoon mustard
> ½ cup white vinegar
> 1 cup brown sugar

Cook on low for 6 to 8 hours, stirring occasionally, until all ingredients have absorbed the flavoring. Serves six to eight.

Cook's Quick Doughnuts

I remember the first time Cook made these doughnuts. We'd experienced a tragedy on the trail drive. One man dead, a dozen missing or dead cattle, missing horses, and my missing brother Chad. To perk the men up while assessing the damage, Cook went all out. He tripled the batch and dropped the dough into hot, sizzling grease in a pot hanging over the campfire. Those doughnuts really hit the spot. I fried up a batch one afternoon at Mirror Lake, and they even turned out.

Start heating the oil (360° is the target temperature. Use a candy thermometer. Or you can use an automatic deep-fat fryer.)

In a large bowl, mix together the first five ingredients:

> 4 cups flour
> 1 cup sugar
> ½ teaspoon salt
> 2 teaspoons baking soda
> ½ teaspoon nutmeg (if desired)

Next, add the following ingredients to the dry mixture, as indicated:

> 2 sticks (1 cup) softened butter. Beat into the dry mixture, by hand if possible.
> 2 egg yolks. Beat until creamy then add to mixture.
> 1 cup milk (add more as needed). Add milk until a soft dough is formed.
> 2 egg whites. Beat until stiff and add to mixture.

Roll out, cut into doughnuts with a doughnut or biscuit cutter, and cook in the hot oil for about 30 seconds. Flip with tongs and cook 30 more seconds. Remove and drain on racks. Sprinkle powdered sugar over the doughnuts (if desired) and cool.

Peach Cobbler

Mother brought this recipe with her when she and her family left Pennsylvania in 1849 for California. Grandfather Johnson was a successful shopkeeper in Pittsburgh, so their family was well supplied for the long wagon train from the east coast to the gold fields. Nobody traveling west had access to fresh fruit, so settlers like Mother's family made do with syrup-preserved fruit in tin cans or jars. Others used dried fruit. Grandmother Johnson "cobbled" ingredients together by dumping sweetened fruit into a Dutch oven, dropping the biscuit mixture on top, and baking it over an open fire. However, Mother insists it tastes just as good baked in an oven.

This is one recipe where you truly throw it all together and it turns out.

Preheat oven to 375°.

> 4–5 cups peaches (canned or fresh)
> 1 cup saved syrup or 1 cup sugar water (for fresh peaches)
> 2 tablespoons cornstarch mixed with 2 tablespoons cold
>   water

Drain the canned peaches, saving 1 cup of the syrup. (If you use fresh peaches, you will need to make a cup of sugar water from 1 cup water and ¼ cup sugar.)

Dump the fruit in the bottom of a lightly greased 8" x 8" cake pan (or whatever you can find).

Heat the peach syrup or sugar water to boiling. Add the cornstarch and water mixture. Cook until slightly thick, about a minute. Pour over peaches in baking dish.

Sweet Biscuit Topping

> 2 cups flour
> ½ cup sugar
> 4 teaspoons baking powder
> ½ cup butter, melted
> 1 egg, beaten
> ½ to ¾ cup milk

Mix all ingredients to form a sticky "drop biscuit" dough. Drop by large spoonfuls on top of the peaches. Bake about 30 minutes at 375°. Serve warm, with warm cream.

Cream
Whisk a cup of heavy whipping cream with sugar and vanilla to taste. Pour over each serving of cobbler. Or serve with a scoop of ice cream.

Iced Lemonade

I remember how Mother and Luisa made lemonade for a rodeo the Circle C was hosting when I was a child. I couldn't figure out how to cut down a recipe for a fifty-gallon barrel of lemonade, so Mother graciously gave me a recipe that makes a nice pitcher. The Circle C not only grows lemons but also has its own icehouse. Packed in sawdust, the blocks of ice stay frozen even during the summer. Now that Memory Creek has its own icehouse, I have ice for the icebox and for iced lemonade and ice cream. It takes several days during the winter to cut the ice on a frozen lake high in the Sierras. After going along on one ice-harvesting trip, I decided that is an adventure I am happy to leave to the men.

> ¾ cup sugar
> ¾ cup juice from freshly squeezed lemons (about 6)
> 4 cups water

In a small saucepan, mix the sugar with 1 cup of the water. Boil to dissolve the sugar completely. Cool. In a 2-quart pitcher, add the cooled sugar water mixture, the lemon juice, and the rest of the water, then stir well. Add more sugar to taste if desired. Serve iced.

ACKNOWLEDGMENTS

I intended to leave Andi and Riley with a new baby at the end of the first short-story collection, *Yosemite at Last: And Other Tales from Memory Creek Ranch*, but the fans did not agree. They begged for another collection, so *Stranger in the Glade: And More Tales from Memory Creek Ranch* has become a reality.

Readers inundated me with dozens of "please write about this" ideas, which I took to heart. "Specter from the Past" (Claire Miller), "Pony Memories" (Kaitlyn B.), and "Count Your Blessings" (Lilly Wiscaver) are the fruits from some of these suggestions.

I want to extend my heartfelt thanks to Andi fan and gifted writer Ellen Senechal for helping me plot the stories "Nanny Riley," "Winning Isn't Everything," and "A Night to Remember." Ellen's insight and knowledge of my story characters were a huge blessing.

Susan K. Marlow

Connect with other Andi fans at AndiCartersBlog.com.

Don't Miss the Entire Circle C Milestones Series

Thick as Thieves
Heartbreak Trail
The Last Ride
Courageous Love
Yosemite at Last
Stranger in the Glade